# Love on the Block

## EMILY REX

To request permissions, contact the author at www.authoremilyrex.com

Published by Park Lane, LLC

First US Edition: April 2026

Paperback ISBN: 979-8-9987408-2-4

Cover: Ink and Laurel

Editor: Elaine York

*To the 45% of female athletes that drop out of sports before age fourteen because of safety concerns, lack of transportation, and body image issues.*

## SMASH HIT: The Pro Volleyball Federation is Back in the U.S.

*Houston Chronicle*

For the first time since the 1980s, women's professional indoor six-on-six volleyball is coming back to the United States. While America's league closed up shop after only two seasons in the 1980s, other countries across the pond have had a thriving, competitive volleyball scene since the end of World War II.

For this inaugural season there will be only six teams in the Professional Volleyball Federation:

- New Orleans, LA *Elite*
- Houston, TX *Moons*
- Las Vegas, NV *Fire*
- Omaha, NE *Shooting Stars*
- Indianapolis, IN *Starfire*
- Atlanta, GA *Storm*

The Houston team, named the Moons after our city's space-centric identity, is made up of a variety of players from here and afar. The starting lineup:

- Temi Cryer (27): *Opposite hitter*
  - Height: 6 feet 2 inches
  - College: Northwestern

- ○ Hometown: Glenwood, IL
- Nashville Green (27): *Outside hitter*
  - ○ Height: 6 feet 1 inch
  - ○ College: University of Wisconsin
  - ○ Hometown: Houston, TX
- Daly Acosta (23): *Middle blocker*
  - ○ Height: 6 foot 4 inches
  - ○ College: University of Minnesota
  - ○ Hometown: San Juan, Puerto Rico
- Danica Marko (31): *Setter*
  - ○ Height: 5 foot 10 inches
  - ○ College: Serbia Federal University
  - ○ Hometown: Belgrade, Serbia
- Simin Zhang (23): *Libero*
  - ○ Height: 5 foot 5 inches
  - ○ College: California State
  - ○ Hometown: Beijing, China

Volleyball season runs from January to the end of May/beginning of June, and all the games will be streaming live on the PVF YouTube channel. You can subscribe and turn on notifications to be updated when each game starts.

Good luck and go Moons!

# Chapter One

## WYATT

## *DECEMBER*

They completely wrecked this airport with construction since the last time I was here. I had to fit my truck in the world's tightest parking spot, and cram myself between the Mini Cooper next to me to get the flowers, balloons, and teddy bear out of my back seat.

My heart races from both my speed and my excitement as I walk quickly through the airport toward the arrivals area. The airport smells like one-thousand different perfumes mixed with body odor and the scent of fresh-baked dough from the Pink's Pizza inside of the terminal. I mentally kick myself over my choice of roses on my way to stand near the door where travelers exit. I had red roses in my hands at the store, but put them back because I read online that they represent love and I didn't want to overstep. So I ended up with yellow, which are supposed to mean friendship.

Finally, I'm in the right place. I rock foot to foot while I wait. The smell of the roses hits my nose and distracts me for one second. Just enough time that when I look up—she's there.

"Nash," I wave. I jog toward her to help with her bags and deliver my gifts. I can't help but devour my first glimpse of her in nearly six months. Blonde hair shining, green eyes like sea glass, she's even more beautiful than I remembered.

Her face lights up when she sees me. "Wyatt!" Her eyes appraise the flowers in my hands, then immediately jump to my chest where my heart beats furiously. "Where did you get that?" She's surprised, but laughing, as I spin for her, showing *Green* printed across the back under the number ten. "I bought one the first day they were available."

"*I* don't even have one yet," she cries as she reaches out to touch the pink jersey. She runs her fingers reverently over the chest where there's a crescent moon, and my heart kicks one big beat under her touch.

I hand her the flowers, then the teddy bear, and finally, the balloons. Her arms are loaded down with my gifts and the half-drunk bottle of water she brought from the plane. "This is all for me?" she asks.

I look around, playfully trying to find someone else they could be for. "I think so, yes," I laugh.

"Thank you," she says, but her eyes are on the roses.

"No problem. How was your flight?"

She shrugs. "You know how it is." I do. I travel a lot for football, but usually we are on a private plane, or at the very least, in first class. I don't know if I could do economy for a long-haul flight like she just did. There's never enough leg room when you tower over people like we do.

I guess being crammed into a tin can, hurtling through the atmosphere at five-hundred miles an hour never really improves with time or experience. But flying private certainly lessens the pain. "We'd better get going. It was a nightmare getting in here; I'm sure it will be a nightmare getting out." I take her checked bag and her big carry-on tote, and together we head toward the parking garage.

My truck waits for us just as stuck as I left it. Could I have gone through the regular pickup line? Sure. But Nash is *back*. She deserves to be met at the baggage claim.

"Let me pull it out, so you can get your stuff in." I turn sideways to get in the driver's seat sucking the hell in out of my gut. I slide into the driver's seat, turn on the engine, and back out just enough that Nash can get in more easily.

When I get out, Nash admonishes me, "You're blocking the whole lane!"

"We'll be quick," I wave her off, then toss her luggage into the bed of my truck. I help her shove the balloons and flowers in the back seat. Looking at all the welcome home paraphernalia strewn across the bench, I realize I may have gone overboard, but I'm just so excited for her to be home.

Once we're on the road, an amicable silence falls over us. I can't count how many times we've done this same airport pickup routine. I'm sure it has taken a toll on Nash. Living so far away from home, from family. Being in different time zones, a ten-hour flight anytime she wants to come back. Looking at her now, blonde hair messy from the plane, no makeup, stolen Houston Hurricanes sweatshirt, you can't see the dedication she has to volleyball. You see a woman with green eyes and a bright smile. One who is unfazed by having missed so much at home while she was in Rome. But I know better.

"Are you happy to be back?" I ask, keeping my eyes on the road. If I look at her too long, I might forget I'm driving. My mind is so desperate to soak her in, to make it click that this is she's really back. My brain's trying to catch up to what my eyes keep confirming is real. She's here. Close enough that the smell of her shampoo cuts through the stale truck air.

She nods slowly, watching the city roll past the window. "It's bittersweet," she says after a beat. "I built a life there." Her voice drifts as she talks about the league overseas, the friends she made, the kind of competition you can't find anywhere else. I let her words fill the space between us.

When she finally goes quiet, I risk a glance. Her profile's lit by the late afternoon sunshine, calm and familiar in a way that hits somewhere deep.

"I'm just glad you came back," I say.

She doesn't answer right away, just gives a small smile. The kind that says everything I need to hear.

And for the first time in months, I feel truly happy.

*Chapter Two*

NASH

"Welcome to your new home sweet home." Wyatt spreads his arms out wide. "Your room is all ready for you."

I want to barrel my way into those arms and have him tell me everything will be all right, but I keep my feet firmly in place.

We drag my luggage through the door of Wyatt's three-story townhome in downtown Houston. "It's like it always is when I visit, I'm just staying way longer." It's so weird that for the last year I've been the one visiting him when this is *my* hometown. Now, I'll be living here with Wyatt while I get back on my feet. Surely nothing can go wrong living with the man you're secretly in love with, yet also in the 'just friends' zone.

"I put more towels in your bathroom for that exact reason."

"Thank you."

"And I've already picked up a six pack of your preferred brewski."

"Can we start there? I don't want to deal with any of this right now." I gesture at the mound of luggage beside me.

Wyatt takes a bow like a Victorian butler. "As you wish."

We ascend the stairs toward the second floor, which is actually the main floor. Everything looks the same as the last time I visited. Weird that he hasn't bothered to hang even one thing on the wall in the time he's been here.

I've only ever stayed here a maximum of like five days, mostly to see him play, but I'm sure living here while I get my feet firmly entrenched on American soil will be fine. We spent so much time at each other's places in college, it was almost like we were living together. There was a month the football house didn't have a working dryer, so Wyatt washed and dried all his clothes at my apartment, so we spent a lot of time together then.

I could have stayed with my parents, but who wants to do that? Besides, their suburb is much farther from the practice gym and game arena.

"The place looks great," I say as I set the flowers on the kitchen island.

"Thanks, I'll probably sign for another year in July when the Hurricanes decide what to do with me."

"Do you like the area?"

"I do..." He hedges, leaving more unsaid than just his simple reply. Seems par for the course in this friendship.

I know Texas was never in his long-term goals. When I met him our freshman year of college at the University of Wisconsin, he never had a plan outside of Wisconsin and being a Green Bay Butcher. That was it for him. His childhood dream. But after finishing his rookie contract with the Butchers, he left last year—heartbroken—to play a one year 'prove it' contract with the Hurricanes.

"Well, maybe you'll buy something here. No rush obviously since now you have a roommate. Besides, I came here to play volleyball," I say with fake sternness, "not to be your personal mover. So stay put for now, huh?"

"Don't worry, I've got no plans on going anywhere as long as you are here."

As he strides toward the fridge I watch, inspecting him, wondering if there was more to what he just said but squashing that wayward thought as soon as it entered my mind. I know the Hurricanes lost in the first round of the playoffs this year, and that must have stung. To go that far and yet not far enough. I know the feeling. We've talked about it enough over the phone, so I don't bring it up now. As I round the island, stepping up to him, I say, "Speaking of plans. What are the plans for this?"

"This?"

"Us," I say, and his eyes go wide. Now that I think about it, my heart is also kind of beating fast.

"What about us?"

"Living together?" I elbow his ribs teasingly. "Roomies." He seems to deflate at my teasing, which is weird. We've always had a lighthearted friendship even when I've wanted more.

"Why would it be any different than when you've stayed before?"

"This will be much longer than a holiday weekend."

"That's kind of a given."

I roll my eyes. "I was just saying." I grab the peanut butter pretzels out of the pantry and start munching. I never like the meals they serve on the long-haul flights, so I'm starving.

"We're friends, Nash. It's not going to be that hard to be roommates."

"What if I want to bring a guy home?" I pop another pretzel in my mouth to cover my own shock at what just came out of me. Why did I say that to him? Why would I want him to think I'm interested in anyone else? If he brought someone home, could I stand to witness that?

Wyatt's normal blue eyes take on a shade of gray. Like the Arctic Ocean when it's trying to sink a ship. "No," he scowls. I don't think I've ever seen that look on his face.

"No?" I balk. "What do you mean *no*?"

"I'm not letting any random man in here. There's a rule for you—no strangers."

"If I know him well enough to fu–" Wyatt cuts me off mid profanity. "I said no." The heat I hear in his voice takes me by surprise. It also makes my stomach swoop. I can only imagine how good that commanding voice would sound when he's telling me to—whoa. Stop that right there.

I put the pretzels back in the pantry, using the three seconds I'm not facing him to let a wave of confusion roll through me at the seriousness in his voice. What was that about? I dabbled in dating during college, though nothing ever got serious. I was too busy with school and volleyball to have a boyfriend. By the time I realized my feelings for him, we were firmly in friend territory, destined to go our separate ways. Same for Italy; though, I may have sampled the local specialty on occasion when the mood struck. Nothing ever got close to serious though, because none of them were Wyatt.

"Okay, geez. I hear you loud and clear." I dust the salt off my hands and move to fill a cup with water. "If you'll excuse me, I'm jet-lagged and gross. I want to get settled in before we do anything else today."

*And before I do something crazy like kiss you. Just like we did the night before I left for Rome.*

Whatever came over him a second ago is gone now. In its wake, he looks a little bashful and unsure. When I walk past him to head up the stairs, I put my hand on his shoulder. I'm going to poke the bear. "Your teammates don't count as strangers, right?" His scowl comes back, brows pinched together, and I duck as he tries to wrap his arms around me.

"You little–"

I squeak as I bound up the stairs, just escaping his grasp. I run all the way to my room. It isn't until I shut the door behind me and lean against it that I realize I left all of my stuff downstairs.

"Shit."

In all of about three seconds of our tenure as roommates, I've already put my foot in my mouth several times. Why the hell would I ask about bringing a man home? Not only am I not looking for that, but I'm going to be way too busy making this league work to waste time fooling around with a guy…

Unless, of course, Wyatt is amenable.

## Chapter Three

### NASH

It's been a while since I was able to give back to my community like this, so I'm thrilled to be here today with the Moons serving food to the unhoused and their animals.

My new team and I gather around a short-haired woman in jeans and a H-Town t-shirt as she explains how the day will work and who the organization is. "Ladies, thank you for being here today. Houston Fights Hunger was established in 2008 and we feed about a thousand people a week between all of our partner groups. Our goal is to meet the citizens of Houston where they are, and oftentimes that's unsheltered throughout the city. How this works is…"

As I listen to her instructions on riding in cars and handing out food and supplies, I glance at the women around me in disbelief. I recognize Daly, our middle blocker. She's six-foot-four and from Puerto Rico. Danica, our setter is an eight-year pro originally from Serbia. Lauren is our opposite hitter and a decorated Olympic medalist. Others on the team are NCAA champions, All-Americans, and National League champions. I may have been looking them up as the team was announced.

My nose tingles at the thoughts of all these athletes on my team. I'm beyond proud to be here with them. I fought for my right to stand among them.

I'm home. In Houston. Playing volleyball. No more ten-hour flights, no more time changes, no more tiny Italian apartment balcony overlooking the cobblestone streets. Playing internationally after college wasn't even a question. There were no other options. My choices were to find a desk job, or leave the country.

Until now.

We are all assigned a car to ride in with a member of the charity. Danica, Lauren, and I are put in the same group and we clamber into our group leader's car. The trunk has been filled with premade meals and gallon bags full of supplies. There's even bags of dog food if they have a furry friend.

"They've thought of everything," I say to Danica in the back seat.

"I know, right. It's super-efficient. I kind of love that."

"I think it's a good way to start off on the right foot as a team." We buckle our seatbelts as our group leader, Ashley, gets the car started.

"Is anyone from here," she asks.

I nod in response. "I am, but I've been gone a long time. I went to college in Wisconsin and then I played international volleyball in Italy."

She laughs as she pulls away from the curb. "I can tell you're all volleyball players."

Lauren snorts when she laughs. "That obvious, huh?"

Danica and Lauren introduce themselves to Ashley as we drive to our first spot. Danica's been all over in her eight years in pro volleyball. Lauren has an Olympic silver medal and is from Colorado, but went to school at UCLA.

As much as I would have liked to hang out with my one other teammate I've played with previously, Temi, I'm kind of glad I'm being forced to get to know the other girls better. I think both Temi and I will be better off this way instead of being able to stay in our comfort zones, which is with each other.

When we finally pull up to the first stop—an underpass somewhere along I-10 West. There's a group of people already waiting. The other players and I kind of take a back seat and let Ashley lead the way. She gets out first, greeting people by name, and the rest of us follow. She gestures at us, "This is Nash, Danica, and Lauren. They're part of the new Houston volleyball team and they're helping out today."

Smiles break out among most of the people, some even say hello back. We gather at the trunk of the car and follow the instructions we were given earlier.

A man with gray hair comes up to me, I hand him a Styrofoam box with spaghetti, bread, and salad. "What drink would you like? We have water, soda, and Gatorade." Wow, I immediately feel myself falling back into my waitressing persona I had when I worked at a Texas Roadhouse in high school.

"I'll have water, please." I turn back to the trunk and take water out of the cooler to hand to him.

"Here you go." He nods in response and retreats back to the curb to sit and eat.

We continue to hand out food, drinks, and supplies. It honestly goes pretty fast, and soon we're on our way to the next spot, and then the next.

The day flies by this way. I guess that's how it goes when you feel like you're making a difference.

On our way back to the parking lot where we started the

day, Lauren asks, "Have either of you done anything like this before."

I nod. "I did when I was younger. The Girl Scout troop I was in volunteered with something like this once a year or so. But it's been a while." Probably too long since I really gave back. Maybe I can make that a priority later, but for me to be able to do anything else, I need to make sure there's a team here for me to be on after this season.

Back in town only a few days and I already find myself at a flag football game. Wyatt and I stand on the grassy sidelines, huffing and puffing, as we watch his teammates in their first rec game of the off season. They mixed up the teams this time and had offense play with their friends or girlfriends, and defense play with theirs. This will be my last pickup game of any kind before the official start of volleyball season.

"What did you think of your first team meeting?" Wyatt asks me as we watch Jaden attempt to play quarterback.

"It was great. The coach is amazing, and the girls are fun. It's going to be an interesting season, though. I can't imagine there aren't kinks to work out in a brand-new league." Despite the fact that Italy has had a professional women's volleyball league since right after World War II, there hasn't been one in the States since the eighties. And that one only lasted two years.

Five years I've been gone. Years that I've loved—don't get me wrong. I just missed so much. I only got to see Wyatt play as a Butcher once in his four years there. I wish I had been able to swing it more, but the distance and our schedules made it so hard. I don't mention it, though. I can't turn back time, and I don't want to poke at anything sensitive when we're supposed to be having fun. When he told me he was leaving to be a Hurricane, I made sure to come home to support him.

"I'm sure a group of pros like y'all can handle it." He waves his hand affably, throwing around the Texan slang I know he just picked up recently.

I cross my arms as I take in the wide Texas sky. "It's sure good to be back. Although, I already tried the gelato they carry at H-E-B, and it was trash compared to the real thing." Wyatt chuckles. "I'm serious," I say, indignant. He, of all people, should know. He is very serious about sweets.

"Oh, I know you are." He pauses, looking at his cleats digging into the short grass. I can feel the shift in the mood, the moment feels like the second before a balloon pops. The tightness of the anticipation. "Now that you're back, I thought maybe we could–"

"That's game! Everyone bring it in for a team photo." If Colin had a whistle, I know he'd be blowing it obnoxiously.

I look back at Wyatt. "We could what?"

His face shutters. Something in his eyes closes off and I can no longer read his thoughts. "Nothing." He guides me toward the field. "Let's go get in this team photo."

I trail him onto the field where Noah, Audrey, Colin, Chrissy, Jaden, Mack, plus some people I just met before the game—and immediately forgot all their names—are standing, waiting to take a pic. I only met Audrey recently when I came back to see Wyatt play at the same time she started dating Noah and began coming around to Hurricane games. Chrissy and Colin strike me as a variant of Barbie and Ken. And it appears that Jaden and Mack are in a fight for the label of class clown.

Chrissy sets her phone up on the tripod, starts the timer, and prances back to the group.

I squeeze in close to Wyatt, the stench of the other men threatening to knock me over. The phone's camera flashes a couple times in quick succession, and Chrissy runs over to check it. "Let's take another." There's a chorus of groans. "Just one more," she cries as she starts the timer and runs back. I look at Wyatt and we make pointed eye contact. Someone's going to have to stop her or we're going to be here all night.

When Chrissy tries to make everyone do a third attempt, it's Noah who speaks up. "I'm sure that one was fine." Out of the side of his mouth where he thinks only Audrey can hear, he says, "I'm sure the first ten were fine." I chuckle under my breath. Those two are so funny. Their relationship started out funny, too. Audrey is his social media manager turned girlfriend—which was a whole thing last season.

"Okay, okay," Chrissy huffs. "I'll send the best of the batch to the group chat." No doubt tweaked, filtered, and edited to high heaven. She turns to Noah and Audrey, mentioning their plans for tomorrow as they wander off. Everyone else moves to gather their bags.

Noah calls after Wyatt. "See you later this week for weights?"

"Yeah, man," he calls back as we both head to the car to go back home.

———

We turn onto Wyatt's street that's filled to the brim with charming townhouses piled on top of each other, and I think I might like to get my own apartment in this neighborhood once I'm settled. It could be a real possibility if the Moons win, and I get my share of the million-dollar prize money. There's not much of Houston that's walkable, but this little area off to the side of downtown is. There's a bar that has trivia every Tuesday night, a huge H-E-B, and a cute little coffee shop all within walking distance from Wyatt's front door. I have to find some time while I'm here to go to trivia night, if even by myself, instead of having no fun for the entire season like when I was in Italy.

When we get inside, we dump our gym bags by the front door and head up the stairs, making a beeline to the fridge. It's then that I realize that the door of his fridge, much like his walls, is empty of any personal items, and for some reason, that bothers me so much. It's not until Wyatt hands me the Italian dressing for our premade salad that it hits me.

"Where's the postcard I sent you from Rome?" I ask, pointing to the empty real estate on the door of the fridge. Maybe he put it away somewhere for safekeeping? But I think a postcard from a different country is definitely something most people would save to look at each day.

"What are you talking about?"

I huff. "I went to the touristy part of Rome where they have tiny shops that sell notebooks, magnets, and postcards, and I mailed you one."

"Well, I never got it. Where did you mail it from?"

"The store had a little outgoing mailbox right outside. The man gave me a pen to use, and I bought a stamp from him. I wrote it up against the brick wall outside the store and put it in the little—" A grin breaks across Wyatt's face, followed by a quiet laugh. "What," I ask. "What's funny about a tiny mailbox?

"There's no way that was legit. That was one-hundred percent a tourist trap."

"Then why bother selling me a stamp?" I cross my arms over my chest. "Explain that."

"To make it look real, obviously." My mouth hangs open like a fish. He's totally right. The worst part is, I had been in Rome over a year at that point. You'd think I would have known something like that with months of being there, but apparently not. Must have caught me at a bad time. Maybe I was tipsy? I don't remember. All I remember was walking along the street, finding that little place, and dragging Temi in behind me. Clocking the realization in my eyes, Wyatt catches my hand and gently pats the back of it. "Don't worry. There are worse scams to fall for than that one."

"Yeah," I nod, but my heart sinks a little in my chest. He never got the postcard that I signed with *all my love*. I would have written more, but spilling my guts on a tiny piece of paper where everyone who handles it will read my thoughts didn't feel right. Even that one small admission never made it here. Wyatt never got it out of the mailbox, held it in his hands, and knew that I loved every second of our kiss at my going away party. He was unaffected by it anyway, so maybe it's for the best.

"You're right. Well, I'm going to get cleaned up for bed. Have a good night, Wyatt."

"You too, Nash."

———

That night I lay in my bed, doomscrolling per usual, when a text from Chrissy pings my phone. I open it and find the photo we took earlier. I pinch the screen to zoom in on myself. I'm a sweaty mess, but that's a regular day for me. And for the guys. It's nice to look at a picture of myself surrounded by people who don't make me look like a freak. I'm a staggering six-foot-one, but that's nothing compared to Wyatt's six-foot-five frame.

I move the screen to look at him closer. His blonde hair is floppy on top, and a couple days of scruff adorns his jawline.

And he's looking right at me.

He's completely ignoring the camera, looking down at me while I smile into the flash. His blue eyes look... full of adoration? That can't be right. We're just friends. So what's up with this? Is this actually the best picture we took, or did Chrissy send just this one to me on purpose?

Five years ago, he kissed me the night of my going away party. The next day, I got on a plane, and we never really talked about it. I thought about it the entire flight. Replaying his lips on mine over and over again. Studying the look in his eyes after, trying to figure out what was going on behind them. When I landed in Rome, I turned my phone off airplane mode, expecting it to blow up with messages from Wyatt either explaining or apologizing, but there was nothing. After twelve hours straight of traveling to a new country, then getting right into the groove of practice while fighting jet lag, I had to pack that memory away and move on. By the time I realized I never said anything either, it felt like too much time had passed. I chalked it up to him being overwhelmed by emotions before his best friend left the country. Since he also never brought it up, he must have thought the same. Something propelled by knowing we would be apart, and that for the next however many years our friendship would be harder than it had been while living two blocks from each other in a small college town in the middle of Wisconsin.

This photo makes me realize just how strong my feelings still are for him. Time and distance have done nothing for my poor heart.

*Chapter Five*

NASH

## JANUARY

"Ow! Why'd you throw it so hard," cries Daly as we beam her with volleyballs after her pass didn't end up in the trashcan we're using as a target. She's still peeking out from behind her arms in case a rogue ball comes her way. Her curly dark hair flows over her shoulder in loose ringlets.

"Why did you miss?" Lauren asks. Her straight brown hair is the direct opposite of Daly's curls.

"Like it's so easy." She motions at her to come over and take her turn at what's supposed to be our friendly icebreaker game. Megan had seen a video online where a player tries to pass the ball into a trashcan, and if they miss, the rest of the team throws balls at them. I don't know how that's anyone's idea of fun, but I wasn't about to be a naysayer on the first day of practice. I breathe a sigh of relief as Lauren goes to take her turn. I still have time before I have to go. It's not that I can't do it. I'm just afraid of getting nervous and missing in front of everyone. I pick up my ball as Lauren gets into a ready stance.

After Lauren goes, Coach calls to us, ending our game and relieving me of having to take my turn. We run over and circle up around her. Standing there, ready to lead us all into a new battle is Ms. Stephanie Etlinger, a pillar of the volleyball community. Earning Olympic medals in both indoor and beach volleyball in the late nineties, since then she's been the coach for the women's Olympic volleyball team. I have no idea how Houston managed to snag her for our first season in a newborn league, but I'm hyped that she's here.

"Ladies, welcome to the first practice of the Houston Moons!" We all cheer. "I'm sure I don't have to tell you all what an honor and privilege it is to be a part of the inaugural season of the Professional Volleyball Federation. I hope all of you are up to the gigantic task of bringing this league to life." We nod, hanging on her every word. "As we get warmed up and start our drills for the day, I want everyone to be patient with one another. This is a star-studded group, and it might take some time for everyone to gel. I don't expect that relationships will form instantly, but it does have to be before our first game against New Orleans in two weeks." She looks at all of us in turn, a glint in her eye. "Lastly, I hope you kept up your conditioning during your break." I groan and turn to look at Temi, who's standing next to me with a ghostly look on her face because, like me, I'm sure she didn't do one ounce of conditioning. I'm so happy she's here with me, though. The chances of us having been on the same team in Italy and becoming friends? Slim. The chances of us leaving that team at the same time to come play on this exact team? Infinitesimal.

Coach blows her whistle. "Everybody, three lines for the belly drill. Let's hustle up!"

*Hell yeah. My favorite.*

We all jog to one side of the court behind the out of bounds line, splitting into three lines. I'm in the first group to go, so I step up and get on my belly facing away from the net, making sure my hands are on the line. I'm in the back-right, Daly is next to me in the middle-back, and Danica is on her right. I remember when I was little and just learning how to play volleyball, we would do this drill facing forward, and my coach would bounce the ball real high, giving us plenty of time to get underneath it. But I'm a career pro now, and Coach pounds down balls at us like the adults we are.

She slaps the ball with her hands one time, our signal to start moving, and I clamber to my feet, turning around at the same time. The ball comes launching our way kind of in between me and Daly. In the split second I open my mouth, waving Daly away with the quick flick of my hand, I say, "I go." I put my arms out quickly, backing up to make sure the ball doesn't hit me in the face. One of the first things I learned in this sport is when to cover your face, but I don't want to do that here in our first practice. I want the women around me to know that I'm in it to win it, no matter how tough we have to play. If it hits me in the face, I want someone to play the second ball right off of it. I recover in time, making the perfect pass to where Simin stands in the setter position. We head to the back of the line, our turn successfully completed. While we stand and wait, we cheer on our teammates and help them read the ball as it comes. The next ball Coach hits goes sailing. "Deep! Deep," I call to Temi, and she shuffles back, getting in a better position.

When I was in Italy, it was soothing to have similar movements and drills as I did in college. That familiarity with the sport I love were the only thing keeping me sane in those first few months.

One Sunday, maybe two weeks after I arrived in Italy and

after all the awe of having a new place to explore had worn off, I woke up with a hollow feeling in my chest. Like everything that kept my soul buoyed had been sucked out. I grabbed my phone to call my mom, but quickly realized it was the middle of the night at home. Suddenly, the full weight of being alone in a foreign country threatened to knock me flat and not let me up. For the first time I realized that I was alone on this continent. I looked at Wyatt's contact for only a split second before dialing.

He answered on the third ring. "Hello?"

"Hi," I breathed. Through the phone he sounded like he could have been next to me, not a cellular connection in what seemed like a million miles away. I instantly felt myself unclench a little. "Isn't it like three o'clock in the morning there?"

"You called." The way he said it sounded like there was no other option besides picking up. My heart had been hurting before he answered, but when I heard his voice so steady and sure, it made it melt a little.

"I miss home."

I heard him roll over, and I couldn't help but wonder if his hair was already ruffled by his pillow. "Home Texas or home Wisconsin?" That's a fair question. I spent my whole life until college in Houston, but the last four years before leaving the States, I spent basically all my time in Wisconsin. Most of it with him.

I loved every second.

"Both. I guess that's why my homesickness is so bad." More sheets rustled and it made me wonder if he turned on a light?

"Did I ever tell you about my high school summer job?"

"No. I thought you worked on your family's farm."

I could hear the nod in his voice as he talked. "I did, but farm chores weren't paid. It was just expected. If I wanted to have spending money, I had to work a job on top of that."

"What did you do in a town that small?" I think about my hometown of Poblocki and its one stoplight. "Did you work at the Pig Wig?" Every time, I got a kick out of the nickname for the local grocery store.

"Nah, not there. For two years I was the mower at the town cemetery. I would go out on Saturday mornings and push the lawn mower around the headstones."

"That's so creepy."

I could practically see the shrug he would give me if we were face to face. "It was honestly kind of peaceful. Almost never hotter than eighty degrees, and when I got thirsty, I drank out of the well." He paused for effect. "Looking back on it, drinking water from a ground well, surrounded by dead people, maybe wasn't my best idea. But hey, it didn't kill me." I laughed out loud. The kind that bubbled in your chest first before spilling from your lips. I hadn't laughed like that since I left. "Maybe that cured all your ailments?"

I smile just to myself. "You know, I think it did. Tell me another?"

"Pa insisted Henry and I learn how to drive in that same cemetery. I asked him why and he told me that if we wrecked the car and died, at least they wouldn't have to take us very far."

"That does sound like Charlie," I laughed.

"He's not one to pull any punches."

I glanced at the clock on my phone. It was about time to be getting up, which meant I'd kept Wyatt up long enough. "I should probably let you get back to sleep."

"I wouldn't have been able to sleep if I had known you were homesick anyway."

"Well, you fixed it for now. Thank you," I whispered, because it felt like if I spoke too loud, it would disturb the peacefulness of the morning here and the middle of the night there.

"Anytime, Nash," he replied, and we hung up, the kiss our unspoken vow that was never mentioned.

For the rest of that day, I carried the warmth of that conversation around in my chest. My memories of Wyatt and Wisconsin and college. It was exactly the kind of story he would tell me when we were driving out to visit his parents, or sharing a shake at Kopp's.

The whistle blows and knocks me out of my reverie. Even though Coach spends the rest of practice running us into the ground, I can't help the little smile I carry from remembering that call. It might have been the first time, but it certainly wasn't the last time I called him at an ungodly hour, just needing to hear his familiar voice in that moment.

We return to the locker room hours later, decimated. I did not, in fact, keep up my conditioning during the off season. "I can't believe we had to run that suicide four times," I complain as I strip off my practice jersey.

"I know. Every single time it was someone different not making the cut," replies Lauren, already dragging her street clothes out of her bag.

Danica pipes up, "It was me at least once, so I'm sorry for that."

A chorus of 'all good's' ring out.

We might be a new team made up of a mishmash of players from around the world, but we all speak one common language—volleyball.

We got our asses ran into the ground today, obviously, but I liked what I saw. Danica has an uncanny feeling for adapting when her set is too close to the net. She never panicked for one second. I've never seen a libero—a team's best passer and scrappiest player—chase down a shanked pass she would physically not be able to get as hard as Simin did today. I look around me and all I see are possibilities and endless talent.

Almost instantly, the homesickness is gone—because I am finally home.

I grunt through my teeth as I lift the bar weighed down with over two-hundred pounds.

"Thirteen, fourteen, and… one more," Noah encourages me while keeping his hands just under the bar for safety, even though my personal best is over three-hundred pounds. I loudly exhale as I push the bar up for the last time. "Fifteen." Noah helps me rack the bar. "Nice job."

I peel myself off the bench and put my hands on my knees, exhausted. "It's crazy how fast you get out of shape after the season ends."

"That's why we're here together," Jaden pipes in. He and Colin are at the squat rack taking turns lifting.

"And," Colin leads, "to interrogate Wyatt about what's going on with him and Nash. Because they're definitely fucking."

"Shut the fuck up," I growl. I thought this was our off-season bros at the gym routine. I didn't know it was a trap.

"You know we can all tell," he says matter-of-factly.

I glare at him. "We're not having this conversation. End of discussion."

Jaden, not one to be put off of anything ever, chimes in. "Great, then we can talk about the fact that you still don't have a signed Hurricanes contract."

*Wow.* The only other topic I absolutely didn't want to talk about today and he had to go and bring it up. "I'm sure the front office just hasn't crossed all the t's or dotted all the i's yet." It's true that I don't know what the front office is waiting on. Another player? More money? Coach's say? No idea. How can I tell them that at the first sniff of interest from the Butchers, I'd be gone? They're good guys. Just because I'm a dick for wanting to jump ship doesn't mean they should have to deal with my selfishness. I know Jaden well enough to know he will take it personally.

Colin, mistaking my neutrality for a brave face, pats me on the shoulder. "I'm sure it's coming. You know how this stuff works. Sometimes it can be so slow."

I nod, taking his reassurance for something I don't actually need to be reassured on. It's no skin off my back. Colin might be the one man who cares about this team the most. As the quarterback, that's kind of his job. I can't express enough how different he is from Clark. Colin would never get mad at a receiver for running the wrong route. He never lets one mistake throw him off the rest of his game. Anyone who plays for him is lucky to have him as a leader. It makes me feel like an asshole that even with him being so great, I still would go back to the Butchers in a heartbeat if they would take me. That is, if their quarterback Jared Clark ever left, which might happen if hell ever freezes over.

"Speaking of taking it slow," Jaden starts, his eyes full of mirth. "Is that why you're saying you and Nash aren't fucking? Cause you're taking it slow?"

"Or is that code for just oral?" Noah asks.

The corners of my mouth turn down in response to their dirty comments, but they continue on apparently, not even needing my input even though they're talking about me.

"I don't know how they could be living under the same roof and just doing oral," chuffs Colin.

I shoot him a mean look. "Don't talk about her like that."

"We're only talking about her the way you wish you could," accuses Jaden.

I huff but don't say anything in response. After a split second it seems my silence has served as an answer to their accusations. "See? I told you," Jaden's grin is wide. I can feel my cheeks heat because, of course, they're all right. We're not having sex, but we would be if Nash wanted it as much as I did.

"All right, let's get back to our workout, guys," Colin calls the group to order.

"Thank you," I say, turning back to the weight rack.

"We have months to bother him about this still," he continues.

"Goddamn you," I mutter, moving off the bench to let Noah sit and take his turn.

If this is what I have to look forward to at these workouts, I might be mysteriously coming down with a cold every week.

Chapter Seven

NASH

We all stand around the parking lot. The January chill clinging to our sweats as we wait for the team bus to pick us up. Our first game is against New Orleans, and we were scheduled to leave at five AM on the dot. A long bus ride being made longer by a tardy driver.

I lean over to Temi where she's rooting through her gym bag. "Where do you think he is?"

"He can't be far now. There's no traffic this early." She shoves her beanie into the corner of the bag. "I could have slept another half hour if I had known it would be so late."

I nod. An un-caffeinated Temi is a grumpy Temi.

Finally, we see it rumbling into the parking lot and we all start picking up our bags.

Coach walks up to the open bus doors and speaks to the man inside.

When she comes back down, she's got a sour look on her face, like she just tried those frozen candied grapes Daly gave me the other day that were so tart they nearly split my face in two. She claps her hands. "There's apparently an issue with the bus, which is why we are running late, but I have to let you know that there is no working bathroom on this bus."

Groans erupt from the team. "What are we supposed to do? It's a five-hour ride, we can't hold it that long," cries Megan, one of our second stringers.

"I suggest you all run back inside now and use the facilities before boarding the bus."

Several women immediately scramble back into the building at Coach's suggestion. I already waited until what I thought was the last second to go, so I'll probably be good. Traveling makes me nervous, so I won't eat or drink much anyway. I typically use all our time before games to catch up on that. It's almost guaranteed we'll make a stop along the way.

When we're all loaded on the bus, just as I suspected, Coach announces that there will be a bathroom break every two hours. "If you can hold it until that point, please try to do so. We are already off schedule and any additional stops will only make it worse."

———

We end up stopping more than every two hours, unloading and reloading, and departing again. I make sure to use the restroom every time we stop so that I'm never pushing it while waiting for the next one. The drive between Texas and Louisiana is the flattest, emptiest, most boring parts of Texas. You can drive an hour without seeing anything but farm fields and pine trees. The trip is dotted by multiple small towns boasting a population of just a couple hundred on their 'welcome to' signs.

It makes me think about Wyatt. Does he ever drive out from the city just to feel the country breeze? Just so he can see more stars? Probably not, he's a busy man. But maybe during the off-season he's tempted to go get a taste of the small-town life he grew up with.

I reel my wandering thoughts back in and focus on the upcoming game.

Since we left late, we arrive at the hotel late. We were supposed to have nearly the entire day to get in, watch film, and warm up, but now we have to run everything on a crunch. It's hectic getting the entire team ready to go that quickly. We have all the regular athlete stuff, but we also need a good amount of time in the hotel bathroom fixing our hair and makeup. That's not what makes us great athletes, but a lot of us focus heavily on our appearance because we know we're putting on a show, as well as a game. Thanks to our delayed bus, we have very little time for that. I have an extensive stretching routine, which normally I start in my hotel room before joining the rest of the team, but I don't have time for it today. I dress quickly, pulling my hair up, and sliding my warm-up gear on over my Spandex. Then I'm ready to go down to the team meal and watch tape.

"This food is way better than what we got at U of M," says Daly, grabbing a plate to start making her way down the buffet.

"Well, it is NOLA. City of soul food," I say as I pick up the tongs for the platter of fruit.

"And soul drink," laughs Temi. "But we won't have any time for fun."

"I'd rather not babysit ya'll on Bourbon Street anyway."

Temi sticks her tongue out at me in petulant response.

With game tape watched and hair and makeup done, we

head down to wait for the bus. I have never wanted to see a bus less in my life, but we shuffle back on to be whisked to the arena to start our pregame warmups.

———

The set comes from Danica high over my head. I try to slow myself mid approach to match the speed the ball is falling, but I already have too much momentum. I'm here now, so I may as well swing. The ball hits the blocker's hands with a resounding *smack* and falls back on our side of the net. Daly drops to try and pop the ball back up, but it hits one of her arms, then the other, then the ground. The ref blows his whistle, calling the play dead and awarding the point to the other team.

Despite my several year friendship with Temi, we still need more work on coming together as a team. Tonight, we're showing that.

"That's on me, guys." She pats her chest, taking ownership of her mistake, as she approaches the rest of the team in the middle of the court. We clap hands and pat butts before returning to our respective positions.

"I like my set a little lower than that," I tell Danica, and she smiles back at me, appreciative of the note. This is just part of the growing pains of a new team. We're getting to know each other on and off the court. Like last week I learned that Daly likes pineapple on pizza and Danica towels off between each toe after she showers. To which I responded that that's her serial killer trait. My serial killer trait is putting on one sock and then one shoe instead of both socks and both shoes. I embrace the quirk.

Our hitting errors are off the charts tonight. They blocked my hit and scored, Temi hit one out of bounds on the cross, and New Orleans is reading our yo-yo serve plan like a book. They're easily digging both our short serves and the deep ones. It's a frustrating game. Any time we come back and get close, it seems like we fall apart a little and lose the momentum.

We manage to push them all the way to five sets, but ultimately still take the L. I knew that playing in a start-up league would come with its own battles—of course I did. I was just blind to how that would directly impact me after spending years playing with one of the oldest, most titled clubs in the world. I know the other team is new, too, but maybe they're working harder or gelling better than we have so far. We'll never know. All we can do is our job the best we know how under the circumstances and improve with every misstep.

After a few words, Coach tells us to get ready to go home. Temi sits down on the bench next to me and starts shucking off her court shoes. I don't even look at her when I say, "Well, that sucked."

"It was our first attempt. We can't base the whole season on the outcome of one game. There will be plenty more in our future."

I sigh and it sounds heavy in the air around us. "This is it for me. If this team doesn't work out, I'm done with volleyball. My only option is that I'll retire and find somewhere to coach." I've had a great career, but eventually my body is going to give out on me anyway, and maybe failing in a fiery explosion would be a sign to quit while I'm ahead of my fucked-up knees and torched shoulders.

"They'll have to drag me off the court," Temi replies. "I'll go back overseas if I have to." Temi moved around a lot as a kid since her dad is an international businessman, so she's used to living anywhere and fitting in everywhere.

"Well, if you do, I'll come watch you play."

I might be done if this doesn't work out, but I'd never leave her hanging.

# Chapter Eight

## WYATT

## *FEBRUARY*

I'm sorting through piles of laundry trying to find my favorite pants—the ones that are athletic but look nice—when my phone rings. I have to dig through another mountain of junk on my bed to find it. Ma's photo beams at me from the screen and I swipe to answer. "Hello?"

"Hello? Wyatt?" Her heavy Wisconsin accent makes it sound like 'yellow'. She always has to ask if it's me since she calls from the only land line left in North America.

"Yeah, Ma. It's me," I assure her.

"Oh, good. I was just calling to check in on you." She keeps her voice light, but I know she's worried about me. This is the third "check-in" this week.

"I'm fine, Ma." Not that it's the truth because at the end of the day, how can I tell her that I got to know my childhood hero, the Hall of Fame quarterback of the Green Bay Butchers, and he was an absolute nightmare human being? He was my childhood hero, at least before he put his hands on me, he was.

But he's still the savior of the entire state of Wisconsin, who led their beloved Butchers to their last Super Bowl win fifteen years ago. Or how do I even admit that maybe I don't technically even have a job right now? Those aren't her worries, though, so I keep those things to myself.

"I'm sure you are," she pauses, giving me a chance to pipe up with what's really going on. When I don't say anything, she continues, "What are you boys up to tonight?"

"Jaden, Noah, and I are going to Nash's first home game." I shove one leg in its hole, balancing the phone against my shoulder. They've played two away games already, so I'm sure they're super psyched for this.

"How exciting! You tell Nashville I say good luck. What a fine young lady." That last comment is strictly for my benefit.

"I will, Ma." I don't mean to sound like I'm placating her, but I told her all this two days ago.

"Who are you bringing to Henry's wedding?" she says it in a way that's supposed to sound nonchalant. Like she could be checking out her nails at the same time, admiring her manicure—if she was that kind of woman, which she's not. "Now that your brother is settling down, it wouldn't be a bad thing for you to take it more seriously. That's why I spoke to Mrs. Patty and we thought it would be a great idea if you went with her daughter. You remember Kayla?"

"You set me up?" Ma has always been involved in my life, but she's never butt in like this before.

"You need a date, don't you?"

And fuck, I might have been flattened by one too many offensive linemen and lost my mind because I open my mouth and say, "I have a date."

"Oh, I didn't realize. You never mentioned a date."

"I didn't think I had to say anything since Nash and I are

living together already." I'm really digging myself in deep right now. Sure, why not? Nash is my date to Henry's wedding and I'm the king of fucking England.

Ma's voice perks up at this. "Nash?"

Might as well put the final nail in the coffin. "Yeah, of course. She's my date."

"How wonderful! I'm so glad," I can practically hear her hands clapping with glee on the other side of the line. "It's wonderful you two are finally together."

"Haha…yeah." This hole is now so deep that I can't even see out of the top anymore, but I need to end this conversation. "Please don't be all weird and crazy around her. You'll freak her out. This is still the same old Nash."

"I know, sweetie, but I want grandchildren."

"Jumping the gun a bit there, Ma. Besides, I'm sure Henry has plans to give you grandchildren." I don't even know if I want kids. *I'm* basically still a kid.

"Well, one can hope for these things, ya know. I'm assuming she'll be staying at the farmhouse with us?"

"Of course." Why the hell not?

She obviously got what she called for and is ready to get on with the rest of her evening. "I won't keep you too long. Like I said, I just wanted to check in on you." Now that Henry is about to legally be Hazel's problem, all of Ma's focus is shifting to me. Ever since I left Vandergriff Farm for college, it's meant way too many phone calls.

"I'll see you at the wedding, but if I can come visit before then, I'll call." Fully dressed now, I search for the keys to my truck. I've still got to pick up Jaden and Noah and get to the stadium. It's a fucking haul—though I've discovered that everything in Houston is. Probably doesn't help that the PVF had to go way out of the city to find a stadium to play in. "I've got to get on the road, Ma. I'll talk to you later. Tell everyone I say hi."

"Will do, honey. Bye."

Adding Ma to the list of people I'm lying to is a horrible feeling, but hell if I was getting set up on a date with anyone who wasn't Nash.

———

I wouldn't say I'm a super recognizable guy. Not many people pay attention to the defensive line. Football players who aren't dating international superstars don't get that much camera time on average. Still, this is Nash's big moment, and I would never do anything to take away from that. The plan is to go in, cheer on the Moons, get a few brewskis in with the boys, and get out undetected.

Jaden elbows me, beer in hand. "You think Nash will introduce me to number fifteen? She's smokin'." I follow his gaze to the court where the Moons are warming up and a woman with dark eyes and beads in her braids, whom I recognize as Temi, is running a blocking drill.

I shrug, "I dunno. Maybe. She and Nash are pretty close. They played together in Italy." Spending hours upon hours at practice and traveling for games will do that to you.

"I'm going to ask her on our way home."

I chuckle. "You go for it." Nothing I could say would stop him anyway. Jaden is indomitable once he's set his mind to something.

Noah plops in the seat next to us and sets a humongous tub of popcorn down at his feet. I hand him his beer and we settle in.

Pretty soon the music starts bumping. It's been a long time

since I was a spectator at a sporting event and not down on the field. It's kind of nice. Though, the nerves are still there. I know Nash wants this team to work so bad. This is my first chance to see her play here. It's her first true home game since her college days. I only got to see her play in Italy once. We took a family vacation and made sure to catch a game in Rome, but since I had my whole family in tow, Nash and I didn't get to spend that much time together besides dinner after the game.

"Where are the cheerleaders?" Jaden asks.

"Why would there be cheerleaders here?" I look at him like he grew a second head.

He gestures broadly around us. "Um, it's a sporting event, i.e., cheerleaders should be here." He looks across my shoulders at Noah like *get a load of this guy*. "I never get to see them. Coach is always like 'keep your eyes on the ball' and I do, but not today. I want to see some skirts and pom-poms."

"Yes, today." I snap. "We are here to support Nash and her team. So you'd better keep your eyes on that volleyball."

"As long as number fifteen keeps swinging like that, it won't be a problem, my man." He pats me on the shoulder, and I shoot daggers at him with my eyes.

The announcer comes over the loudspeaker, letting us know that the game is about to begin and to please rise for the singing of the national anthem. I've done this hundreds of times in my life, from high school football to now, and it never fails to make my blood run faster through my veins. It's like my body knows that this is the signal for go-time. As my blood starts buzzing, I have to remind myself that tonight we're in the stands and I am only here to watch.

Our plan to lay low only lasts until about halfway through the second set. There's not a ton of people in the stands tonight, and there are only so many bodies for the camera man to pick on. I guess I really shouldn't be surprised that he quickly found us. Not only are we three big dudes (well, two…Jaden isn't that tall) crammed into these little seats, but we're making tons of noise. It probably took someone running audio or video about ten seconds to clock us as Hurricanes players.

The next time a team calls a timeout, we show up on the big screen with a navy blue and white border around us and Houston Hurricanes in huge red letters. Jaden waves, eating this shit up.

He leans over to me. "Nice of them to get our team colors up there."

Things devolve quickly after this. Several people from our section turn around to look at us. We wave politely at them trying to discourage them from coming up. I promised myself that I wouldn't take anything away from Nash, and getting what little crowd there is in our section turned away from the court to stand in line for a picture is definitely taking attention away from the Moons.

The second an older lady with a Hurricanes shirt on starts coming up the concrete stairs, Noah takes control of the situation. He turns to me. "I've got this. You watch the game."

There's not much time left in the timeout, but for the remainder of it I watch Noah as he intercepts the lady—and anyone else—who had been coming toward us.

"Are you Noah Fox?" she asks, obviously starstruck.

"That would be me."

"And who is that behind you?" She's trying to see around Noah to get a look at me and Jaden. Jaden can join in if he wants, but I'm here for one person only..

Noah, smart as he is, turns her attention back on him. "Would you like a photo?"

Her eyes light up at his offer. "Oh, yes. That would be amazing."

As the woman gets her phone out, I turn back to the game where the teams are taking their places on the court once more.

Nothing, and no one, will take my focus off of Nash tonight.

*Chapter Nine*

NASH

"One, one," I call as the pass goes to Danica. Right before it hits her hands, I call louder. "Outside, outside!" I'm already in position, locked and loaded for my approach. If the set doesn't come to me, I'm the decoy in this play, so I'll be swinging at nothing trying to fool their defense.

I step forward, arms in front of me, gaining momentum as I swing my arms back behind me. Danica is sending it my way so it's go-time-show-time. On my last step I close my feet and swing my arms back in front of me, letting the power bring me up in the air.

"You've got two," Temi hollers. I try and move my swing to hit around the two blockers, but their middle has edged me out for my cross. I try and adjust at the last second to hit down the line, but as I'm landing, the ball comes right back down at me.

It's like slow motion. Me and the ball both coming down at the same time. Instinct kicks in and I shoot my arms out to try and pop it up from where it falls along the net—a drill we've done at least a million times. But I step on someone from the other team's foot and start to lose my balance. My body pitches to the side as the ball hits my arms, and instead of going over my head and behind me to the waiting passers, it shoots to the right, runs along the net, and then falls to the ground.

The whistle blows and the referee signals a point for the other team. Immediately, I'm incensed. "She's over the line! That's illegal." I'm yelling but I don't know if it's out of kinship with my team, or fury at the refs for not calling it. "That's our point." And we desperately need it. This game is tied up tight at eighteen all in the third set.

Daly comes up beside me as I'm about to start up again and puts a hand on my shoulder. "Those are international rules, babe." I go completely still. I swear my blood stops moving through my veins. The air stalls in my lungs.

"What?" I'm supposed to be a professional volleyball player, and I can't keep up with the rules of the country I'm currently playing in? What is wrong with me? How am I going to convince the entire country that they want this league to live on after this season when I'm making stupid mistakes like this?

"Overseas it's a fault if they're so far over that they're not touching the line, but here it's legal as long as they didn't interfere with your play."

"They did, though!" I gesture wildly at the net, speaking rapidly. "I stepped on them and couldn't get the ball up."

The referee's been listening to me this entire time, and to his credit he thinks I just need an explanation of the rules, when what I really need is a lobotomy to save myself from this embarrassment. "Miss, your attack was complete, the ball falling was part of their block. It's not interference."

He blows his whistle again.

Well, I guess that's the end of that. A strangled laugh escapes my throat, but I don't have much time to regroup before Coach calls me. "Green, sub out!" I jog to the sideline and touch hands with Lauren. "Where is your head tonight?"

"I don't know, Coach."

"I need you to sit on that bench and fucking find it."

"Yes, ma'am."

I take my seat next to Megan and grab my towel off the back of the chair to mop the sweat off my face. Of all the games to make that horrible mistake, it had to be tonight when we're at home.

…With Wyatt watching from the stands.

My eyes make their way to him, and I'm surprised to find a small line forming at the beginning of his row.

*What the…?*

I see Noah holding his hands up at a young man as if keeping him from scooting down the aisle. Noah signs a hat and takes a selfie with the kid, then the next person in line comes up. I look two seats over at Wyatt, whose eyes are locked onto the court. I watch him, on the edge of his seat, as he watches Temi winding up for the kill. Despite what's going on right next to him, it's like nothing else exists in the world. As if he can feel my gaze on him, his eyes swing from the court to me. I keep my face straight, not feeling even a small smile after my massive mistake, and he must see it because he gives me a thumbs up. I nod slightly in response and focus back on the game.

Because I have to focus on what's important—and right now that's my career, so Wyatt will have to take a back seat along with my feelings.

———

"I think the Hurricanes in the stands got more time on the jumbotron than we did," Megan huffs as she throws her clothes into her locker. Even though we won the game, the vibes are a little low because of all the attention Wyatt and the guys got. I knew they were coming so I expected them to get some attention, but basically live-streaming Noah signing hat after hat was a bit much. I can't blame Megan for her frustration even though my heart is begging me to go to bat for them. They were here to support me; they didn't ask to be the center of attention.

"It was nice of them to come," Temi says as she takes her court shoes off and begins working on her ankle braces.

"They knew exactly what they were doing," Megan spits.

*That's it.*

"I don't think making enemies of the other Houston athletes is a good way to start this season, do you?" The words come out sharp as a tack. My need to defend Wyatt is stronger than my need to smooth things over with her.

Megan looks properly scolded. "Geez, I just meant that the minimal amount of people who came were there to see us, and that's what they should have got."

"We've got to earn the right to a full crowd," says Temi.

"Exactly," I say in agreement. I'm not sure how we're going to manage it, but winning our first home game of the season is a good start.

*Chapter Ten*

WYATT

The Houston Moons end up winning their first home game thanks to their defensive specialist's digs and Temi's kills.

The crowd is on their feet to cheer. But it's not a roar… It's more like a purr.

I was so absorbed in the game, watching Nash's every move, I failed to realize that the stands never really filled in as the game went on. On the bright side, the ones who did show up made tons of noise. Hopefully, the Moons were so focused on their foes that they didn't notice a semi-empty house. Volleyball's still a new professional sport in this country, so more crowds will come.

Noah can see the crestfallen look on my face and puts a hand on my shoulder as we shuffle out of our row of folding chairs, "It's just the first game. I'm sure it'll fill up as the season goes on. Don't worry."

I look back at the court where the teams are gathering to head back in the locker room. "I know. It's just that this is everything to her."

I can tell by the tightness in her shoulders and the drawn

look on her face that the car ride home is going to be a terse one. I think that's partly why Nash and I get along so well. Athletes are a different breed. We aren't happy with just winning if we didn't play to the best of our abilities. If we felt like we were a hindrance to the team, the win doesn't matter.

We exit the stadium quickly. Jaden, Noah, and I pile into my truck and pull it around to wait for Nash.

I turn to Jaden. "Get in the back."

"Why?"

"You know Nash has to navigate." I can't listen to directions and drive for some reason.

"Oh, does she? Or do *you* need her to be shotgun?" A sly smile spreads over his face, but when I shoot him a look, he slides out of the truck and shimmies into the back with Noah.

When I spot her lugging her gym bag toward us, I hop out of the truck and take the bag from her. "Good game!" I say, wrapping her in a tight hug.

"The Moons? Yes. Me? No." She moves around the truck to hop up front while I toss her bag in the bed.

"Great game, Nash," echo Jaden and Noah from the back. They're squashed together even though this is a king cab.

"Thanks for coming, guys." She obviously doesn't want to continue this conversation with the guys here. If she wants to say more, she will during our post-game ritual. This was something we started sophomore year of college when our season coincided. After either one of us had a home game, we'd head to the local Culver's for a burger and a scoop of the flavor of the day.

I put the truck in drive and slowly pull away from the curb, steering us toward the city. "Where to first?"

"I'm starving," Nash chirps.

"Take us to my house first," Noah says. "Audrey waited for us to eat."

"Okay, dope."

We settle in for the drive back to downtown, but the quiet doesn't last long.

"So you're going to give me number fifteen's number, right?" Jaden says, the look on his face like a dog with a bone.

Nash and I groan in unison. She and I are on the same page, as usual. "Not a chance, Jaden." Nash leaves no room for possibility with that reply and I just chuckle.

When we pull up to Noah's house, the guys hop out and we wave to Audrey, who's standing at the front door waiting for them.

"'Night, guys! See you later!" Nash calls from the passenger window as Jaden and Noah let themselves in to Noah's house. She turns to me. "Thank God. I couldn't take another second of Jaden wanting me to play matchmaker. Like, no, I do not know what kind of dudes Temi is into and I won't be giving you her number."

"For real. The man has no off switch."

"He's kind of adorable, though."

I shake my head and turn the truck toward Whataburger.

Our game day tradition has always been a burger and fries. Here it's Whataburger, in Wisconsin it's Culver's. I'd never admit it to anyone here, but I think Culver's is better.

"So, how does it feel?" I ask, one hand slung casually over the wheel.

"Honestly, it's bittersweet. I got used to Rome, but it never truly felt like home," she sighs. "I would be a liar if I said I wasn't disappointed in the turnout tonight." She leans back in the seat, and she looks so small against the size of my truck, despite her long frame. Like the lack of fans in attendance was her fault, that drawing in the big crowds is somehow resting on her shoulders.

"I get that. I still kind of feel that way about Texas. There's fun stuff here, but it's no Wisco."

"Texas and Wisconsin are similar, if you really think about it. They both have a very specific type of culture and vibe," she says.

"Yeah, here it's cowboy hats, rodeos, BBQ, and country music. Wisconsin has beer, cheese, dairy cows, and the Butchers."

"At least Wisconsin respects volleyball. The stands at U.W. were packed for every home game. I was psyched to play here, but I can't ignore how empty the stands were tonight—and at the professional level," she says, dipping her head, trying to hide how disappointed she really is. "I just really want this to work. How are we supposed to build a league from scratch if we can't fill that little arena? If we can't get bodies in seats, why would they bother to put us on cable? How are we supposed to play for Houston knowing they canned their WNBA team after winning four back-to-back championships? It's just not friendly out here for women's sports."

I palm the silver chain around my neck, thinking. "Well, as long as you guys keep playing great, the people will come."

"From your mouth to the fans' ears."

# Chapter Eleven

NASH

I'm not one hundred percent sure Wyatt understands the sting of a quiet home game. Football always draws a crowd, and he's been able to play in two of the biggest football states in the country. Not just any football team, one of the oldest professional football teams whose stadium is entirely made up of season ticketholders. It's actually part of your Wisconsin legacy to be put on the waiting list for them before you're even born.

I'm trying not to let my sour mood seep into my favorite tradition, but it's a tall order tonight.

Whataburger's bumping since it's late on a Friday night, and one way or another, everyone ends up at Whataburger after midnight, apparently. I order a number one with everything on it, and Wyatt orders the same thing with a double patty. We get a chocolate shake to share and squeeze ourselves into a booth with our little orange order number tent sitting on the table. We have to sit offset from one another; our miles of legs not meant for regular people-sized tables.

"We used to steal the shit out of these in high school," I say, holding up the little plastic number card. "We put them on the dash of our cars." Wyatt laughs like I just told an inside joke. "What?" I ask incredulously.

"You say that literally every time we come here."

I gasp. "I do not!"

"It's cute. It's like you can't help it." A small smile splits my lips, and I look at Wyatt over the top of our shared shake. He's dressed nice—for him. He's one of the most casual guys I know, but tonight he's wearing a Dri-FIT Nike polo and tan joggers. His chest and arms bulge at the seams, and his hair is cropped close at the sides, but the length in the front folds over his forehead, pulling your line of sight to his crystal blue eyes. He's built like real Wisconsin corn stalk. Thick and huge. Like he was destined to either play lineman or throw around bales of hay.

I take a long sip from the chocolate shake they already served us and then hold it out for him. "What was up with all those people in the stands? It looked like Noah was directing traffic."

"I thought we were flying under the radar pretty well until they flashed a video of us on the big screen with the Hurricanes logo on it. Then every football fan in our section, plus a couple ones over, were coming up to us trying to get photos and signatures. Noah sacrificed himself so that I could watch the game." He takes his turn sipping the dessert.

"That's crazy," I say, but it's not very convincing. I don't want to admit that I'm jealous that they're the kind of athletes who get noticed. It's not Wyatt's fault that he plays the most profitable sport in the world. I guess I should have just been born a man. At my height I would have made a great football player. Too bad I fell in love with the feeling of flying through the air, hand making perfect contact with the ball as I snap my wrist on the follow through. There's a small silence between us, but I'm not going to break it with my envious thoughts, so I let it simmer.

It stays long enough that Wyatt taps his phone to wake the screen. I catch sight of his background photo. "Is that our pic from flag football the other week?"

He chuffs like he's been caught. "Yeah, it is. Why?" When I look at it again, I remember when Chrissy first sent it to me; when I saw the look on Wyatt's face as he stared down at me and not at the camera. The soft smile that, to an unknowing person, could look like more than friendship...

I bite at the inside of my cheek, thinking. The way the crowd cheered for them when they were shown on the jumbotron...Megan being so mad that they were the focus... What if we made their popularity work for us instead of against us? If he was there as a supportive boyfriend instead of a football player, would that—could that—benefit the Moons? And the attendance and recognition of us as athletes?

This is nuts. If we pretended to be together to bring fans to the games, everyone would see right through us. Not to mention, why would Wyatt want to fake date me? We kissed one time and never talked about it again. He probably isn't attracted to me, and the look in his eyes in that photo is platonic fondness and nothing else. Still...

I couldn't help but think about the people who were waiting patiently in line to get a chance to meet Noah. I want that. I *need* it. You'd think I was an investor with how much I cared, but I have more than money in this game. I have my whole life, and all my heart and my soul.

That's priceless.

Wyatt squints at me. "What are you thinking? You have your scheming face on."

"No, I don't."

"Come on, tell me. I'm your best friend."

I hesitate, then lean forward conspiratorially. "You would help me with anything, right?"

His eyebrows scrunch up. "I mean, theoretically, yes. Anything. As long as it's nothing illegal. But if it was illegal, maybe—if you really needed me."

"What about getting fans to our games?"

"I meant what I said: if you're there, people will come."

I lean back in the booth, arms crossed. "I'm not sure I believe that. I think I might need to take matters into my own hands."

"What do you mean?" Now he's officially suspicious.

"I mean, if the PVF can have even one fraction of the fans the NFL has, we'd be set."

"And how do you plan on doing that?" I look pointedly at him until he gets the hint. "Oh, you want me and the other players to be the draw."

"Actually, what do you think about being my boyfriend," I say, and he immediately chokes on his drink. He coughs, bumping his chest, trying to dispel the liquid. "My *fake* boyfriend," I quickly clarify as he takes a gasping breath. Wow, I didn't realize the mere thought of being with me was enough to end a man's life by choking to death.

"Jesus."

When the teenage employee steps up to our booth holding our food, we both jump like kids caught with their hands in the cookie jar.

"Thank you," we mutter, not making eye contact.

Once she's gone and our burgers are unwrapped, I decide it's time to get back to the topic at hand. "So, will you do it?"

"What makes you think we can fool everybody?"

"Please," I scoff, "Everything a girlfriend would know about you, I already know." I mean, yes, I was just doubting our ability to pull this off about three seconds ago, but he doesn't need to know that.

A grin splits his lips. "True."

I take a huge bite of my burger as we just stare at each other. Game days always leave me starving.

"What would the rules be?"

"What do you mean?"

"In the movies there are always rules for this sort of thing." He points his fry at me. "Like no kissing. At the very least, an end date when we call it off."

"The end of volleyball season?"

"That's only a few months away. How much could we accomplish by May?" He chews for a second while he thinks. "What about July? After my brother's wedding? You could be my plus one." Why are the tips of his ears pink right now? Is he embarrassed to be talking about this? Or is there something else going on?

"I'd love to visit your family, but how is that going to help my team?"

"We could each get two events. Like I could pick Henry's wedding and one other thing, and you could make both of your choices volleyball things."

I chew slowly and nod. Then quirk my brow, confused. "What's in it for you?"

"I may have already told Ma that you were my date." He fiddles with the lone fry in his hand.

"Wyatt!" I can't believe he would do that! But wait...aren't I pitching to him basically the same thing right now?

"She called me before the game and told me that she was going to set me up with someone and I panicked. I can't go to my own brother's wedding with a blind date. I didn't think you'd say no anyway. And it will help get my parents off my back. They won't worry about me so much if they think I have a girlfriend. You'll be saving me, really. Plus, if you're there, they won't want to talk so much about my leaving Green Bay."

"Remind me, why won't you tell them you punched Jared Clark?" Seems like a lot of this worrying could be fixed if he was honest with them.

He holds up his hands. "Whoa. There were no punches thrown. He pushed me and it immediately got broken up."

"Even better then. That just makes him look like more of an ass."

He shakes his head in disappointment. "You've been gone from Wisco too long if you don't know why. As long as he's the starting quarterback of the Green Bay Butchers, my lips are sealed."

I eye him curiously, not completely believing him. He waits me out.

"Okay. It's a deal. We'll start right now. Tomorrow, if anyone asks—we're dating. It's new, but obviously we've known each other a long time." Like this is going to be so easy.

"That's your plan?"

"Do you have a better one?" I cross my arms and wait. When he doesn't have a response, I continue, "That's what I thought. The Moons won't be hard. Temi knows our history, and everyone else is just getting to know me." I put the now-empty shake to my lips and slurp, trying to get more out and making tons of noise. "The Hurricanes will be harder." He's only been on the team for one season, but just like volleyball, spending all that time with each other primes them to get all up in your business.

"I don't think so." He raises his eyebrows at me, asking a

question without asking. "People want to believe in romance. If we show it to them, they'll believe it."

"I guess that's true."

"Two for you, two for me." I wipe the salt from my fries off my fingers on a napkin and then offer my hand to Wyatt over the table. "Deal?"

He takes my hand and shakes it. "Deal."

I may have just agreed to the death of me.

# Chapter Twelve

NASH

Warring emotions swirl within me as I step under the hot spray of the shower. I wet my hair, then lather it with shampoo.

On one hand I'm pissed at myself for how I played tonight, on the other hand I'm infatuated by the sight of Wyatt in the stands. I forgot how spoiled I was when I had him at all my home games at U.W. Every year that passes, my fondness for our college memories increase.

After I rinse the shampoo, I run the conditioner through my hair. I rinsed off in the locker room before we left, but I don't like to wash my hair there. I need my own toiletries. While the conditioner sits for a second, I look at all the products I've got lined up in the shower. Just a month and a half of living here and it looks like Ulta exploded. Razor, shaving cream, body oil, hair mask…Wyatt's body wash? I recognize the classic masculine five-in-one. He's been buying the same brand and scent since I met him in college. It's cool and clean and manly. I rinse out my hair, and the feeling of the conditioner running down my body has me reaching for my washcloth. I grab my regular vanilla and lavender body wash, but right before turning it over on the cloth, I pause. How nice would it be to go to bed smelling like him tonight? To get cozy under the covers and be wrapped up in the overwhelming scent of Wyatt. I wouldn't even have to find an excuse to steal a hoodie from him. He wouldn't suspect a thing.

I put my body wash down and pick his up. The front shows a bear with its claws out like it's taking a swipe at you in front of a snowy forest background. Typical man shit. I pour some onto the washcloth in my palm and rub it to a lather. I close my eyes as the fragrance mixes with the shower steam and coats my whole body. With my eyes closed and his scent surrounding me, I can almost imagine that this might be what it feels like to share a shower with him. If we were actually together, would we shower platonically? Both of us washing our hair at the same time. Taking turns standing under the spray. So comfortable with each other that we aren't fazed by nudity. It doesn't turn sexual every time because there are so many other opportunities for sex, which we make good use of…

*Well, this was a huge mistake.*

———

Even though I'm freshly dressed and still stuffed from my burger and fries, I lie in my bed staring at the ceiling fan as it spins.

Every time I close my eyes, all I see is me arguing about the center line penetration again. I play it over and over, looking at it from every angle. I don't know what that ref was smoking, but their foot obviously interfered with my play. I know I could have popped that ball back up.

*Doesn't matter in the States, though.*

*And I can't change the past.*

I roll over and hike my thigh up, trying to get comfortable.

I stare at the wall now.

My mind drifts toward Wyatt and the deal we just struck over burgers and fries. The way all good deals are made. It's crazy, isn't it? To think that not only could we pretend to be boyfriend and girlfriend, but that it may be enough to bring this team the recognition that it deserves? That Wyatt's presence alone will magically fill a stadium with people who, as of right now, have no idea we exist. I guess I'm just lucky that he lied to his mom and needed my help just as much as I needed his.

Wyatt, who has never told me no.

Wyatt, who kicks his friends out of the front seat because he knows I like to ride shotgun.

Wyatt, who towers over me with his dirty blonde hair and corded muscles.

Wyatt, who...is sleeping twenty feet from me. Who technically owns the bed I'm lying in wearing just my panties right now...

I need a glass of water.

I kick off the comforter and reach for an oversized t-shirt to pull over my head.

The house is dark, but not pitch black. Light from the streetlamps seep in through all the big windows, bathing the house in a warm glow, illuminating my path to the fridge.

I grab a cup out of the cabinet to the right and start filling it with water from the little dispenser.

"Nash–"

I jump at the voice, spilling the water all over the floor as the plastic cup clatters against the hardwood. I whip around, expecting a murderer.

"Oh my God, Wyatt. You scared the shit out of me." I grab the towel hanging from the oven handle and start mopping up the water.

"I'm sorry." Wyatt coughs into his hand and I remember that I'm not wearing any pants. Just my high-waisted bikini panties with cherries all over them. I bolt upright, drop the towel, and finish mopping the water up with my foot. "What are you doing up?"

I set the cup on the counter and lean against it, still not looking at him. "Couldn't sleep."

"I never did understand how you could drink a coffee right before a seven PM game."

I turn to face him, and my mind goes momentarily blank at the amount of skin I see. Athletic shorts hang loose around his waist, the soft light of the fridge emphasizing a very muscular stomach. "It's not the caffeine," I say finally. I could drink a gallon of coffee and go to bed no problem. "It's the game. I just keep replaying it in my head. Every stupid mistake I made tonight." I hold my hands up like I could grab a volleyball and start all over.

"Everyone has off nights."

I snort sarcastically. "Maybe players on teams with built-in fans do." I look right into his blue eyes knowing jealousy is plain as day on my face. He watches me right back. "But I don't."

"It's not like if you don't win the championship this year they'll cut the team."

"You don't know that." My voice rises. The restlessness

that spurred me out of bed is at its peak right now. "No one knows that," I say again, quieter. "I'm sorry. I didn't mean that. I'm just stressed. And tired–" Wyatt steps up and wraps his arms around me, hushing the negative thoughts rushing through my brain.

"Hey. The stadium was not empty. I was there." He puts his hand on the back of my head, holding me to him. "And I promise that I'll never let a home game be empty. I'll be at every single one, and if there's one I can't make, I'll send twenty Hurricanes in my place." I sniff against his bare chest. I think he's already taking his fake boyfriend duties too seriously. Or maybe that's just him being my best friend.

"Thank you." I lean back to look up at him. There's not many people I have to physically look up to. I love how being wrapped up in him makes me feel small. My fingers move against his bare chest of their own accord…

Alarm bells ring in my head.

I step back. "Thank you," I start, "For being there for me." I put another step of space between us so I can breathe without feeling the warmth emanating from him. "I'm so lucky to have you as my best friend." That is probably unnecessary to say, but I need to remind myself that we are faking it. Because right now, under the cover of night, together in his kitchen, it would be too easy to convince myself that this is more.

I watch as he rolls his lips together. "You're welcome."

I start backing out of the kitchen. "I should try and get some sleep."

His left hand holds onto the edge of his shorts in a tight grip. "Yeah, you should."

I turn and head up the stairs. For some reason I worry about my pace. I don't want to go too slow because I'm still only panty clad, but I don't want to make it look like I'm literally running away from him. I'm not. I'm running away from the heat his huge hand on the back of my head stirred in my belly.

The whole walk of shame up the stairs I say over and over again: This is what's best for the team. That's all.

# Chapter Thirteen

## WYATT

I laid awake a long time last night, images of Nash in just my t-shirt and her panties danced in my head relentlessly. Something else tugged on my mind that I can't quite put my finger on. Something that was different.

This morning, I'm more in the mindset of kicking myself in the butt for agreeing to let her move in with me. Even though it's not permanent and we're best friends—it's torture. Seeing her like she was last night, or how she is right now as she comes down the stairs to the kitchen—with pants on this time, thank fuck—all sleep rumpled and yawning. I'm sure she didn't sleep well either given how worked up she was over their game.

"Good morning," I say, and she jumps like she didn't even know I was there. Stealth is not an easy feat at my size.

"Oh, good morning."

"Did you sleep well?" In response, she just takes a coffee mug out of the cabinet and picks the biggest coffee pod off the little rack. "I'll take that as a no."

Now that she's just on the other side of the counter from

me, I'm reminded of the thing that was different about her last night that I couldn't quite place. We sit in silence as the coffee machine whirs to life and fills her cup. Without her miles of long legs on display, I can finally think about what it was about her last night and this morning that's different. The smell of coffee mingles with something else, and then it hits me. "Why do you smell like me?"

She goes ramrod straight. "What do you mean," she asks, but she's looking at her coffee.

"You smell like my body wash. I just figured it out."

She turns to me, clutching the mug like it's her lifeline. Her eyes meet mine, then the floor, then her mug, then me again, before she says, "Uhhh…"

"I just thought there was something different about you and I couldn't put my finger on it until you walked past me just now."

"I, uh–needed it." She nods like she's agreeing with herself. "I ran out of mine, and I didn't realize it. You have a spare one of yours in my bathroom, so I just used it. Sorry."

"Don't be sorry." It feels good as fuck to smell myself on her even though it's disappointing that I didn't have anything to do with it, and she didn't get it from sharing a shower with me. "That's what it's there for?"

Nash's nose scrunches a little at my response. "You have a lot of women showering in there?"

I nearly hop off my barstool. "No!" I settle myself back down. "I mean, no. I don't. But it's the guest room, so there should be extra supplies in there for any guest who might need it." Why am I always putting my foot in my mouth around her? I used to know how to be a normal person.

She snorts into her mug like she finds my distress amusing. "Well, mystery solved. I'm going to get dressed now."

———

Thank God Nash is out of the house most of the rest of the weekend with Temi because I spend the entire time barely paying attention to anything. My mind completely on my new deal with Nash.

So I'm going to fake date a woman I really have a thing for to bring attention to her professional volleyball team, which she loves more than anything. What could possibly go wrong?

Actually, scratch that. Half my mind is on my new arrangement with Nash. The other half is using all its might to not picture Nash in my kitchen in *my* t-shirt and her panties. Maybe I was wrong about living together. Maybe I can't do it, and it won't be like it was when she just stayed a long weekend. At least then there was an end to our arrangement.

Even if that's true, what am I supposed to do now? Kick her out?

I sit at my eat-in breakfast bar, thankful Nash already left for practice, and scroll through my phone while I polish off the last of my protein shake. It tastes like shit today. I miss the cafeteria at the Hurricanes compound. I miss Ma's cooking, too. I would kill for a tater tot casserole on a wintery day like today. My eyes refocus from my food-induced daydream when they catch Jared Clark's name in the headline of an ESPN article. I skim it, my empty shake in the other hand.

CLARK: I wasn't my best, but a bad season for me is a good season for most quarterbacks.

I snort at his comment. *What a dick.*

I don't like to talk about why I left Green Bay… Nash is the only one who knows the truth. The day it got physical between us, I knew I had to tell her because I couldn't stand to play under Clark for a second longer. He's three-hundred percent competitive. He's a damn drama queen prone to playing hero ball. He chokes in the NFC championship game every year. He's the opposite of everything I believe myself to be as a football player—steady, centered, humble, and unflappable. All of that led to a shoving match in the locker room at the end of my last season. He shoved me first, but of course it doesn't matter. He's QB1 and I'm just a defensive lineman. I'm lucky the rest of the team separated us before a punch could be thrown.

I love Wisconsin, but the entire state is dedicated to the Butchers. I'm not sure if it's just state pride or if it's because they're the only "fan-owned" team in the league, but everywhere you go people talk about that week's game. The majority of them keep their singular share of the team over their fireplace mantel like a prized family heirloom. He can do no wrong in their minds. He's the family patriarch. He's a hero. Who was I? A young kid from a farm in the middle of nowhere. To say that I didn't think his football skills made up for his shitty personality? The last thing I wanted to do was kick the hornets' nest on my rookie contract. Had I said one negative thing about Jared Clark, I very well might not have played another season in the NFL.

So I kept my mouth shut. I looked the other way when Jared wanted to practice his own hand signals with the receivers instead of the ones Coach came up with. I ignored the way he blamed the entire offense when a play didn't go the way he thought it should. I never said anything to him on the sidelines when he would come and pout during games we lost. I didn't judge him for his lone wolf mentality. Even though I think he's the reason we haven't been to another

Super Bowl—I still said nothing. I simply let him be, while quietly trying to soothe the disappointed child inside me who had his poster hung on the wall and dressed up as him six Halloweens in a row.

When Coach called me into his office and told me to pack my bags for Texas, I didn't argue, I didn't fight. I took my ticket out of there and didn't tell a soul about what had really happened. Some days I feel strong, and I think I can shoulder this weight like Atlas holding up the heavens for all eternity, but sometimes I look around and realize no one else understands. No one understands why a farm boy from Wisconsin left his dream team without a fight. I think what it boiled down to was that I would rather everyone continue living their dreams than shatter them with what is most likely just my opinion.

I close the app on my phone and roll my eyes. The dude has an ego the size of Texas. I don't need to see anything else.

*Shit.* I jump up when I see the time. I'm already late to meet Noah and Jaden at the gym. I shove Clark into my mental box with all the other shit and lock it down tight.

Hm, that thing is probably getting pretty full.

## Chapter Fourteen

NASH

"So, you guys are together?" Simin asks as we stretch, getting ready for another killer practice. It felt good to win our first home game, but it's a long season, and we need to be prepared for anything.

"We are," I say, putting my right foot against my left leg and leaning over it. "Wyatt is my boyfriend." It hurts my stomach to say that when this is all fake, and I want so badly for it to be true.

"Since when?" Temi eyes me from her side stretch. She's the one I knew would be the hardest to convince. When we met in Italy, the kiss was still fresh on my skin, and I confided in her quickly.

"It's recent," I say, avoiding saying anything specific.

"But what about…" she starts.

I switch legs. "We were out for our usual burgers after the game last Friday and we finally talked about the kiss."

"What kiss?" Simin asks, confused.

"The kiss they shared before she left to play volleyball in Rome," Temi fills her in.

"Right," I say, putting both legs out in front of me and folding over them. I talk with my face almost touching my legs, which makes lying easier. "I said that I felt something, but when he didn't mention it ever again, I thought he felt nothing, and he said that he thought the same about me. Once we established that that wasn't the case for either of us...." I pause here and let them fill in whatever they want to think happened. I decided on this story because it seems best to stick as close to the truth as possible.

"Wow, you guys are horrible communicators." Simin laughs at the stubbornness of it all while she stretches her shoulder out.

"We're working on it." By lying to everyone else, too. Coach blows her whistle, and we all stand to do moving warmups. We line up at the base line and wait our turn to skip to the net and back. "It's perfect timing, too, because in two weeks it's the NFL Honors and Wyatt is getting the award for most sacks."

"That will be so exciting and glamorous," Simin exclaims, then launches up into a one-legged skip leaving me and Temi behind at the line.

Temi smiles at me and it makes my throat burn with worry. "I'm really happy for you guys."

"Thank you." I'm not sure what else I can say without my conscience taking over my body and spilling all the gory details. I imagine saying it out loud: *it's all fake.* Then Temi would look at me, disappointed, not only for lying, but for stringing Wyatt along. This is too much to ask of a best friend —both her and him. The NFL Honors will be on national TV. Everyone will see us together and it will be a hell of a lot to unravel. But this is something I have to do. If I don't try absolutely everything to get this volleyball league up and off the ground, I'll regret it for the rest of my life. Obviously, they've hired a staff, but just like volleyball is a team sport, this is an all-hands-on-deck situation.

Coach's whistle blows again, knocking me out of my spiraling thoughts and making me realize it's my turn. I almost held up the line. That's no way to get to a championship game. Worrying about the future on the sideline —especially when it's a future I can still change.

# Chapter Fifteen

## WYATT

The NFL Honors are always hosted in the same city as the Super Bowl. I'm a little pissed to be in Dallas for the awards show when we could have been here for the game if the Hurricanes hadn't blown it in the playoffs. But I'm also relieved that I'm here with Nash. I guess I'm lucky she wanted to make this her first event of our deal so I don't have to fly solo.

The drive up here was nice. It gave Nash and me some time to go over the plan for tonight. I think she felt guilty about hijacking my speech, but I would have mentioned her even if we weren't faking a relationship. Slipping in the Moons will be easy.

What won't be easy is hauling all this luggage from my truck into the hotel. When I pull the third bag out, I have to say *something*. "You know we're only here for one night, right?"

Nash looks around like she's trying to find the answer to my obvious question. "I know."

"Then why do you have ten suitcases?"

"There's only three bags! And my dress takes up one on its own!" She cries. "Men never understand the importance of overpacking." She looks pointedly at my suit in its dry cleaner bag and my single backpack.

We manage to shuffle all our shit into the lobby to check in. The hotel has gigantic chandeliers, and the smell of BBQ wafts through from the in-house restaurant. I make a mental note to check that out before the event. They never serve enough food at those fancy places. I'd have to eat ten of those fancy event dinners to feel anything.

The receptionist, a middle-aged woman with heavy makeup and dark hair, greets us as we walk up. "Howdy, welcome to Hotel De Armas. Can I get your name to check you in, hun?"

I step up to the counter. "Wyatt Vandergriff."

Her extra-long nails click clack on the keys as she types. "Okay, I see you right here. Perfect." She reaches for a key card and a pen, smacking her gum as she smiles at Nash over my shoulder. "Here you are, hun. That's room 313; you're going to want to take the Aggie hallway to the Longhorn elevator and go up to floor three."

My stomach drops to my balls. "One room?"

"Yes, sir. The NFL booked one king-size room for those in attendance. I'm sure they assumed any plus one was a partner? Unless otherwise specified." She looks back at Nash, carrying her long dress bag. She's smiling at me because for all intents and purposes, we're together. We look like a couple; we are supposed to be a couple. I did not consider what that might entail when it comes to sleeping arrangements. The thought makes my face heat. I want people to look at her and think we're together, and for our plan, that is important, but for some reason it makes my stomach flip. I chance a glance at Nash, and she just shrugs her shoulders.

I take the card from her outstretched claws. "Thank you," I glance at her nametag, "Helen."

"You're welcome, hun. Ya'll enjoy your stay."

We gather our stuff and turn to walk away. As soon as we're a couple steps out of hearing range, I say, "I'm so sorry. I can take you to another hotel and pay for your room there if you want. I had no idea this was one room, I swear."

She laughs and puts a hand on my arm. "Relax, Wyatt. We're already sharing your house. We can share a room. There are no secrets between us."

I laugh, but it comes out breathy and nervous. "Totally. Not weird at all."

———

Sharing a room with the woman you're fake dating, but harboring real feelings for, is not as fun as it sounds. I got about three minutes in the bathroom before she was kicking me out, claiming she needed the entire two hours we have to get ready. She took her toiletries, a hair weapon of some kind, the dress bag, and many other odds and ends in there with her. Leaving me to lie on the king-size bed and flip through the cable channels. After getting sucked into the basketball game that was on, I'm shocked when I notice how much time has passed.

I grab my suit out of the bag and start to get dressed. I'm going to have to get in that bathroom to fix my hair one way or another. I could do it at the very last second, but hopefully Nash doesn't make me wait until then.

I'm tying the laces on my fancy shoes when the bathroom

door opens. I'm immediately hit with a tsunami of smells from all the products.

Then I see Nash and I forget how to speak.

"Huh. W-wow. You look–" I put my arm behind my head trying to recover my grasp on the English language. "Beautiful."

She runs her hands down her body, fingers dancing over black sequins that hug tight to her hips, and my eyes follow down, down. Until they stop at the top of the slit that starts terrifyingly high and reveals miles and miles of tanned leg. *Shit.*

"Is it nice enough?" she asks. Hearing the insecurity in her voice makes me want to lavish her with praise. "It was hard to find something on such short notice. I can't exactly wear something off the rack with my height."

"It's perfect. Really, Nash. You look gorgeous. I'm not even going to have to do anything tonight. Once the camera gets a load of you, everyone will be talking about the PVF."

Her cheeks burn a beautiful pink as she ducks to grab her shoes off the floor. "Will you help me with these? It's a bit hard to lean over in this dress."

I move toward her and take the heels out of her hands, then I get on one knee in front of her to bring her bare foot up to my leg to balance. I slip the silvery heel over her foot and begin working the tiny buckle. The sting of her heel pushing into my thigh is a torturous pleasure. When I clasp the other one, I make the grave mistake of looking up at her, hands still circling her ankle. Our eyes meet over miles of smooth legs as time marches on with the two of us frozen just like that. Letting go of her is like trying to release a live wire. My eyes are glued to her face, but she averts hers, looking for her clutch.

Yeah, it's going to be a long, long night.

# Chapter Sixteen

## NASH

I'm quaking in my silver strappy heels as our driver gets closer to the theater where the honors are being hosted—from the chill or the nerves, I can't tell. I keep my hands folded in my lap to hide their shake, and to keep from reaching out to touch the lapels of Wyatt's all-black suit. His hair is perfectly mussed, and the cologne he's wearing fills the car with the heady scent of man. I look out the window of the backseat as we pass through downtown Dallas so I don't have to make direct eye contact with Wyatt. Reunion Tower passes by, and I wonder why I can't shake these tittering feelings. I haven't had any problems with my stupid heart since our kiss, and now I can't seem to calm the butterflies in my stomach. Was it just easier when we were continents apart? Did the distance allow me to focus on our friendship and not the physical spark between us? Maybe it feels stronger now because of my lengthy absence.

"So," Wyatt starts, and I jump, "we should probably hold hands."

*How does he know?*

My eyes go wide. "Now?"

"When we walk the red carpet." He side eyes me like I'm a criminal giving a cop the thousand-yard stare.

"Oh. Right."

"At least some kind of formal hand position, like I'm escorting you."

My breathing is shallow and feels like there's nothing in my lungs. Like they're starving for oxygen. "That would make sense. I mean, I wouldn't want to trip or anything." My eyes are everywhere—on his face, out the window, at the driver, at my manicure. I can't settle them or my mind. My brain is showing flashes of me falling on my face, my heels too much for my giraffe-like frame.

Wyatt takes my hand and holds it in his on the seat between us. "Hey," he soothes. "It's going to be okay. You look beautiful. You're a professional athlete, too, and you belong here. I will not let you fall in front of everyone."

I take a deep breath. "Okay."

"Do you trust me?"

"I do." More than anyone.

We arrive at the drop-off for the theater way too soon for my liking. I need another four-hour car ride to calm my nerves. But in seconds my door is being whipped open and an event employee holds out his hand to help me from the car. I take it and immediately look around for Wyatt. I don't trust myself to stand on my own for one second. He's there so quickly, the gentleman basically puts my hand right in to Wyatt's.

He looks at me, and in his eyes I see readiness. I try to reflect that in mine when I give him a slight nod. He looks forward and plasters on his best interview smile as we move into the masses. Behind the scenes is like a beehive absolutely buzzing with people going hither and tither. People dressed in all black speak into headsets. Other athletes and their partners stand all around us waiting for their turn.

When it's our time to walk the red carpet, a woman comes up to us. "What are your names? For the cameras."

"Wyatt Vandergriff and Nash Green." She nods at Wyatt, and we move forward.

The lady calls our name to the photographers as we position ourselves in front of the custom backdrop. Instantly the flashes start. The photographers are calling, "Wyatt!" Trying to get him to look their way.

I'm smiling so hard my cheeks hurt. The flashes from the cameras put spots in my vision. I have no idea how long we stand there. Eons, probably. The only thing keeping me standing, as I knew it would, is Wyatt's arm tightly clutched in my hands.

He shifts me forward to put an arm around my back. I let my other hand dangle limply for a second before putting it on his chest. "Is this okay?"

"More than okay." His voice is husky, and the lights are still blinding, but I can't hear the call of the photographers anymore. I can only see the ocean in the blue eyes staring back at me.

Wyatt's eyes catch the next guests moving in behind us, signaling our time to leave. He moves me back to his side, holding his arm out for me to take once again, and we move farther down the carpet where interviewers are vying for attention.

Wyatt answers all the questions lobbed at him with grace.

"Out of these three great players, who would you cut, start, and bench?" one asks.

"Do you think athletes or rappers have better jewelry?" follows the other.

We move through them, trying not to step on any landmines. Most of the reporters ignore me, like I'm just arm candy. Which is fine by me, even though I knew exactly who I would have started, cut, and benched.

Finally, *finally,* we reach the end of the road—er, the carpet—and are ushered inside to find our seats.

One hurdle cleared, countless more to come.

# Chapter Seventeen

## WYATT

Every five steps someone stops us to say hello, making it feel like it takes one-million years to get to our seats. My dress shoes are squeezing the life out of my feet, and I'm damn ready to sit down.

We greet player after player, coaches, and wives. The onslaught does not stop until we are literally at the entrance to our row. I guide Nash ahead of me with a hand on her lower back and we collapse into our seats.

"I think the hard part is over," I whisper to her, so close I can smell the sweet scent of the shampoo she uses. "Now we just have to sit here and listen."

"Until it's your turn," she says.

I nod. "Then it's show time."

She crinkles her brow at me, giving me a look. "What's that supposed to mean."

I tilt my head like a curious puppy hearing a funny noise. Coming with me to this event was her idea. "The whole reason you're here—my speech." I realize how that sounds and sputter, "I mean, I would want you here no matter what. I'm so glad you're here. I would have thanked you in my speech anyway. It's just better that you're with me."

*Everything is better when you're with me.*

A small smile splits her glossy lips, and I have to hold onto the armrest of my chair to keep from launching myself at her and giving us a redo on our kiss. "What are best friends for?" she says, not realizing it's the lightning bolt needed to kill my inner thoughts. I suck in a deep breath, trying to calm my racing heart.

Finally, the lights dim.

The NFL Honors is not like the Emmys or the Grammys. Lady Gaga isn't here in a meat dress to pump up the party, and no one is going to interrupt the MVP winner's speech. Overall, the vibe reminds me of trying not to fall asleep in a pew on Sunday morning growing up. Nash and I sit shoulder to shoulder, and I'm hyperaware of her presence. I thought it would go away after a couple weeks of her being permanently home, but it's not dissipated one bit. I think it's my new normal.

We listen to variations of the same speech as everyone who wins thanks their wife and their parents and their teams. After we make it through the bulk of the speeches, it's time to start fully paying attention again.

Unlike MVP, where the winner doesn't know if they've won until their name gets called, the Sack Leader Award automatically goes to whoever had the most sacks on the quarterback during the season—which was me.

"With a total of eighteen-and-a-half sacks and twenty-seven quarterback hits, the winner of this year's Deacon Jones Sack Leader Award is..." The emcee pulls a card out of a small envelope and reads, "Wyatt Vandergriff, Houston Hurricanes."

The crowd cheers politely as I rise and move through the

aisle toward the stage. I shake hands with the previous year's winner as he hands me the trophy. It's heavy and the metal feels cold in my hands. I turn toward the microphone and look out over the crowd as best I can with the stage lights blinding me.

"Thank you," I clear my throat. "It's an honor to receive this award. First, I would like to thank my coaches and my team. This would not be possible without the rest of the defense. They make my job easier and my days more fun. I'd like to thank my parents who instilled their farmer's work ethic in me. And lastly," my eyes search the audience for Nash, "I would like to thank my girlfriend, Nash. As a fellow athlete, you're able to support me in a way no one else can, and as a member of the inaugural Houston Moons women's professional volleyball team, you inspire me. It was brave of you to leave your family and play overseas, and it shows your courage to return and play in an unproven league. I know that you will soar to great heights here, and I think if you wanted to, it would be possible for you to brighten the stars on your way to hang the moon. I look forward to many more years together." I hoist the trophy over my head in salute. "Thank you."

When Nash throws her arms around me as I sit back in my seat, I can't help but feel like that speech felt a little too true.

# Chapter Eighteen

## NASH

I excuse myself to the ladies' room so I can check if I accidentally ruined my mascara with the rogue tear that slipped loose during Wyatt's speech. Something about seeing your best friend in the whole world say such amazing things about you in front of America… It's got me feeling some type of way. But it's literally what I asked him to do. Part of our deal was that he go up there and announce that he was my boyfriend. He was just acting the doting partner like he was supposed to. He's not one to break a promise, either.

I'm washing my hands when a small voice pipes up next to me. "Miss Nash?"

I turn, shaking the water off my hands before reaching for a paper towel, and see a girl, probably around eight, with a sparkly periwinkle dress on and silver Mary Janes. Her hands are clasped nervously in front of her. "That's me." My smile is friendly.

"You play volleyball?" she asks.

"Yes, I do. I've been playing since I was about your age." Her eyes light up.

"I want to be a volleyball player when I grow up. I want to be an Olympian!"

I throw my damp paper towel away and put my hands on my knees. "I have teammates who are Olympic gold medalists, and they wanted the same thing."

"Eliza…" Her mom emerges from a stall dressed in silver taffeta. "Don't bother this nice woman."

I laugh. "Oh, it's no bother. It's a pleasure to talk to a future Olympian." I wink at the girl, and she practically vibrates with excitement. "If you can ever make it to a game, I'll sign anything you want, and I'm sure my teammates will, too." Eliza now clings to her mother's dress, tugging on the fistful of it she has.

"Mommy, we have to go."

I smile at her mother, hoping to display my platitudes for having started this up. Hopefully this isn't a 'puppy for Christmas' situation where she won't talk about anything else for months on end until her parents finally give in. But hey, my goal is to fill the stands even if that means I have to do it one chair at a time.

I slowly back toward the door. "So nice to meet ya'll."

I take a big breath when I'm on the other side, looking at my feet, trying to find my balance again. I'm not great at interacting with people like that, but if I want the PVF to be as big as the NFL, I'm going to have to get good at it.

"Tough time?" Wyatt chuckles and my head snaps up. He hands me a champagne flute, "Drink up. I found a photo booth."

He holds his other hand out for me, and I take it. It feels so natural to be led through the crowd, his hand rough in mine. In college he always took me through the packed bars just like this. All around us, guests are dressed in their formal attire as they stand around cocktail tables or wander toward the bar. Small appetizers are passed around, and Wyatt and I make eye contact, both knowing we will end up with fast food after this, the portions they provide too measly.

We come up to the photo booth. There's a table stacked with props—silly hats, huge sunglasses, and feather boas, but we walk right past them.

"Cute one, Charlie's Angels, number one, and awkward prom?" I ask, ticking each pose off on a finger as I confirm our traditional photo booth pics.

"You know it." He straightens his tie as I move to step into the booth. I smoosh myself into the far side. My bottom barely resting on the smallest edge of the seat. When Wyatt steps into the booth, the entire area is immediately filled with his cologne. Despite my squeezing, he can barely fit one thick thigh on the tiny seat. "Tight fit," I say, trying to make light of the fact that I can feel just how solid his thigh is, like cement next to me. I'm puzzled by the blush that creeps up his ears.

"Now," the guy manning the station pops in, breaking up whatever the hell that was. "You're going to want to push the button when you're ready to start. It will flash a count down before each picture. Four pictures in total." Little does he know, we're pros, so instructions aren't necessary.

The countdown starts and we move to our first position. The camera flashes. We quickly move to pose number two: Charlie's Angels. A classic.

Camera flashes and we're off again. Both of us hold one hand up with the 'number one' finger sign and close one eye in a still wink, a la Ricky Bobby from *Talladega Nights,* our favorite funny movie.

The camera flashes. We're one shot away from orchestrating a perfect photo strip. We normally do the awkward prom pose standing up. I open my mouth to say so as the clock ticks down, but all that comes out is a yelp as Wyatt pulls me onto his lap. I watch on the little screen as he smiles with his arms wrapped around my waist.

When it's over, we start untangling to climb out. I can't help but say something. "That was new."

He shrugs, but he's smiling. "Thought we could change it up a bit."

We've done these poses what feels like countless times, but tonight it feels different. It feels like we aren't standing in a downtown Dallas theater, but on the edge of a cliff, and his arms are the only thing keeping us from tumbling down.

We move to the side to get our physical and digital copy of the photos. When the guy hands it to me, I can't help the grin that spreads across my face.

"These might be our best ones yet." I laugh, the strip in my hand.

He takes it from me and puts it in his pocket. "Let's go find some of those little pieces of toast," he says, taking my hand again.

"Bruschetta" I say pointedly.

"Tomato, potato." He waves me away. "They're too small no matter what they're called."

He can never remember the word, and I never want him to.

We stand around a tiny cocktail table covered in black tablecloths and eat the little appetizers. A player I don't recognize steps up behind Wyatt, tapping him on the shoulder to get his attention. As Wyatt turns to greet the man, I take him in. Red hair cropped short to his skull, full beard (also red), and hands covered in tattoos that I can also see creeping up his neck.

"What's up, man?" He claps Wyatt's back.

"Nothing much," he responds as if we weren't just on television.

"Congrats on the award. Well deserved. I know our quarterback hates playing you guys."

"Thanks, man." He gestures toward me. "Have you met my girlfriend Nash?"

"Can't say that I have." He holds a tatted hand out to me. "Adam…nice to meet you."

I take his hand. "Likewise, Adam."

Another guy comes up to us and greets Wyatt, pulling him away from our conversation.

"You play volleyball?"

"I do. Wyatt and I met in college when I played at U.W."

"And what are you up to now?" I don't know if he meant for this to come off weird, like I *couldn't* still be playing, but it rubs me the wrong way.

"Still playing volleyball." I nod slowly, like *what a weird question*. Did this guy not pay a lick of attention to Wyatt's speech less than a half hour ago where he specifically mentioned that I play volleyball?

"Oh," he looks genuinely shocked to hear this. "That's great. I didn't realize that women still played once they finished college."

Wyatt is finished with his conversation with the other guy and then returns to our conversation, thankfully. "What's up?"

This guy and Wyatt are obviously friends, and I don't want him to get stuck with his foot in his mouth, so despite my initial ick, I decide not to say anything to Wyatt. "We were just talking about the new women's volleyball league."

Wyatt's eyes light up. "Isn't it so cool?" This question is directed at Adam, but it's apparently rhetorical as Wyatt continues, "After all this time, finally, ladies can play stateside."

Adam recovers quickly. "That's so great. Can't wait to see it on TV."

"It's only streaming live on YouTube right now, but..." Wyatt crosses his fingers, "hopefully in the future they will be on cable."

"I'll tune in for sure!" He points to the near-empty drink in his hand. "I'm going to grab another. You guys good?"

We both nod and Adam walks off throwing a "great to see you" over his shoulder as he goes.

I don't think Adam is an asshole, I think he was just uninformed on the goings on of professional volleyball. Hell, maybe *any* women's sport? If I'm going to take it upon myself to make sure this league is a success, then I guess it's my job to inform men like Adam? He lives a life where the whole world is obsessed with his sport. He can sneeze and hit a football fan anywhere he goes. It's been this way long before he was even born. So I have a chance to make volleyball the same.

"What's the plan now?"

"Did we check all the necessary boxes?" Get the award, make the speech, shake hands, hit the passed appetizers, perfect photobooth shoot... I think so.

"Yup." Thank God.

"Are you hungry?"

"Of course." He holds his hand out to me. "Let's get out of here."

As Wyatt leads me through the thinning crowd toward the valet stand, I take in the last of the glitz and the glamour around us. My feet are throbbing from these heels, and my hair hurts from being pinned. As fun as it was to get all dressed up tonight, I think I like Wyatt better at home on the couch in his usual athletic clothes. He looks edible in his tailored tux, but I know it's not him. The confidence he carries himself with here is practiced; whereas, at home, it comes more naturally to him.

Then it hits me. We're not going back to our home tonight.

We're going back to a hotel room with only one bed.

# Chapter Nineteen

## WYATT

"You'd better tip him big," Nash says as we get out of the car.

"Yeah, I'm getting it for him," I reply, digging through my suit pants for my wallet.

"Just the tip?" she starts, and I might be exhausted from a long night, but I still meet her call and refrain.

"Just for a second."

"Just to see how it feels." She finishes, and we smile at each other like buffoons. I basically throw some cash at the driver who was kind enough to take us through a drive-thru before ushering us back here.

We walk arm in arm into the hotel, my other hand loaded down with the Taco Bell bag filled to the brim with goodies. I don't know whose idea it was to feed a theater full of football players finger foods, but they should be fired.

It doesn't hit me until the elevator is already ascending toward our floor that we are about to return to a hotel room that's going to be uncomfortably tight. Nash and I have never shared a bed. There has always been a couch for me to crash on.

We pad our way down the long, carpeted hallway, quiet in the way that you have to be when you're coming back to your room really late and you're trying not to wake anyone up.

As I let us in the room, I decide to cut it off at the head. "I'll sleep on the floor tonight. It was my fault we didn't get two rooms, or at least two beds."

"We can share the bed. You shouldn't have to sleep on the floor on your award night." She sits on the edge of said bed and starts to take her jewelry off.

"No, I'll be fine. It's no big deal."

"We've been friends forever, it's not weird," she insists, patting the bed next to her.

And I am a weak, weak man. "If you're sure. You can take it back any time tonight and kick me out."

"I'm sure." She stands and spins around so her back faces me. "Now, help me out of this dress."

I am cursed. That's the only explanation for how I got myself into this situation. I'm finally hearing words fall from her lips that I've always wanted to hear, and she thinks everything I said about her tonight is fake because this relationship is fake. God is trying to smite me.

I take the delicate zipper in my hand and slowly trail it down the dress. The bare skin revealing itself inch by decimating inch. It goes on for miles.

She's not wearing anything underneath it, either. I bite down on my lip to keep my breath from brushing over her bare skin. She holds the front of the dress to her breasts and steps away from me. "Thank you." And she's gone. Back in the bathroom.

I hear the shower turn on and I give myself a second to stand there and calm myself. I'm about to lie next to her all night. I need to get my body under control before she comes out. It's rude to pitch a tent next to your best friend. Who you're fake dating. Alone in a hotel room. With one bed.

By the time I have everything calmed down and I've laid out our burritos to eat, she comes out of the bathroom wearing tiny shorts and another shirt she stole from me. I duck into the bathroom as quickly as possible and splash cold water on my face, considering even a cold shower.

I can do this. It's just like every other time Nash and I have ever hung out as friends. Hopefully, I won't even be conscious in bed because we are supposed to be sleeping. I change, carefully putting my suit back on its hanger. Luckily, I brought a pair of basketball shorts comfortable enough to sleep in; otherwise, I would have been in just my boxer-briefs. I contemplate taking a really long time in here to avoid facing Nash again, but I decide it's not worth eating soggy burritos over.

When I step hesitantly out of the bathroom, Nash is already cross-legged on the bed with a Burrito Supreme in one hand and the TV remote in the other. She flips the channels so quickly I don't know how she even knows what's on. "I saved you all the Fire sauces." She stops to push them to my side, and instantly sounds of carnal pleasure come blasting from the TV. "Oh my God," she screeches, lunging for the remote and fumbling it trying to change the channel. I watch in disbelief as a young couple is naked on a bed together. *Holy shit*, it's one of those soft-core porn channels that you can rent at a hotel.

Finally, she flips the channel to a sports talk show and heaves a sigh of relief. She looks at me, cheeks flushed with embarrassment. "Someone before us must have paid for it." The pitch of her voice goes up at the end of the sentence, making it sound like a question.

I lift one brow at her in mock accusation. "Oh, really? The porn isn't yours?"

"Stop! You know I wouldn't–"

"Were you holding it for a friend?" I tease.

She throws a Mild sauce at me, and it hits me in the chest. "Wyatt!" she scolds, but it's full of giggles. "It was an accident."

I hold my hands up in surrender. "Okay, okay. I believe you. I just want to eat my Cheesy Gordita Crunch in peace."

We scarf down our Taco Bell while the random broadcaster on TV talks about the latest hockey game. I think the exhaustion from the day has finally hit us now that our bellies are full of massive amounts of Nacho Fries. When we're done, I collect all our trash back in the bag and shove it unceremoniously into the tiny hotel room trashcan. That was a nice break from thinking about sharing a bed with her, but now it's time to face the music.

I excuse myself to the bathroom once more to brush and floss, and when I come back out, Nash is already lying on her side scrolling through her phone. I lift the sheets and slide in next to her and lie on my back, staring at the ceiling.

"Thanks," she says quietly, like if she spoke too loud, it would disturb the moment.

"For what?"

"For tonight. And for agreeing to help me. It really means a lot that you'd do this for me."

"I'd do anything for you," I say, looking her way. Her smile is soft as she rolls to reach over me to switch off my lamp, flushing the room with darkness, pressing herself up against me. I would sell my soul to have Nash's body flush with mine and have it be real. I have to keep reminding myself that it's not. Nash is single-minded. There's no room in her life for any love other than volleyball, which is obvious because how else would we have ended up in this scenario if not for her love of the sport?

"We'd better get some sleep. It's a long drive home tomorrow, and the rules of I-45 state that you have to have at least one near-death experience on the way." She rolls back to her side, settling in the covers. I lie still, messing with my necklace, not wanting to keep her awake with my inevitable tossing and turning until I hear her breathing even out.

It's a long time before sleep finds me.

## HOUSTON HEATS UP: Local sports stars spark a new power couple.

*Tea Spill Tribune - Houston*

*Hottie Hurricanes player spotted with a new gal, see inside for all the pictures and our scoop.*

Houston Hurricanes defensive lineman, Wyatt Vandergrif (27), was spotted at the NFL Honors over the weekend with a local woman named Nashville Green (27) who is currently a starting hitter for the Houston Moons women's volleyball team.

When he won Sack Leader of the Year, he said this of Green, "…it would be possible for [her] to brighten the stars on [her] way to hang the moon, if she wanted to."

Eagle-eyed fans spotted the couple earlier in the month,

enjoying late night Whataburger, cuddled in a booth sharing a milkshake, and the lineman only had eyes for her.

While we don't know much about her (yet), we can't wait to see this new pair light up the downtown skyline.

# Chapter Twenty

WYATT

I wake up to sunlight streaming through the crack in the hotel curtains and something perpetually buzzing. Nash's slender leg is thrown haphazardly over my thigh. She must have rolled around during the night because she fell asleep facing away from me. It felt like a defensive measure—from what, I'm not sure. Maybe last night was more than she could take. Maybe being with me in public like that was harder than she thought it would be. I hope that isn't the case, but she was unreadable last night. She starts to move in her sleep, and I freeze, not wanting to disturb her. Her leg starts moving farther up my thigh and I have to bite down on my lip to keep from making any noise as she just barely grazes my junk with her knee. Oh fuck. I'm being split in two. Half of me is a little worried she's going to knee me in the balls, and the other half is ready to go to war to earn more of her touch. I don't want it to be an accident. I want it to be purposeful.

The noise starts up again, startling me out of my lustful thoughts. For a second I think it's a fly whizzing by my ear, but when I look at the nightstand for something to swing at it with, I realize it's my phone. I think about ignoring it and trying to go back to sleep, but as I watch, ten new texts come in, so I give in to my curiosity. What could everyone possibly be talking about this early on a Sunday.

Oh, fuck. It's me.

The group text with me and my Hurricanes teammates seems to be the most persistent, so I start there.

COLIN

GIRLFRIEND?

JADEN

WTF IS GOING ON?

MACK

Why is everyone screaming?

COLIN

Wyatt just called Nash his girlfriend at the NFL Honors.

MACK

OH SHIT

JADEN

Exactly!

COLIN

Wyatt, you little bitch, you better respond.

MACK

No need for name calling, man. You're going to scare him off, and then we'll never know.

Okay, maybe I should have been less heavy handed with the drop on this—given them a heads up somehow—but how could I when I know this whole thing is fake? Honestly, it was easiest for me to just say it to everyone, and no one, at the same time.

Another text comes through.

COLIN

We're waiting

MACK

Are we really that surprised?

When did these guys, who I didn't even want as my teammates, get so in my business? As a matter of fact, when did this group chat even start? When did we become…friends.

I start to type back.

It just sort of…happened

I mean, true.

COLIN

And why didn't you say anything?

It's really new. I didn't want to jinx anything.

Also true.

She's with me right now and we have a long drive home, so chill out.

JADEN

You can explain at the gym.

I will.

I collapse back onto the overly stuffed hotel pillow, letting the phone fall to my chest. At least I was able to buy myself some time to think and make a plan before I see them on Thursday. It seems like an oversight on my part that I never thought about what this agreement would mean when it came to them. My parents are going to be easy; hence my mother's joy over the phone. My brother might be suspicious, but he's so busy, he probably doesn't care. They're also many states away, so they're not going to be able to get up in my face about it until June when I bring Nash to Henry's wedding. Colin, Jaden, and Mack will be the only ones in the near future to get a good whack at me at Ironsides during our workout in just a couple days.

Great, I can't wait.

# Chapter Twenty-One

## NASH

"I've got to pee."

"Again? We just stopped in Buffalo." Wyatt's been driving us the four hours home and I think I'm about to push him over the edge with the amount of pit stops I've needed.

"We're almost to Madisonville; we can stop at Buc-ee's!" I explain. "This is a very important Texas tradition. A road trip is not complete without it."

Wyatt turns his blinker on for the exit with the huge beaver on the sign, but that doesn't stop him from complaining. "I don't see what the big deal is. It's just a gas station."

"Just a gas station?" I scoff. "Get ready to live."

The automatic doors swing open for us as we walk in, and I watch Wyatt's eyes go wide. "It's huge!" He looks from one thing to the next in quick succession—fountain drinks, jerky station, tie-dye beaver t-shirts, ready-made meals, and miles of snack aisles.

"I told you so." I smirk at him. "I'm going to the ladies' room first. I'll be right back."

By the time I come back from the immaculate bathrooms, I

find Wyatt ordering a pound of habanero teriyaki jerky from the counter, his hands stacked with snacks. He has sweet Beaver Nuggets, fudge, brisket tacos, and a bottle of specialty hot sauce. All gleaming with the beaming beaver mascot. Plus, regular candy, chips, a Dr. Pepper, and a Gatorade.

"I see you found your way around?" I laugh.

"There's a Reese's in there for you somewhere."

"This is enough candy for a week," I tease as I sort through it.

"Not for me."

I laugh. "True. It might last you two whole days, though."

"Worth it, right?" Jerky hangs out of his mouth as he talks.

I nod emphatically. "Totally."

We pay for all our provisions and get back on the highway, falling into a comfortable silence. My sixteen-hour country music playlist is still going strong. It carries us down the highway to nineties classics and new radio hits.

"Speaking of Texas traditions…" he starts. "I've been thinking of my second event for our deal. You got the first one, and I think I should get the next."

"Okay, shoot. What are you thinking?"

"As much as I love Wisconsin, I think I'm ready to give Texas the chance it deserves. I've been here nine months, and I haven't really done anything. I just go to practice during the season or the gym with the guys in the off season. I've been to a few restaurants and Colin and Noah's houses. That's it."

"Consider me your official tour guide, then." I take a fake bow.

"I was thinking about going to the rodeo…would that be a good place to start?"

My face lights up at the suggestion. "Oh my God, yes! That's actually the perfect place to start." I hold my hands out in front of me. "We'll get you Texas lessons." I tap my chin thinking about everything he would need to fit in there. He's honestly not that far off, having grown up on a literal farm. That's more country than most people in Houston ever get. This might be the south, but we're still the third biggest city in the country.

"I don't know if that's necessary."

I hold up a hand to silence him. "Class is in session."

"Right now?" he asks, surprised.

"We have at least an hour, and I already have everything you need to know right here." I tap a finger to my temple. "First lesson." I lean back in my seat. "The *h* in Humble is silent and the *u-y* in Kuykendahl is actually an *ir* sound."

"Why do I need to know that?" He peers over at me.

"The fastest way to tell if someone isn't from around here is what they call things. For example, they change the name of a highway, and we all refuse to comply."

His brows crinkle in confusion, "Okay…"

"Another thing about highways is you must be doing eighty miles an hour at all times or get in the slow lane so people can pass you." He looks pointedly at his speedometer. "You've got the next rule down pat." I gesture around at the truck we're riding in. "Drive a lifted truck and never tow anything with it."

"Hey! I have a farm truck back home that does tow things."

"Yeah, but that's Wisconsin. In Houston, everyone drives trucks, and almost no one needs them."

He lifts his head proudly. "At least I already have cowboy boots."

I laugh. "Wrong-o. Your cowboy boots are actually used. We have to get you a new pair of Lucchese's that you'll only get out of the box for country concerts and the rodeo."

His head hangs in defeat. "Being a Texan is hard."

"We'll invite the whole gang!" I put a comforting hand on his arm, "Don't worry, I'll help you through it." I can see longing in his eyes and I'm sure he's thinking about Poblocki. It hurts my heart knowing he misses home so much. "Well, I don't want to overwhelm you with the rules, so that's enough Texas lessons for today."

# Chapter Twenty-Two

## NASH

"This cannot keep happening to us," Temi groans as we all stand back and look at the net that resembles the Leaning Tower of Piza. Practice had started like any other day. We went to the locker room to put our stuff away, got our court shoes on, and then we came out to get the net set up. I can't say for sure how many times I've set up and broken down a net in my life, but it's a lot. Something like three to five days a week, eight to ten months a year, for the last twenty years? How many is that? I don't know, I'm horrible at math.

"Let's double-check the storage closet for the crank one more time. Maybe we just missed it," suggests Daly.

"You think you missed it, Temi missed it, and I missed it?" I ask incredulously. That's like three pairs of eyes.

"Let's make Danica look for it. She's a mom, so if it's there, she'll walk right in and find it."

We all turn away from the net and I yell for Danica, who's still in the locker room. She comes out with a confused look on her face. "What's wrong?"

I point at the net behind me, normally taut across the top,

it's now completely sagging in the middle. "No one can find the crank. We thought maybe you could use your mysterious mom powers," I explain.

She heads in the direction of the closet where we've already brought out the cart that the poles and net are stored on and searched high and low for the missing metal piece.

I can't help but be annoyed that we're wasting time at another precious practice because of a malfunction out of our control. Maybe the founders of the league are forward thinkers and have enough money piled away to fuel this thing for four or five seasons before they have to pull the plug, but I don't want to take that chance.

When she's not out in just a few seconds, I know she's not going to find it. The motherly power to find missing things works almost instantaneously, or it doesn't work at all. I'm not surprised when she comes out empty-handed. "I have no idea where that little sucker got off to."

Temi looks at me. "Who was here last?"

"I think there was a high school tournament here over the weekend. They must have accidentally misplaced it or walked off with it." I gaze at the net halfheartedly. With its big dip in the middle all sunken in, it looks a little halfhearted, too.

"Crazy that they would take like the most important part. It basically ruins the whole thing," says Daly.

"Yeah, what are we going to do for practice today if the net isn't competition height?" Simin asks, looking at the rest of us.

"Oh, it's competition height all right...if you're ten and under," Temi jokes and the laughter of my teammates breaks up some of the negative thoughts inside me.

Coach comes out of the makeshift office and sees us all standing around. "What are you all waiting for?" We split in half, Temi and me going one way, Daly and Danica going the other in a dramatic reveal of the fucked-up net. "Christ on a bike. You don't have the net up yet?" She checks her watch. "We're already twenty minutes behind."

We're silent for a beat, having an unspoken conversation between us about who is going to tell Coach that the net is missing a key piece. I'm trying to make this my team, so I'll speak up. "The crank is missing; can't get it up all the way. There's no way to tighten it."

She looks at each of us in turn, then up at the ceiling. "Well, ladies. We'll just have to make do."

I hate those two words. As a female athlete, I've heard them more times than I can count.

When the net is broken—we make do.

When the bus is late—we make do.

When the court is taken—we make do.

When the high school bake sale only made enough money to send one team to state and they gave it all to the boys instead of splitting it evenly between us—we made do.

I didn't have to make do in Rome. There was money and fans and support there. But here in my home country, in my home *city*, I'm back to making do.

I'm so fucking sick of *making do*.

# Chapter Twenty-Three

## WYATT

If I had known when I agreed to these team workouts at the end of football season that they would become an interrogate Wyatt fest, I would have declined.

Unfortunately, it's too late for me, and I find myself, once again, at the squat rack with Jaden, Colin, Mack, and Noah being battered with questions. After the sixth one in a row where none of them even let me get a word in edgewise, I finally snap at Colin. "Don't you have a wife to get home to?" I look at the rest of them. "Girlfriends?"

Jaden laughs. "Furthest from it."

"Okay, not you." I look back at Noah.

"Audrey and Chrissy are actually together today. Something about Chrissy needing a girls' day." His smile is like a cat struggling to keep hold of the canary it caught. "So, no. I don't have anywhere to be. I have literally all day to stay here and lift weights with you guys. Now, stop deflecting our questions."

They all came so fast I can't even pick one out of my brain

to answer. "Start over. Ask them again, slower this time. I can't keep track when you all talk at once."

"So we were right? You guys are sleeping together and now you've finally figured your shit out and are official?"

"Basically, yeah."

It seems like everyone is about to start up again with more questions, but Colin takes charge, as he should. He's our quarterback, after all. "No offense, dude, but when you first got here, it didn't really look like you wanted to be here." He pauses. "I don't mean to play football, I mean with us."

It was that obvious? I thought I kept a pretty good smile on my face even though it was damn near one-hundred degrees when training camp started. I thought we were all miserable? I didn't know you could pick my misery out from the next guy and compare it. "It's complicated."

"Because of Nash?"

I'm immediately struck with the need to defend her. "No. She's the easiest thing in my life."

Noah holds up his hands trying to break the tension. "Let's try something else. You've been here nearly a year; why are you interested in doing this now?"

"Yeah, when I invited you to go to NASA with us you said you didn't want to go," Colin adds.

"I might have hated this city when I got here. But this is Nash's home, and now she's back and I know she wants it to be for good. With her I feel like I'm open to seeing what Houston has to offer."

"And you didn't feel that way about any of us?" Jaden gestures at the guys currently in Ironsides gym. "Asshole," he mutters.

"I didn't know you when I first got here. It's not even been a whole year yet, so chill out. I do like you. I like all of you—

against my better judgment." I huff a laugh. How am I going to explain this to them? I think… I'm going to have to tell them it's not real.

I need them to come to games with me, and if they're right about how grumpy I was when I got here, maybe they won't want to help knowing it's for me. But they'll help when they realize it's for Nash.

"Guys, we aren't actually together," I blurt, and the entire gym goes silent. Even the music seems to fade while they all stare at me slack-jawed. "That's why we weren't together before now, and why it doesn't make any sense because it's fake."

"What do you mean fake?" Noah's brows are pulled so close they could cross.

"She wants to use the Hurricanes name and popularity to bring fans to the Moons games. She thinks if people know we'll be there, they will be more likely to come. I agreed to it if she would be my date to Henry's wedding. We get two events each, Henry's wedding is the last one, and after that we'll just amicably break up."

Jaden and Mack make eye contact, but the silence continues. I don't know what spurs me on, but I can't shut up. "And when I told her I might be interested in experiencing more Texas things now that I'm getting my footing here, she offered to show me."

A snort immediately burst out of Mack. I shoot him daggers with my eyes and he sucks it back in.

"Texas lessons?" asks Noah.

"She's going to teach me how to fit in. She's going to take me to the rodeo, get the right boots, et cetera."

"Why do you feel like you don't fit in?" Fuck Noah and his therapy sessions making him get in touch with his feelings. He can be as in touch as he wants with his own stuff as long as he doesn't call me out like this. Why was I so against liking it here? There must be something to enjoy; otherwise, why would anyone even live here? It's certainly not the weather or the natural beauty…

"When I was a kid, I was a Green Bay Butcher every year for Halloween. My entire family is made up of Butchers fans. It was my lifelong dream to play for them. And I did."

"But now you're here," says Jaden.

I nod at him. "Now I'm here. It's because a player and I had a difference in views about how to be a part of a football team. So when my contract was up, I left. Easy as that." I didn't name any names, but I think they can read between the lines. "But I don't think it was all that easy because when I came here, I didn't have the same love for football as I did when I was wearing the jersey I had always dreamed of. I met my biggest hero, and yeah, he pretty much sucked. I lived my dream and it's over. What do you do with the rest of your life after that?"

Colin puts a comforting hand on my shoulder. "You keep going—and instead, you become the hero you wanted him to be."

"He's right," Jaden adds. "After a loss, there's nothing to do but get up the next morning and go back to practice."

"And I'm no Jared Clark," Colin says in a self-deprecating tone. "So don't put me in the same category as him just because we play the same position."

*Yep. Definitely read between the lines.*

"I would never." And it's the honest truth. In the nine months I've known him, he's proven himself to be nothing but a team player.

"You still love the game, don't you? Even if the jersey isn't the one you pictured yourself wearing?" Jaden looks like if I said no, it would crush him.

"Football always has been, and always will be, the most important thing to me," I reassure him.

Noah puts his hand on my shoulder. "I think you need a clean slate. Wipe all your past hesitations away and just let whatever happens happen." I think Noah does this shit on purpose. There's something about him that makes you want to spill your guts when he's around.

"With Nash and with us," Mack adds.

I just nod because my eyes are a little prickly, and I do not want any of these guys to see me like that, even if we did just become real friends. In the way that things always go when you're a group of dudes, the conversation is over without another word, and we all go back to watching ourselves lift in the mirror as we count our reps.

## *MARCH*

"What is that?" Nash asks me as we meet at the front door to get picked up by Chrissy and Colin.

"It's…my hat?" I put my hand on the offending object. "What's wrong with this hat?" I've had it since college. It fits perfectly, and it's soft in the worn kind of way.

"It's so ugly. You're supposed to dress nice for this." She picks up a tiny purse and puts tiny things in it.

I look down at my button-up shirt and the shiny new boots she took me to get earlier this week. "I am dressed nicely." She looks up from stuffing her minuscule purse and gives me a once over that I'm sure is meant to be discerning, but all I can feel is the weight of her gaze. I feel like a male peacock, like I should start an interpretive dance just to earn the privilege of being seen with her tonight.

She puts a hand on my shoulder. "I'll pick you one out when we get there." She nods as if she's agreeing with only herself because I haven't said anything. "Then your outfit will be complete."

The Houston Livestock Show and Rodeo is two weeks of carnival rides, food, and concerts, all headlined by a rodeo with huge cash prizes that's held at the end of March every year. I remember when the lineup was announced in January, and it was the talk of the locker room. Everyone critiquing the big names headlining the nightly shows, who they were disappointed wasn't coming, and who they wanted to see. It's prefaced by a cook-off you can't buy tickets to—you have to know someone. There's also a wine competition, a livestock auction, and lots of scholarship opportunities for rising students interested in this industry.

I've been to my fair share of rodeos in small towns scattered throughout Wisconsin, but I've never seen anything on this grand a scale. Did I mention it's at the Houston Hurricanes' stadium? And it's standing room only every night for two weeks straight.

We park in a secret parking garage on the backside of the stadium that Chrissy knows about and walk in through the back gate of the compound. Nash and I are dressed up, but it's got nothing on Chrissy. She's covered head to toe in denim and rhinestones. Beside her, Colin looks like a depressed cowboy in black jeans, black button down, black hat, and black boots.

I don't even recognize the stadium. Normally, the whole place is empty when I arrive for a game and is empty when I leave. Today it's absolutely swarming with people. There are people dressed up like us, but others walk around in t-shirts, regular jeans, and Vans, holding some sort of fried food on a stick. It's a welcoming atmosphere, like a party where the whole city's been invited to come as they are and enjoy good food and entertainment.

I'm too busy taking in the sheer amount of people swarming around us. There must be a hundred-thousand people here. I've never seen the Hurricanes grounds like this. It's been completely transformed. There's a carnival complete with a Ferris wheel in the parking lot. The convention center is within walking distance of the stadium and full of booths selling belt buckles and a bunch of other stuff.

"Where to first?" Chrissy asks. We all look at each other waiting for someone to make a suggestion.

Mouthwatering scents waft from a long row of food stands all lined up side by side under a tent. My stomach rumbles. "How about food first?"

"No carnival rides?" Chrissy asks.

"I'm not about to lose my head on one of those traveling metal contraptions," says Nash with a laugh.

"Food it is." We all head in the direction of the white tops between the stadium and the convention center.

Nash bumps me as we walk, "What are you thinking?"

"I'm thinking BBQ baked potato." I point to a stand claiming to have award-winning pulled pork. "And we share a funnel cake."

"I meant about this being your first event of our deal."

"These are just my friends, though." I think I'm going to lay it on extra thick. The guys are in the know, so they won't think twice when I go overboard with flirting. They'll probably be pleased, actually.

"Maybe those are the people we need to convince the most. Plus, you're a Hurricane wherever you go." I glance over to where Chrissy and Colin are in line for a foot-long corn dog.

"You're right." I hold my hand out for her, and she takes it, but it hurts a little knowing that this show of affection is only because of my status and not because of what I mean to her. I straighten my shoulders. It doesn't matter that she needs my name as a Hurricane. I can enjoy being with her just the same.

We cram ourselves at the end of a picnic table otherwise occupied by a family trying to enjoy their meal. Colin sets three beers in front of us. Chrissy has one of those huge plastic frozen margarita tubes. Nash points to her. "That better last you all night."

She takes a long pull. "What's it to ya?"

It feels good to sit after all that walking. The parking lot to the main building must be a half-mile long. These cowboy boots are nice, and they cost a pretty penny, but I find myself missing the ones I brought from home that are perfectly molded to my feet.

Jaden sits down next to us and puts a plate with a burrito the size of his head on the table. Colin's eyes go wide. "What is that?"

"It's called the lineman," he looks at me playfully. The size difference between us is easily seven inches and close to one-hundred pounds. "It's got brisket, mac 'n cheese, and BBQ sauce, all wrapped up in a warm tortilla."

"Disgustingly gluttonous," mutters Chrissy.

"Amazing," whispers Noah, who is now eyeing his grilled chicken quesadilla like it's disappointed him greatly by simply being basic.

Jaden takes a massive bite out of his burrito, and the rest of us dive into our food as well. The sounds of my group eating and drinking, passing chips and queso around, Colin trying to get Chrissy to share a bottle of water that Chrissy doesn't seem to have much interest in mixes with the sounds of the thousands of people milling around us. Some glance at our table as they walk down the aisle between the food stands and the rows and rows of picnic tables, looking for their friends or family who hopefully saved them a seat. Most rove right over us, but a few get an eyeful of Colin and end up doing a double-take. I stare at them as they move from one face to the next, three pro football players crammed into the little table. Then when they meet my gaze, it's hard. It says don't even think about it, pal. They look quickly away and move on, back to searching for a spot. It's so packed right now that people are sitting on the curb with plates of food in their laps.

Someone walks by us with a confection so crazy looking, it makes me do the double-take this time. Nash sees me looking at this triangular sweet on a stick and answers my unspoken question. "Fried pie on a stick. I've had the key lime before. It's to die for."

"Should we get one of those?"

"The stand is out by the carnival, or at least it used to be. I don't know if we have time." She taps her phone to check the time. "We've still got to head to the shops."

"Funnel cake is fine." I know that's what she really wants anyway.

"That's right there." She points behind my shoulder to a stall that says Junkfood Junction over it. "I'll go stand in line."

Nash comes back with our funnel cake piled high with powdered sugar. She has forks in her hand, but we both forgo them for our fingers. I break off the first piece and offer the steaming treat for her to take from my hand, my eyes daring. She does. Leaning in to take it gently from me, her tongue brushes the pad of my finger, and it takes every ounce of me not to pull her to me for another life-altering kiss. She groans at the sweetness of the cake, and now I am truly suffering. My other hand grips the table for dear life.

Between mouthfuls of fried heaven, Nash looks at me with

a mischievous twinkle in her eye. "It's time for your next Texas lesson."

I look around us. "In front of everyone?"

"Yes," she says emphatically, "because for this one I'm going to need some help." She pauses for dramatic effect. "Every Texan is trained to respond to a call. Do you want to hear it?"

A smile splits my lips as I lift my beer to take a swig. "You know I do."

She looks at Audrey and Noah, who I know are native Texans. "Deep in the heart, okay?" They nod and she clears her throat. Then she absolutely belts, "The stars at night are big and bright–" Everyone around us pounds on the table four times in quick succession. A small chorus of, "deep in the heart of Texas," breaks out around people's eating.

"What sorcery is this," I say to Nash as the crowd around us is all smiling and elbowing each other. Some of them are still carrying on the tune.

"It's the call and response of the state. Everyone knows it." She smiles at me, and I can barely stand the warmth in her eyes, the pride she has in showing me all of her favorite things about living here when I'm secretly planning to dip at the first sign of Jared Clark's retirement announcement.

I don't want her to see the doubt in my eyes, the way that I still have one foot out the door. Luckily, Chrissy saves me. "Time to shop?" We all nod in agreement and set off from the food tents to the convention center.

———

The first thing you're hit with when you walk in is the smell of animals. I have no idea how they get the smell out for the other fifty weekends a year. The next thing you're hit with is how insane it is to get full-size hot tubs, mattresses, and trucks in here. There're also booths boasting custom hats, belt buckles, dog treats, cowhide rugs, and new and used lassos. This isn't even the stadium. This is the secondary building on the premise. That's how big this place is. I never really appreciated it until now.

"I didn't realize there was a market for used rope," I say, bemused, and Nash laughs and grabs me by the hand to drag me to a sweet-smelling booth two stalls over. This one offers a truly exceptional variety of roasted and candied nuts.

"We'll take one of the créme brûlée pecans, please." The man hands Nash a bag of nuts, still warm from the pan. I get my wallet from my back pocket and hand a card to the gentleman.

Nash glances at me. "Why are you paying?"

"My girlfriend doesn't pay when we go out." I obviously haven't been laying down the law enough with her. She should know I'd never let a lady pay unless we agreed to splitting the bill in some way that's even. But this is a date.

The man gives her the nuts and she hands them right to me. I immediately open them and pop one in my mouth. "We just had dessert," she scoffs.

"I think the words you're looking for are 'thank you'." I dip my hand into the bag and grab a few. "You know I've got a sweet-tooth, sugar." I smirk as I lick the stickiness off my fingers. I know we're faking it, but I can't help it when I know it will turn the tip of her nose pink like that. Her eyes drop to my lips where I'm licking off the sugar left behind, and then quickly back up to my eyes. That's the first time I've called her a pet name. I think she likes it…

Being out and about is the perfect excuse to be like this

around her. The playing and teasing that old Wyatt never thought would be possible is within present Wyatt's grasp. It's the way I would be with her if this were real, and it's the best way to make it believable to anyone watching our interactions. If this happens to make our friendship go tits up, I may as well enjoy every second of it.

This place must be the size of ten football fields because behind all the shopping stalls are rows upon rows of cattle waiting to be shown. There's also two mini arenas complete with bleachers for onlookers.

"Why are there cows here?" Jaden asks as we walk perpendicular to the first row of cows and their handlers.

"These are FFA students. They raise a cow all year and bring it here to show. The hope is to win a title and/or sell the cow at a high price at auction," Nash explains.

"The kid gets the money?"

"No, it goes toward scholarships and education programming. They didn't have FFA where you grew up?"

"They did, but nothing like this." He gestures around us at the hundreds of steers waiting to be judged.

"You ain't seen nothing yet."

"Guys," Chrissy whines, "cows are boring. And sad." She looks at Nash. "They're all going to get eaten. I want to go see the cute bunnies."

Nash hooks her arms through Chrissy's, and they lead us toward the front corner. The only place we haven't been.

The girls ooh and ahh over the show bunnies of all different breeds, petting the soft pelts of any who will let them. I hear gagging, and when I turn to see what's going on, I find Colin staring at the birthing pen in the southeast corner. They're live-streaming a cow giving birth by using a huge projector to cast it on the wall. I pretend to cover his eyes and the girls dissolve into giggles. "That's so gross," Colin exclaims.

"I grew up on a farm. I've seen it all." I put my arm around his shoulders and steer him away from the miracle of life.

Once we get back to the entrance where they display the kids' art competition, Chrissy asks, "Okay, is there anything else we want to see? If not, we should start heading to our seats for the show."

Nash perks up. "Oh, I almost forgot! We have to get Wyatt a new hat."

Chrissy picks my 'gross' hat off my head and my hands immediately move to smooth down my hair. "This one is covered in sweat marks."

I snatch it back from her. "It's from working." I gesture at the crowd of overdressed people around us. "Not like these people would know anything about that." Maybe some of them do know. Maybe they work on a farm and are just here to enjoy the food and the music, but I highly doubt that.

Nash takes my hand. "Come on, I saw a stand over by the hot tubs that had nice ones." She looks at Chrissy and Colin. "Do you guys want to come?"

They look at each other, then shake their heads. Chrissy says, "No, we're going to check out the wine garden. We'll meet you at the gates to get in?"

"Sounds good."

The hat booth Nash was talking about is literally a wall of hats behind a folding table. A man with a curled mustache greets us as we walk up. "What're ya'll lookin' for?"

"I need a new hat, apparently." I'm still holding my old hat in my hands. Why does it feel like replacing it is a betrayal? To Wisconsin? To my hometown? The Vandergriff family farm? I don't know.

Nash points to a hat on the wall. "Can we see that one?"

It's out of his reach, so the gentleman moves to take it down with a little pole. It's stiff and golden. The folds at the top crisp. "Here you go, Miss."

She hands it to me, and I plop it on my head. "What do you think?"

"Let's try one more." She points at another hat. This one is more of a bone color, but similar in shape to the first one.

I take the first one off in my right hand and set it on the table. Then put the second one on with my left. Nash taps her chin with her finger, thinking. I flex my muscles to really give her an idea of just how good I can make this hat look. I watch her eyes dart from the hat to my biceps as they strain against the material of my button down, then back to the hat again. She has to clear her throat before she says, "I like the second one better. The color brings out the blue in your eyes."

The man selling it looks at me, silently asking me what I think. "We'll take the one she likes."

"Need a box?"

"No, sir. I'll wear it out." I hand Nash my old hat and pay.

When I turn around, new hat in hand, I almost choke. She's wearing my old hat. It's so big it's barely above her eyes, but I can't help the way my cock stiffens just slightly at the sight of it. That's the only explanation I have for my next sentence. "You know what they say? Wear the hat, ride the cowboy." I wink at her. She stares dumbly back at me. Just like when we bought the nuts, the tip of her nose turns pink. I need that little spot of color like an addict needs their next hit. It's the only thing telling me there might be something more than fake dating friendship going on between us. It's all I have to hang on to.

We stand close as she fixes the band of my new hat. Our

breath mingling between us. I love how easy it is to look her in the eyes. My high school sweetheart was average height for a woman, and it was a pain having to get to her level all the time. I never have that problem with Nash. She's the perfect size for me. I bet she'd fit me like a glove in bed, too.

The moment between us seems to last forever. For all I know, we could have already missed the rodeo and concert while we stood here.

"Sir?" We both jump ten feet in the air. "Your receipt?"

I turn to take it from him, using the split second to hide the blush coloring my cheeks before turning back to Nash. "You good?" For a second, I can see she thinks I'm talking about the cowboy cliché I was spewing, but she quickly realizes I meant to catch up with Colin and Chrissy.

"I'm good."

"Lead the way."

She nods, and we head toward the main stadium.

To get to your seats, there's a six-story concrete ramp on the side of the building. If you were in the nosebleeds you'd have to walk around and around and around. Luckily, we don't have to go all the way up. When we walk through the opening from the concessions area to our seats, my jaw drops. I have never seen the field like this. Gone is the green AstroTurf. The entire thing is covered in dirt. Tons and tons of it. Not the kind of dirt you find in the garden, either; instead, it's finely ground stuff that's almost dust. The whole arena is buzzing, the energy palpable. This is a different kind of action than football, and the feeling in the air reflects that.

"The HLSR has eight rodeo events," Nash informs me as we scoot down the aisle to take our seats. This rodeo has way more stuff than the ones I attended in little towns around

Wisconsin. "My favorite is barrel racing, but I think bull riding is the most well-known."

"And the most dangerous," supplies Chrissy.

We watch round after round of rodeo events. When a bull rider gets bucked off after just a second, we laugh when the big screen shows the score: bull riders - 0, bulls - 1. Dudes being stupid on bulls is cool and all, but nothing gets my blood pumping like barrel racing. I can see why it's Nash's favorite. The women look ethereal on the back of their steeds. The horses dance at the gates as they wait for their signal to go, and then with all the power of a wild beast, they bolt out of the tunnel and toward the first barrel. I can't imagine how the women keep their seat as they guide their horse around the second barrel and the third, their legs kicking out wide as the horse picks its speed back up for the dead sprint back to the tunnel. Watching a cowgirl with her hair flowing behind her as she encourages her horse to go faster and faster is something anyone can appreciate.

We scream for the Exxon wagon as they race against three other sponsored chuck wagons around the arena. The carts careening to one side as the four horses take them zipping around the curve. Next a big group of teenagers comes out to stand in the dirt in jeans and matching t-shirts. Volunteers adorned with fancy rodeo vests make a tunnel from the entrance to where the kids wait, ropes in hand.

The announcer comes over the loudspeaker. "Are you ready?!" The crowd screams, and a torrent of calves, spry and quick, run out into the arena. After a short count, the kids are let go to start their chase.

"Why do they want a cow?" Jaden asks.

"If they catch a calf and get it back into the starting box, they get to keep it and raise it for their FFA animal that year instead of having to pay for one themselves," I answer.

Jaden bumps me on the shoulder with his elbow. "I wish we could have just caught a college scholarship."

Nash barks a laugh. "It's not as easy as you think." She points to where one kid is hunched over, hands on knees, already puking up whatever they had for lunch. Jaden's nose scrunches in disgust at the sight of vomit. We watch as a rodeo volunteer comes and escorts the kid off to the side.

It takes about fifteen minutes for the kids who are trying to catch a calf to get a hold of one. "You have to get a harness on the animal and drag it back into the square outlined in white chalk that they started in. If they don't cross the line, it doesn't count." Some of the kids grab one quick, get it harnessed, start running it back in, and are done in less than ten minutes. Others take fifteen minutes just to grab onto the tail of the cow and are dragged behind it for yards until they can right themselves. By now most of the kids and their caught calves are back in the square where volunteers come and immediately help control the animal while the kid signs paperwork. There are a few left trying to get their cow moving, and there are lots more kids with no cow at all.

"Look," Chrissy shouts, pointing to the northeast corner of the arena. We all follow her line of sight and see a young woman, one hand on the harness, the other on the calf's tail, pulling with all her might trying to get the beast to move. The announcer has seen her, too. "On the count of three, let's give Kelly a little encouragement! One, two, three!" The crowd goes wild. People are screaming, whistling, and clapping as Kelly digs her heels in and tries to get the animal to move. She's probably thirty feet from the safety of the white chalk, but that's a long way to go when you're pitting your strength against an animal's, even one so small. A few of the young men who have given up on catching a calf come toward the young woman fighting for her life. The crowd cheers again as the boys get on the other side of the calf and start pushing. Between her and them, there's no way the calf can stay still. It trips over its wobbly legs and starts moving. With a little momentum and encouragement from the kids, and from the crowd, they're running. The smile on the girl's face is a mile wide, even though her hair is dirty from getting dragged. We cheer again as she crosses the white line and people swarm her, taking the rope and the calf so she can catch her breath. She hugs the two boys who came to her aid and signs her name on the paper claiming her calf.

That is definitely something the little rodeos up north don't have.

We also don't have mutton busting. While the staff works on bringing out the huge mobile stage for the concert, everyone's attention is directed to a small pen in one corner of the arena where rodeo volunteers put little kids on the back of sheep and let them go. They're all so cute with their little helmets and chest protectors on. Adults plop them on the sheep and then help them back up when they fall off.

The crowd noise rises up and up as one little boy rides his sheep the full twenty feet to the end of the pen without slipping off.

I lean toward Nash in delight, the biggest smile on my face. "This is awesome!"

"I thought this wasn't your first rodeo." She winks at me.

"It's not, but this is way bigger than any I've ever been to."

She cheers for the next kid, a little girl with pigtails waving awkwardly at the camera in her face after her ride on the fuzzy sheep. "And the concert hasn't even started!"

We watch as an interviewer walks up to the winning girl, dark hair a mess from the helmet, and asks, "How did you hold on so long?"

"I practiced a lot," she says with the lisp of a kid who's missing their front teeth.

"How did you practice? Do you have sheep?"

She shakes her head, "I rode my daddy i-in the living room." The crowd roars, a mix of applause and laughter rolling through the dusty air.

She hands the girl her belt buckle prize. "Well, all that practice paid off—make sure you share this buckle with your dad, okay!"

The crowd goes wild.

# Chapter Twenty-Five

NASH

It's impressive how they keep this show on the road. When one thing is done and they're setting up for the next, they make sure to keep the crowd entertained. Sometimes they have a game on the big screen where you can text to play trivia questions about farm animals. When the kiss cam starts up, I'm delighted. We roar with laughter when the camera shows a girl in her twenties next to a guy with a ballcap on and she starts violently making a 'no' gesture with her hands. The man points to her and mouths 'that's my sister'. The camera changes quickly after that as the audience roars with laughter. The next victims are an older couple who are obviously married, and we all whoop when he kisses her passionately.

The next face I see on the screen is *mine*? What the hell?

I almost fall out of my chair as I watch me and Wyatt on the camera. Time stops as I take in his broad smile on the screen right over where it labels him as a Houston Hurricanes player. I glance at myself for a millisecond and see "Houston Moon" under myself in bright pink script. I'm still looking at the screen, so I see Wyatt's hand move toward my face in real time as he places it on my cheek and pulls me closer. Our lips meet, and I know the crowd is going wild, but I can't hear them over the rush of blood in my ears. I kiss him back, giving him every part of me I've been wanting him to have. His lips are warm against mine, and I get a quick taste of the powdered sugar he missed with a napkin. I've been kidding myself for the last nine years. Convincing myself that I can live without this affection from him for the rest of my life... What was I thinking? Wyatt only breaks the kiss when Noah nudges him with an elbow. "Dude, the camera cut away."

Wyatt kisses me one more time, and if I didn't know any better, if it wasn't just wishful thinking, I would think that maybe it was to show me that he doesn't care that the camera isn't on anymore. That he's kissing me because he wants to this time. When we pull away again, I try to read his eyes, but he just seems pleased with himself. Is that because he can see the flush of pink in my cheeks from having the life kissed out of me, or because he's doing his job as my fake boyfriend, getting me the attention I need in front of everyone here?

I startle in my seat as the announcer booms over the speakers. "Ladies and gentlemen, the lights will be going out shortly." It's the same guy it's always been since I came here as a tween. His voice is deep and easily recognizable from the rodeo circuit. A trickle of hesitant cheers once again ripple through the crowd, raising the hairs on the back of my neck in anticipation.

It's been years since I've been to the rodeo, but I have great memories of coming every year as a kid. From grades five through twelve, I went to at least one night of the rodeo. In high school, I usually went with a group of friends or the guy I was dating at the time. I've missed it so much the last nine years while I've been gone. It's no Roman Colosseum or Trevi Fountain, but it holds a special place in my heart.

And something about being here tonight with my friends, new and old, makes me feel like I can fly, like anything is possible. For the first time since I got back, I really feel like I'm home. At rest. I'm not afraid to have a spark of hope. That this league will be successful. That this hare-brained scheme is going to work. And it's not going to ruin us. That we will still come out on the other side of this best friends like we've always been.

The spotlight comes back, shining bright on the far entrance, and the crowd begins to rile itself up again. It starts at a dull roar, but when the snout, then head, then ears of a horse appear through the gate, it kicks up to a galloping cheer.

The newest star in country music, who happens to have grown up about an hour north of here, rides out on his horse. He waves to the crowd on his way to the stage.

"That's the kid one of your college teammates went to high school with, right?" Wyatt yells in my ear so I can hear him over the strums of the first song.

I lean in and yell back, "Yeah, he wore rhinestone jeans and everything, apparently." No one is surprised he made it here. Except, maybe him.

I turn to the stage and start to sing along. The sad lyrics paired with the heavier drums does it for me every time. I'm belting about my lover leaving me for another man, lost in the music, when I catch a glimpse of Wyatt's face out of the corner of my eye. He's watching me watch the show.

"What?" I ask.

He shakes his head with a smile on his face. "Nothing." I

elbow him in the ribs. "You just look so beautiful." The lights from the slowly spinning stage fly over our faces in their rotation.

I feel his words hit me like a kick in the gut. Like a kill shot to the face, the ball bouncing off my nose. Maybe it's the energy from the rodeo, maybe it's the thrill of the concert, or maybe it's Wyatt's words that make me feel like he looks so good in his boots and new hat. I've seen him done up a hundred times before. Just last month he was in a full suit at the NFL Honors, but tonight, I must have dust in my eyes because he looks different.

Sexy different.

I physically can't help myself from touching him, so I reach out to straighten his collar.

He grabs my wrist with his hand. "Nash…" His voice is hesitant, but his eyes are full of hunger.

We're already neck deep in this. Why not add a couple more feet of quicksand? "I want–"

"Thank you, Houston!" The crowd whoops and hollers in response. "I'm just a kid from Conroe with a guitar and a dream. You made them come true." The band picks up again, playing along with him as he moves back to where a staff member is bringing his steed.

Colin leans over to us and yells, "Time to go. It's going to be a pain to get out of here."

I look back at Wyatt again, the words I was about to say still stuck on the tip of my tongue. If I chew on them any longer, they'll get stuck in my teeth like the saltwater taffy they sell at the zoo. But he's watching the singer canter away on his horse, decidedly not looking at me.

In the quiet, exhausted walk toward our car, I decide it's for the best that I didn't get to finish that sentence. If Wyatt was interested in something physical, he would have said something after kissing me at my going away party.

But he didn't.

And he still hasn't.

# Chapter Twenty-Six

NASH

The second we walk in the door, Wyatt kicks his boots off and bolts for the shower, saying goodnight over his shoulder. On the way home he looked like he was doing everything in his power to not give me a chance to say what I'd planned to, even though I no longer wanted to. In the car, he immediately turned the music up, claiming he wanted to play the songs we didn't hear during the concert.

I'm already hyped up from the buzzing energy of the rodeo. The masculinity of the bull riding and steer roping, but what pushed me to my clothes feeling too tight to be able to sleep was the sound coming from Wyatt's room. I could hear him turning on the shower. The sound of water running over a hulking, strong, naked body… Nothing on except that chain he never takes off.

Am I about to masturbate to my best friend?

Yes, yes, I am. It will be my little secret.

I lift up the sheets and climb into my bed. My head hits the pillow, and I feel the kind of relief that only comes from lying down after spending a long time in motion. It's a good relief, but it's not enough, so I slide my panties down my thighs, just a little. I don't need to be fully nude to slide my hand down my stomach, finding my clit. Just the first soft touch sends a bolt through my body. A need for pressure, a desperation to be filled, but I won't get the toys out tonight. Not knowing Wyatt is still awake in his room down the hall. I just need a quick and dirty orgasm to help me relax after a fun night and a long week of practice.

I rub patient circles around her. Letting my wetness coat my fingers as I go, making every movement smoother. I tease myself until I can't take it anymore. I put the pressure on and increase my speed, feeling the flesh move under my finger. My other hand goes under my shirt to barely brush my nipple. I don't want to picture tan skin, blonde hair, bright blue eyes, and that goddamn cowboy hat, but I can't think straight this close to an orgasm, and he's there. It's out of my control.

As the tide rises in me, kept on course by my fingers which are experts in my own pleasure, I crash toward release like waves against the cliffside.

"Oh fuck." I can't keep the words from spilling from my lips.

# Chapter Twenty-Seven

## WYATT

While I tried to get dressed after a head-clearing shower, I felt the need to come apologize for being such a dick after the show ended. I hadn't wanted to push her. I don't want my feelings that have been there for years to influence anything for her. I didn't know if I'd be able to hold my tongue—or my distance—if she said something that tipped me over the edge.

A clearer-headed Wyatt reminded me that she doesn't deserve the silent treatment for not speaking her mind. Friends should be able to talk about anything. So after I towel dry my hair, I wrap it back around my waist and walk the three steps it takes me to cross the landing to her room. I came to apologize, but what I see nearly kills me.

The door is just barely cracked, and I can hear sheets ruffling like she's awake.

"Nash?" I whispered.

And wait.

No response.

I put my hand to the door, hesitating. I don't really want to wake her up if she's already asleep.

"Wyatt." My body goes ramrod straight. Every single muscle locked into place like I'm preparing to take a hit.

She's awake, all right.

I clamp my hand over my mouth to keep myself quiet. I can't stay here. I cannot get caught creeping like this. She wouldn't want me to hear what she sounds like when she's about to come. My sad badge of honor still says 'fake boyfriend', so I shouldn't bear witness to what's happening in her room.

I take my hand off the door like it's hot to the touch. I can feel my vision go narrow. I bite down on my lip to keep the whoosh of my breath from making any noise. I shut my eyes so that I don't accidentally get a glimpse of something I can't unsee…that I would never want to unsee.

But somehow, it's worse with my eyes closed. Without sight it's like her moans are coming from right next to me instead of within the room mere feet away. Like she could have been up against this door, underneath my weight, legs wrapped around my hips instead of in the bed where she's oblivious to my presence.

With what feels like a swift kick to the teeth, I realize that I'm standing in the hall in nothing but a quickly tenting towel and I should absolutely not be here right now. I back away from the door, tripping over my own two feet in my haste, the bath towel around me slowly losing its grip on my hips. I right myself and hold it up with one hand as I stumble back to my room and close the door as quietly as I can.

Back in the safety of my room I should feel relief from each little gasp and moan I overheard, the very sounds I mentally stole to tuck away and have for myself when I didn't earn them, but I don't. I can hear her cries echoing through my mind like the cheers of the crowd echo off the roof of the

Hurricanes' stadium. It rolls through me, forcing a shiver down my spine.

I'll never be able to sleep like this, so I go back in the bathroom and turn the shower back on. I put a new towel out since the one I just used is soaked, and with my tail between my legs, I step back into the shower.

I choke a little when I wrap my fist tight around myself. I normally try to keep my mind from wandering to Nash when I have my cock in hand, but after tonight… to hell with it, I let my mind wander. I let the leash go that I usually hold tight to. Because *she* wanted me to be her fake boyfriend. She picked out a new hat for me to wear. She was the one who was about to ask me for something when the concert ended and all the lights came back on, breaking whatever trance we had been in. I'm at war with myself. My gut tells me there's something else between us outside of this fake relationship, but she never suggests anything that would make me know for sure. So tonight, I backed away from her room, brought myself to my lonely shower, and indulged in replays of the sounds I just witnessed and the kisses from earlier tonight until I am spent.

# Chapter Twenty-Eight

## NASH

The sun rises the next morning faster than any morning has ever come. Faster than I came last night thinking about Wyatt.

Our friendship is real.

Our relationship is fake.

My attraction to him is…palpable.

I roll out of bed and get dressed.

I'm greeted by the smell of coffee first. Wyatt has a mid-tier espresso machine. It takes pods, but its own brand of fancy pods. It's a splurge for someone who grew up on a farm drinking burnt brewed coffee every day.

His back is to me when I get down the steps, and for a second, I just stand on the landing watching him. He moves methodically through the kitchen, putting milk in the frother, and a new cup under the machine.

I could have stayed in this moment of peace forever. Stood here until time passed us both by, but we're living together. I can't avoid him forever. Besides, it's not like he *knows* what I did last night. I just have to act natural, and he'll be none the wiser. "Good morning."

Wyatt turns to me and there's a look in his eye that I can't read. "Good morning."

"You look like you just saw a ghost."

He looks at the mug on the counter and then back at me. "Uh, yeah. I almost dropped this mug, but I caught it in time."

I side eye him as I move toward the cupboard for a water glass. I don't know what's wrong with him. Maybe he's hungover after the rodeo? But he didn't have much to drink. Not nearly as much as I saw him drink when we were in college.

I open the fridge and pour myself some water. "So…what did you think of the rodeo last night?" He's staring at the machine as it pours a steady stream of creamy coffee into the mug below. It's like he's not even in this room with me right now. "Wyatt?"

He startles out of whatever he was thinking about. The tips of his ears turning pink and his gaze not meeting mine when he replies, "It was certainly something." He clears his throat and turns to me. "Is it that packed every night?"

I nod. "Basically, from the first night to the last."

"Did you have fun?" The tone of his voice is teasing. Like he's telling an inside joke I should totally get, but for some reason I don't.

Now it's my turn to look down at the cup in my hand. Unfortunately, the water doesn't give me very much to study. I did have fun last night, both at the concert and after…

*Act natural, Nash.*

Is pointed eye contact as natural as avoiding eye contact, or does it also look strange? "I did. I love hanging out with the whole gang, and the vibes are unmatched."

Letting myself slip and imagine him while I flicked the bean last night was a horrible idea. We are already fake dating yet real roommates, so I really don't need anything to get awkward between us. Well, more awkward.

You know what? No. It's not awkward. Plenty of people have a thing for their best friend. They literally make movies about it. I'm not doing anything wrong.

I drain the rest of my water and put the glass in the sink. Thank God I have a mani/pedi appointment with Temi today; otherwise, I might sit in my guilt for the next two hours, instead.

"Well, I've got to go get ready to meet up with Temi. I'll be back later."

He's still looking off in the distance at something I can't see. This time it's out of the window over the kitchen sink that faces the street below. I lean over his shoulder looking for whatever has his attention, but I don't see anything. "Dude, why are you being so weird?"

He startles like he didn't realize I was standing right next to him. "I'm not being weird. I just didn't sleep well last night and I'm not fully awake yet."

I point at his coffee, abandoned on the counter while he daydreams. "Good thing you've already made your coffee then."

"Right," he says, but it's choked.

I head back toward the stairs. "I'm going to get dressed now. Don't fall asleep mid-sip and accidentally drown in your latte."

His returning smile is small, not the big grin that I'm used to getting from my teasing, but I let it go. Like he said, he's tired. Everyone is allowed a little grace.

Even someone like me—who's hooked on their best friend?

# Chapter Twenty-Nine

## WYATT

*APRIL*

"This technically doesn't count as part of our deal," Nash says as we pull up to Jaden's house on a sunny afternoon in April.

"And why's that?" I ask as we get out of my truck.

"I would have come regardless. I don't miss a crawfish boil," she explains. It's the height of crawfish season, or so I've been told. I've never had it before. "This is perfect for your Texas training. It's like a holiday season in spring. An excuse to get together and celebrate without the pressure that comes with Christmas or Thanksgiving."

"And what exactly *is* crawfish?"

"Think of it like if a shrimp and a lobster had a baby. Except they're only this big," She holds her fingers about four inches apart.

"I don't like lobster," I say, skeptical.

"I know, and it's a shame. Don't worry, crawfish just taste like the seasoning they're doused in."

We let ourselves in the front door to a packed house.

People are everywhere holding beers, chasing kids, and picking at the snacks proffered on the kitchen island. I lead Nash through the house looking for Jaden. He explained to me that being from Louisiana made him the designated boil master. Even though this isn't an official fake-dating event, to the knowledge of everyone here, we're still together.

We step out into the late spring sun and spot Jaden standing over a cooler with a sack of crawfish. He's showing them to the woman next to him. They both turn to us, and I'm surprised to see Nash's teammate, Temi. I guess Jaden found a way to get her number after all.

"Oh my God, hey!" Nash embraces Temi, her braids swinging over their shoulders. "I had no idea you were coming!"

"Jaden didn't tell me you'd be here either!" She looks at him, playfully stern.

Nash turns to me. "This is my boyfriend, Wyatt."

Goddamn if I don't like hearing those words from her pretty pink mouth. They taste like the sweetest sugar-coated lie.

I hold my hand out for her to shake. "So nice to finally meet you!"

Jaden hefts the sack of crawfish out of their cooler and sets it in a big plastic tub. "Wyatt, can you help me with this?"

"You betcha." I move over to him, and he hands me a knife to cut the sack open. Then he grabs the hose and puts it in the bucket, filling it with water.

"They're dirty little fuckers. Gotta give them a bath before we eat 'em." We slosh them around in the water as Jaden says, "Most people don't do this step, but I don't think anyone likes their mud bugs actually muddy."

I shiver a little at the idea of eating something like that.

There's nothing like this in Wisconsin. The closest we get to Cajun food is Friday fish fry. "I guess I'll only be eating the ones you cook."

"Grab all that seasoning over there for me."

I turn to the table next to the two huge pots sitting over propane tanks. I grab lemons, butter, and a colossal-size tub of red stuff that looks like cayenne. I hand it over to him thinking he'd sprinkle the now-boiling water with a chef's hand, but to my surprise, Jaden starts dumping everything in. He opens the spices and pours half of them in. "That's so much!"

He side eyes me. "We're making thirty pounds plus fixins'." I take in a breath to say more about his flavoring decisions—even though this is my first time at a crawfish boil—but I inhale some of the Cajun spice floating around us and dissolve into a coughing fit instead. It seems to last forever as Jaden nonchalantly continues squeezing lemon after lemon into the pot, throwing the citrus carcass in after. "Those spices will get the back of your throat," he laughs, completely unaffected by seafood boil war zone we're in.

When I finally recover, Jaden stands by the bucket full of creatures. "Help me dump them." I move to take the other handle, and we walk it toward the first pot, the one with no seasoning. "First, we boil them; then we will put them in the pot with the seasoning and let them soak in all the flavor. The longer they sit, the spicier they'll be, so I'll let you try them before I pull them out. You can tell me if you like the heat level."

"Sounds good," I say as we upend the bucket into the pot. I stand back as Jaden stirs it with a wooden paddle that's way too small to actually move a boat, but way too big for indoor cooking.

As we watch the pot boil away, I glance over at Nash and Temi, their heads are close together as they talk.

I wonder if they're talking about me, and if so, what Nash is saying. Has our fake-dating events and our Texas lessons affected her feelings for me at all? I was attracted to her the second I saw her in that wood-paneled living room freshman year of college. Just how does one go about changing platonic feelings into something more? Is it something you have to have instantaneously when you first meet like I did? Or can it grow over time?

I have a bad feeling I'm going to find out either way.

"How did Jaden get a hold of you?" The boy was bull-headed, but it obviously works for him.

"He DM'd me on Instagram." She laughed. "I kind of liked that he wouldn't take no for an answer."

"I didn't think it would be cool of me to give out a teammate's number. You never know what kind of crazies are out there." We watch Wyatt and Jaden pull one crawfish out of the pot to taste test the spice. "Jaden is a good guy, though. I wouldn't scare any of my friends away from him if they were interested."

She gives me a shy glance. "I might be." I teasingly bump her shoulder with my arm.

"I would love to have you in the stands with me cheering the boys on. Especially now that I'm state-side, I'll be able to go to way more games."

"Well, now that you're officially dating, I'd imagine you'd go to as many games as possible."

"It's a blessing and a curse that football and volleyball season are at completely different times. The downside is there's only like two months a year where neither of us are in season."

"You're going to have to be flexible. That's for sure."

"Right now, I'm most concerned about our season and making sure there's a team to play for next year, and the year after that."

"It shows in how you play."

"I just don't understand why volleyball hasn't gotten big here like it has in so many other countries. What is it that hockey, football, baseball, and basketball have that we don't? It's fast-paced, it's action-packed." I pause, thinking. "Is it the lack of contact? That can't be it. Baseball isn't a contact sport."

"Women's sports have always had to fight harder for recognition. I think now's a great time for us to go big, though. The WNBA is in their prime with their new draft class. They've proven that women's sports *can* garner the views."

"We have to find a way to get a piece of that." I look out over the party, teeming with athletes and their wives who are the new influencers. "For people to pay attention to us when it's not Olympic sand volleyball."

"We're going to make it, Nash. We're starting to put it all together." We better. Or I'd better get my resume polished for the first time since high school.

The boys make their way back to us and I can't help but look over at Wyatt while he walks, he's got on a fishing-style shirt, billowing in the wind, blowing the floppy part of his hair around as he runs his hand through it while talking animatedly to Jaden. I get to have my best friend here. I want him to stay in Texas. I want him to embrace it. Maybe even love it for however long he stays with the Hurricanes.

Traditionally, crawfish are eaten standing up. When Jaden approaches the newspaper-covered table with the metal boiling basket, I whip out my phone to take a video. This is my favorite part of a crawfish boil. I hit record as he tips the basket over and thirty pounds of crawfish plus potatoes, garlic, corn, sausage, and mushrooms pour steaming onto the table. No plates, no utensils, just crackers for the garlic, which gets creamy and delicious from being boiled with Cajun seasonings.

Everybody digs in immediately, picking up one crawfish and beginning to disassemble it, or using their arm to sweep a small pile toward them. I take a potato and a corn for myself. The corn soaks up more spice than anything else in the pot. It'll set your mouth on fire, and I'm eager for the burn. I look at Wyatt standing still next to me. He's staring blankly at the crawdad in his hand.

"Like this," I say, taking the tail in one hand and twisting it away from the body. He mimics me with his own. I peel a few shell segments back to reveal more of the meat. "Now pinch the tail and pull the meat out." Mine wiggles free and I show him the little piece of meat.

His eyes go wide. "That's it?" He takes in the huge pile in front of him. "I'm going to have to eat like a million of these."

"This is a social meal; you're not supposed to get full on them. Eat more corn and potatoes. If you're still hungry later, we can pick something up."

"What now?"

"Now, you *can* eat it, but I don't like the idea of eating shit, so I peel off the mud vein. That's controversial, though—true Cajuns eat it all." I discard the grossness and pop the clean tail in my mouth. I pick up the body and put it to my lips. "I do suck the head, though."

My gaze meets Wyatt's as I pull the juices from the chest of the crustacean. When I discard it, my lips glisten with spices, and I lick them clean. Wyatt's pupils blow wide, and he quickly looks away. "Show me again."

I pick up another and start the process over.

Wyatt downs three more potatoes, and I tease him when he tries the corn and has to start gulping beer. "I forgot the only spice they use in Wisconsin is black pepper!" I pat him on his back as he coughs up the spice. That shit tickles the throat. "You poor thing. Thank God you're here to learn what good food really is."

He throws a crawfish shell at me. "What would I do without you?"

I can't help myself as I say to him, "It's a good thing you don't have to find out, dear boyfriend."

# *Chapter Thirty-One*

## WYATT

## *MAY*

Even though I'm a proud NFL player, I love it when the crowd boos the commissioner as is the tradition during the draft. I heard that it started after a Super Bowl team got caught cheating and their fans booed at the next draft, and then everyone else just jumped in.

This year it's being held in Detroit, and Jaden, Mack, Colin, Noah, and I are watching it at Colin's house. It'll go on for about three days, but we'll just watch the first couple rounds. As someone just one season out of their rookie contract—and currently without a contract at all—it's interesting to look at all the new young faces who are having their dreams come true right now. We're all curious to see what new talent is going to be joining us for the next season. I do find it harder to watch than it has been the last couple years. I used to be that kid waiting to hear his name called, desperately hoping that I would get drafted at all, and underneath that hoping it was the team I dreamed of playing for. The me who's watching right now is a bit worried that it's May, and I still don't have a contract signed and delivered for next season with the Hurricanes. I might not have wanted to play here, but I would rather play literally anywhere than not play at all.

Wings are piled high on plates in front of us, overflowing with different flavors, carrots, celery, ranch, and bleu cheese as well as fries, onion rings, and potato wedges.

"I bet Trenton Wilder goes in the first round," Jaden says, smacking his lips as he licks garlic parmesan off his fingers.

"No way," Colin snorts, "his completion to interception ratio was way too close as a quarterback."

"I think it'll be Jason Amara," Mack adds. It seems like every year the guys coming out of college get bigger and faster. In today's world, you basically have to be a freak athlete to play in the NFL.

When the special ding that signals the start of a team's time to put in their draft pick plays, we all stop shooting the shit and pay attention. I'm not surprised to see that the Cheetahs are picking first since draft order is determined by how good a team does during the season, and they went four and thirteen. The Hurricanes will be toward the back since we made it to the playoffs last year, and the Butchers should be somewhere in the middle. They didn't have a great season, but they didn't have a horrible one either.

"With the first pick in the draft, the Jacksonville Cheetahs select Deondre Harris, cornerback, University of Connecticut." We watch as the selected player stands from where he's seated with his parents and walks toward the hall that leads to the stage. On the way up he stops and is given a hat for his new team. The crowd goes wild when he puts it on and confidently steps foot onto the stage. Confidence that is not misplaced seeing as he just went first overall in this year's draft. It's good company to be in. He accepts the jersey handed to him by whoever the team sent to represent them and holds it up for the cameras. The cheering continues after he says how excited he is and walks off stage, and the next team is on the clock to make their selection.

And so it goes. We watch as name after name is called. Some seem like they expected it, others seem surprised. A particularly controversial quarterback is often shown when he is not drafted. He's supposed to be a favorite to go early because of the recognition he brought to his college, and the fact that his coach is also his dad and an ex-pro. So far, he sits uncalled.

Finally, it's the Butcher's turn. I'm on the edge of my seat, but trying not to show it. I don't think that many guys keep up with their old teams the way I do, and I don't want it to seem weird that I'm so interested in who they draft.

The sound rings again. "With the twenty-sixth pick in the draft, the Green Bay Butchers select Jason Amara, quarterback, University of Utah." The TV cuts to a scene of Jason Amara in his living room surrounded by his parents. I guess he didn't think he would get drafted in the first round since he didn't travel to be there in person. Maybe that's the kind of humility that team needs.

Then it hits me. Why are they drafting a quarterback when they have the king of Wisconsin still playing for them? Is there something going on that they're not talking about in the press? The Butchers are known for drafting a quarterback early on, before their current franchise quarterback is really ready to retire, and letting the new guy learn behind the veteran. That works if you're a down to earth guy from the poorest part of the South, but I have a feeling it might not go over as well with a prima donna from California.

Then again, that could just be my dislike talking.

"Wow, good for him." Mack has half a wing in his mouth, but it doesn't stop him from speaking.

Jaden is scrolling through his phone, no doubt keeping up with the social media posts about each player. "Did you know he was only five-foot-three when he started high school?" Damn. That's one hell of a growth spurt. He's got great size now at six-foot-three. It's ideal for your quarterback to be tall enough to see over the offensive lineman in front of him.

Everything goes on around me: Mack gets another beer, Jaden takes a handful of fries, the next five teams draft their players, and I just stare at the TV, not really seeing who gets chosen because I'm thinking about the Butchers' choice. There's change on the horizon there, and it might be good for me.

As of right now, I have no commitment to the Hurricanes. Until I sign my next contract with them, I'm free to go anywhere that wants me. The Butchers have just made a move big enough to make Jared Clark leave, and before I sign back on to my first team, I can do everything in my power to help make Nash's league successful.

I might be delusional, but things just might be finally looking up.

*Chapter Thirty-Two*

## NASH

I'm quickly learning the harsh reality of playing in a brand-new league.

I walk onto the court for the start of practice and see chaos. There's a team already there, all right. But they're standing on either side of the half-court line throwing big red rubber balls at each other.

Daly walks up behind me and quickly takes in the scene. "What the fuck is going on?"

I gesture at the players. "Dodgeball."

"I see that," she says flatly. "But why are they here during our time?"

"Let's go see."

We walk over to where Coach is talking quietly to who seems to be the dodgeball team manager. She's pulled up to her full six-foot-four inches, ready for confrontation. I just catch clips of their conversation, "Scheduling disaster—I can't believe you allowed this to happen."

A couple of us are standing around waiting to see if we are

going to actually get to practice; a few others are warming up like they're sure we will.

Coach storms away from the other man, clapping to bring us all in. "There's been a mistake in the scheduling of the court time." She takes a breath.

Temi speaks up, "They're in the weight room too?"

Coach nods. "Apparently, this is a joint practice between two teams. There's one in the weight room now, and later in the day they will switch. Normally, I would have a backup plan, but since I'm not from around here, I'm not sure where we can go on such short notice to have any kind of workout." She looks at us for suggestions or ideas. Coaches are supposed to have an answer for everything, to never crack under pressure or let anyone see them flinch, but this season hasn't come without challenges, and we need to stick together if we want to make it.

"Let me call a friend," I say and step away from the group and into the locker room to grab my phone. I unlock it and go to my favorites, hold it up to my ear, and listen to it ring. Time and time again I find myself leaning on Wyatt when things go sideways in my life, and this time is no exception.

"Hello?" Wyatt answers.

And he never fails to come through when I need him.

"Hey," I hedge.

"What's up? Shouldn't you be at practice?"

"I am, but there was a scheduling issue and the Average Joe's are here, instead. We need somewhere else to go, and I thought maybe you might know someplace that can accommodate us last minute?"

"I think Ironsides is usually closed on Mondays, but I'll call and get them to open for you. He owes me a favor. I'll text you the address."

"Oh my God, you're a lifesaver. We cannot afford to miss a practice. Even just catching half of a workout is enough."

"It's no problem." I can hear the tease in his voice when he says, "Anything for my girl."

Tell me why my stomach did a little squiggle when he called me that? Why did I have to press my lips between my teeth to contain my smile? "Bailing me out, once again."

"It's not bailing if I want to help."

I toe the tip of my court shoe at the ground. "Nobody heard that anyway. So your boyfriend charm is wasted on me alone." I hear everyone in the main gym speaking over one another and say, "I've got to go let everyone know we're moving out." If I stay on this call with him any longer, I'm going to be flouncing out there like a little schoolgirl.

When I come back out of the locker room, my teammates are putting their warm-up sweats back on over their practice gear and changing out of their court shoes for a variety of other footwear, as if they've given up hope on having a practice today. They turn expectantly to me. I hold my hands out like I'm about to tell them I found the golden ticket and we're all going to meet Willy Wonka. "I've got a place. I'll text the group chat the address and we'll all meet there."

"Where are we going?" Temi asks.

"How did you find something so quick?" Lauren adds on.

"Wyatt trains at this gym with some teammates, and he said they're usually closed on Mondays, but he is going to call and get them to open for us."

An actual cheer that makes me feel simultaneously like a hero and a fraud, breaks out. I wave them off. "Yeah, yeah, yeah. You can thank me if this actually works."

Temi runs up to me. "Wyatt did this?"

I shrug. "He said the guy owes him a favor."

"Either way, that is so sweet of him."

I try to hide the smile and blush combo spreading across my face. "He's a sweet guy." And I am walking the tight rope between us. The thin line between making a good thing even better and ruining something that's been so important in my life. The cherry on top of that shit pie is that I'm also lying to all my new teammates, who I feel like are becoming my good friends.

I try to not let those thoughts linger as we get to Ironsides gym and acquaint ourselves with the space. I check my texts one last time before abandoning my bag. There's one from Wyatt.

WYATT

Let me know if you need anything else.

If he only knew what I really wanted from him…he might change his mind about that comment.

———

When we wrap up our weight room session, the owner of the gym, an older man who's ex-NFL, comes out to greet us. "Ladies, I hope you enjoyed your time here. I'd like to extend a discounted offer to you for your off-season gym needs. Just let me know if you're interested later on." We all nod our thanks.

Coach speaks up, "Thank you for letting us use your space on such short notice."

"No problem, always looking out for H-town's athletes when I can." It's at this moment that Wyatt strides through the front door. "Wyatt," John, the owner, greets him, "Great to see you."

I walk to Wyatt's side, intent on thanking him myself for saving our practice. "John, this is my girlfriend, Nash."

"Oh, that's how you know this lovely team," John says, unsurprised. I reach out to shake John's hand. He's built like a truck and his head is shiny bald.

"Nice to officially meet you."

"You, too. Let me know if you need anything else. I'll get out of your way so you can pack up." With that, he strolls back to the office he came from. I assume he has work to finish since we disturbed his off day.

I reach down to grab my bag, but Wyatt beats me to it. "Let me." And I do.

I wave goodbye to the girls, and we head out the front door of Ironsides. The weather isn't unbearable yet, but the wind that blows is warm, hinting at what's to come. Wyatt reaches for my hand as we walk toward my car. We basically don't go anywhere in public not connected anymore. My body was tired before Wyatt showed up, completely exhausted from dead lifts, but now I can feel it light up in his presence. Starting from where he's touching me and moving up my arm. It's getting harder to ignore how natural this feels. Like what I imagine a caterpillar must feel when making its cocoon. I think it knows it's doing the right thing and that it will be protected while it morphs into something beautiful, and I silently wonder if whatever this is between us will also change into something equally as wonderful.

I unlock my car, and Wyatt throws the bag in my backseat. We stand awkwardly for a second, unsure of how to leave things. He came to my rescue once again. How many times does he have to do this before I consider him my official knight in shining armor? He's certainly not the freshman I once knew, all shaggy-haired and gangly. I take in his full lips that surround his bright smile, light stubble gracing his cheeks. Somewhere during the last five years while I was gone, Wyatt has become a grown man.

I can't help but tongue my lip. "I'll see you Friday for lunch?" I lean back against the car, and he leans in toward me. So close I can smell his cologne, sharp and masculine.

"You will." I have the sudden urge to kiss him, and I have to grip my keys so tightly in my hand that it hurts. He must be able to read the look on my face because he asks, "Penny for your thoughts?"

Something has been weighing on my mind. "When this deal is done and everyone's gotten what they wanted, what's going to happen to us?"

"We'll still be friends, right?" he says honestly.

"Yeah," I say. "It's just–" Wyatt takes my hand and momentarily stops me.

"I think things will work out exactly the way they're supposed to."

"That's cryptic as fuck."

He laughs. "I know." He takes one step closer. "You trust me, right?"

I gulp like a cartoon character. "I trust you," I say, but my eyes go right to his mouth. I'm sure he notices because he goes completely still for a second. Like if he allowed himself to move an inch, he would unleash on me. My heart pounds in my chest and I wait for him to move, to decide how far this is about to go in this now-empty parking lot. No one we need to convince is around. Then again, no one is around at all. If we kissed now, it wouldn't be for show, wouldn't be for stress release. It would be kissing just because we wanted to. Do I want to take this further? Would our friendship survive if we didn't work out?

Wyatt takes a measured step back. Giving me space to catch my breath.

*I guess I'll never find out.*

# Chapter Thirty-Three

## WYATT

The next home game for the Moons is on a Saturday in early May, and the place feels packed. That's probably because the entire Hurricanes team is here, including the sixteen-man practice squad. I didn't give anyone the option to refuse. I told them they could bring anyone they wanted, but they had to be here tonight.

There's about eighty of us here, give or take. We absolutely overwhelmed the concessions before finding our seats. I stand in the middle handing out noisemakers to anyone who will take one while the teams warm up below.

I hand a water bottle full of little rocks to a rookie. "I want this section to make so much noise it sounds like the entire arena is full."

He nods and takes another from me to hand to the girl he brought. I look at her, realize I'm probably being rude, and mutter, "Nice to meet you. Welcome to the Hurricanes." Then I amble off to the next group to see who I can entice with some hand clappers on a stick.

I have to pull my shirt away from my chest again. Chrissy

assured us the paint we used was body safe, but it itches like a son of a gun. I can't wait to have the cool air flowing across my heated skin.

Finally, the announcer starts talking and lets the crowd know it's time for the national anthem. "Please rise if you are able and remove your caps for the singing of the national anthem by Claire Young."

We all rise, and as a group we are pretty intimidating. I wonder if we are moving the needle in favor of the Moons with our sheer size. A young lady steps out to sing the national anthem and we cheer politely when she's done.

*Here we go.*

"The starters for your home team, the Houston Moons," bellows the announcer.

I gesture at all the guys around me to get up. Nash is probably so focused on the game she hasn't even noticed all of us up here in the Moons colors.

She's fucking about to, though.

When he starts calling the names of the players, our chunk of the crowd goes wild with the noise makers we brought. I see some of the other team physically flinch. Each starting player has a palm-sized volleyball they throw into the crowd, and they all come our direction.

"Starting at outside hitter from the University of Wisconsin, at six-feet, one-inch tall…"

I look at Jaden, Colin, Noah, and Mack. "Now!"

We all whip off our shirts just as Nash's name is called. "Nashville Green!"

I scream until my lungs are burning, spinning my noise maker in the air.

"Let's fucking go, Nash!" Jaden hollers from my right.

Nash steps up to throw her swag and looks right at me. We

are front and center, and she whips it at me. It hits me in the chest, and I juggle my arms trying to secure it. She twirls her pointer finger around, a laugh glossing her lips.

I look at Colin in confusion. "What's she saying?"

Audrey turns around below us and barks a laugh. "You're out of order, idiots."

Chrissy turns at the sound of Audrey's laugh and puts a hand over her mouth. "Wyatt and Noah, switch places."

I look at Noah with a navy-blue O on his chest and realize we've been spelling MONOS. "Ope, lemme scooch right past ya there."

Once we're in the right order, Nash gives us a thumbs up. She turns to face her team, greeting the next player called. When Temi's name is called, I elbow Jaden, and when she whips her little ball at him, I whoop a laugh. Seems like his persistence is paying off.

I hope mine will pay off, too.

# Chapter Thirty-Four

## NASH

For the first time stepping out onto the home court, I can feel the energy emanating from the stands. The United Care Center is absolutely buzzing, and it's everything I dreamed it would be.

The bass is thumping in my chest as we line up at the outline of the court, waving as the crowd cheers. This is what we've been missing the whole time. Other stadiums we've been to have felt full, cheering for the other team. It's more than just home court advantage. It's seeing the pride you take in your city returned to you by its people.

I soak it all in as we go down the line taking turns throwing our ball into the boisterous crowd. Some seem to be targeting a particular fan, others just launching it and seeing where it lands. I nearly drop mine when I look for Wyatt to throw it to him, and I see him shirtless with a huge N on his chest. I throw my ball, beaming it at him. Wyatt barely has time to catch it and bobbles it a bit before finally securing it. My eyes go down the row once, and then again trying to make sense of the word. I can see the looks on their faces when they realize they're not in the right places. There's some shuffling in the stands, and finally they're in the right order. They whip their shirts in circles over their heads as they yell. I laugh when I see Colin say something to him that makes Wyatt smile. Probably something like, "That's why you play defense."

When the referee blows his whistle, we all move to our starting spots. I can't hear the announcer's commentary, but I can guess what they're saying, "The Moons are the top blocking team in the league, finding success setting the pins and patrolling the middle." They would be right. Daly is six-foot-four. She makes her sidestep to either the opposite or the outside look easy.

My heart is beating fast, normal for me since a brown sugar espresso is part of my pregame routine, but my overall nerves are closer to the surface tonight than usual. It feels like the stakes are higher than they've been all year.

I put—not all, but most of—my eggs in tonight's basket. I called in so many favors to get the entire Hurricanes team here. I've asked Wyatt for so much lately, and all I've been giving him in return is Texas lessons, my friendship, and a singular kiss, which feels measly in comparison to what this sort of attention could do for the Moons. Between Wyatt and his teammates, and the fans that are here of their own accord… we need to put on a show.

Those thoughts continue floating around in my mind as we settle in for the first set.

"The implementation of the electronic line judge has increased the speed of the game by eliminating the need for human line judges and challenges," Jaden recites, and we stare at him like he just grew a second head. This man is all football all the time. No room for anything else in his mind, but now he's spouting volleyball jargon like he's an expert? "What?" He shrugs. "I did some reading."

The look Noah gives me is knowing.

The speed of the game is mesmerizing. When you get to the nitty-gritty, football is a lot of standing around. If you recorded an entire game and fast-forwarded through all the commercials, time-outs, ref calls, and waiting in between plays, you would watch about thirty minutes of actual football, even though a full game is technically four, fifteen-minute quarters. Between the automatic replay technology, the electronic line judges, and the fifteen-second serve timer, volleyball has almost no downtime. Those things keep the next point coming, but the speed of the ball itself is bewildering. It's almost like the puck in hockey. The velocity of the hits, and the rapidity of the serve-receive is mind-boggling. You can't take your eye away for a second or you'll miss it.

I watch Nash the whole time, obviously, but in the moments when my focus widens and takes in the entire team, I watch in awe as they shift in sync. When it looks like the other team's outside hitter is going to hit it down the line, they all shift one way. When it looks like a cross court hit, they all shift the other way. Like a school of fish, always on the lookout.

They're close to putting this game away, if they can push through and win the third set. The score is too close for comfort to try and put this away in three. The Fire is up to serve.

I cup my hands around my mouth and start to chat. "Houston Mo-ons." I clap five times after, and people in the crowd around me pick it up. We've got to make them second-guess something that should be muscle memory. Like when the crowd behind the uprights tries to distract the opposing kicker and makes them miss. All of the Hurricanes are screaming and twirling/shaking/slapping their various noise makers. The regular fans around us catch on and add their voices in. The cacophony thundering through the gym is like one of Houston's powerful summer storms.

The ball hits the tape at the top of the net and tumbles its way over, but the Moons were ready for it. Lucky serve. You never get that twice in a row. Bumping a tipped-over ball that short is tough, and the setter is forced to bump-set. The ball goes too far back for the opposite hitter, forcing the D ball. It doesn't cause quite as much confusion among the Fire as the Moons would hope. Their defense stays disciplined reading around their blockers. They're able to get a beautiful pass to their setter and she lofts it toward the outside. I'm not gonna lie—their hitter's swing is majestic as she flies through the air. She's nothing compared to Nash, of course. But even I knew it was a good swing, and I'm not surprised when it beats the block and tumbles down the Moons' side of the net. Their point.

The same player, number eight, goes back to serve again.

If we made her stumble once, we can do it again.

I rally the crowd once more, raising my hands in a 'pump it up' motion. We get as loud as we can. This set is getting way too close for comfort.

This time her jump serve hits the net. I look up at the scoreboard. Twenty-three all.

Chrissy turns to us. "What if they tie at twenty-five?"

I open my mouth to answer, assuming none of my other teammates are going to know the rules, but Jaden beats me to it. "They'll keep playing until someone wins by two."

I point my thumb at him. "What he said."

We watch with bated breath as the Vegas player goes back to serve. When the ball hits the net, we all expel our held breath.

It's Nash's serve and it's basically on her to win. A serve error like the Fire had will effectively end this game.

Nash steps back to the line, bouncing the ball as she goes. A hush falls over the stadium.

I've seen Nash play tons of times, and I still can't get over her serve warmup. She takes the full fifteen seconds. I count along, like the dance mom's on that show she made me watch for a whole weekend once while she was sick, as she bounces it five times, spins it toward herself twice, then picks it up, and spins it twice more. I motion along with her. She once told me that in high school someone made fun of how long her warmup was, pressuring her to change it, but then she got benched for missing too many serves. She went back to this routine and hasn't deviated since.

She tosses the ball and pounds it to the other side. I can see it float side to side in the air from where I'm sitting, and I feel bad for whatever player ends up having to field that ball.

It goes to the back right and the player chases it down behind her. She reaches one arm out in an attempt to get it, but it flies right over and lands just barely in.

"Ace, baby," shouts Jaden as the Hurricanes group swarms like a disturbed beehive.

Game point.

Nash's serve again.

The world's longest warmup again, but I'm so glad that in a moment like this she has it to rely on, to steady her, and focus her mind.

"Dude, what is she doing back there," asks Mack.

"Shut the fuck up. Don't jinx her," I snap.

She pauses for one second, then tosses the ball high over her head, taking a couple big steps. By the sound the ball makes when it connects with her hand, I just *know* it's a good one. It sails right over the top of the net, barely any arc for the other team to get under. It's perfectly positioned. The middle back dives for it, but misses.

It's an ace. Two in a row to win.

"MOONS WIN," the announcer calls over the loudspeakers, but I'm not paying him any attention. My eyes are locked on my best friend whose teammates are coming over and shaking her by the shoulders and patting her butt.

My legs move without my permission, and I'm hurtling, unthinking, down the stairs toward the court, down the little ramp that leads to the hardwood and jogging to the Moons who are now a tangled pile of limbs.

Someone puts a hand on my chest. "Excuse me, sir. You can't–" But I don't even let him finish. Colin will come behind me and smooth it over anyway. My one-track mind is taking me straight to Nash. She turns from Temi at the last second and sees me.

"Wyatt, oh my God." She's breathless from the game, and I'm sure the winning. I wrap my arms around her waist and hoist her into the air.

In that moment, when nothing matters except what exists between us, it's the easiest thing in the world to touch my lips to hers.

# Chapter Thirty-Six

## NASH

When Wyatt sets me back down, my knees feel like Jell-O. Winning a home game with the stands packed, and then getting the life kissed out of me by him is an emotional roller coaster I don't ever want to get off of.

"You were amazing." Wyatt's face is still so close to mine, and I realize with a sudden fierceness that I want to kiss him again. And again. The thought that maybe I can spend the rest of my life kissing that face is a terrifying one. His lips felt the same as they did before: soft and warm, but this moment was different. A kiss before leaving the country is a low point. A kiss on camera for a laugh at the rodeo is lighthearted. A kiss after winning a big home game is the highest I've ever felt.

I look around the stadium, buzzing with fans, and the whole Hurricane gang coming behind Wyatt, then look back to him. "Thank you." I can't find any more words, but I hope he knows that I mean for being my best friend, for doing this for me, for bringing his teammates here. For asking a favor of them when just a year ago he wasn't thrilled to be a Hurricane. For kissing me like I've never been kissed before.

His eyes search mine. What they're looking for, I don't know. "Nash, I–"

"Photos!" Chrissy yells. "Get together, guys. I want all the Hurricanes and all the Moons." She motions with her hand, telling us to all squish together. We stand in front of the net, under the bright lights, arms around one another. Wyatt scoots in next to me. His right arm over my shoulders. I look up at him and I'm hit by the memory of us at flag football. It's crazy to think that photo inspired all this. Now we're all together on the hardwood of the volleyball court, hopefully on our way to a winning season, smiling and sweaty. At the beginning when I was full of uncertainty and unease, he was there. Here he is again today, holding me up while I climb to the top.

"Say Houston," Chrissy calls. Several H-Town hand signs —hand facing you, just the pinky finger and pointer finger up —appear around me.

"Houston," we say together, smiling at Chrissy's phone camera.

When Chrissy is satisfied with the pic, the Hurricanes and the Moons mingle. It's a bit hysterical seeing some of the shorter football players getting towered over by the volleyball goddesses.

Someone taps me on the shoulder, and I turn to find Colin, Chrissy, Noah, and Audrey. They each hug me in turn, and I feel bad cause I'm super sweaty.

"You did so great!" Audrey has a brand-new Moons shirt slung over her shoulder. She must have just bought one from the merch table.

"This is my first volleyball game, but it won't be my last, that's for sure," Colin says.

"Thank you, guys, for coming."

"Of course," says Noah. "We support all women's sports."

Audrey nods her agreement. "I loved watching you play! Your moves out there are how cool I think I look at yoga, but I definitely look nowhere near as graceful as y'all."

"I'm sure Noah doesn't think that."

"He doesn't," Noah says. Audrey looks up at him with so much love in her eyes that it chokes me a little. What must it be like to have that? To bare your soul to someone and have them accept you for exactly who you are? When I had to be overseas, I couldn't let myself want that, but now that I'm home and I'm hoping for permanency…maybe I could?

Wyatt puts his hand on the small of my back. "We can stand here all night, but I'm ready for my post-game burger."

I start to head toward the locker room to get changed and grab my stuff. "I'll be right back." My stomach growls and I'm shocked at how hungry I am all of a sudden.

Whataburger with my best friend—I mean, faux boyfriend—is calling my name.

## Moons Chase a Championship!

*Texas Sports News*

The 13 and 3 Houston Moons are on the hunt for the championship. Their upcoming games against Atlanta and Omaha will be crucial to securing their trip. The 12 and 5 Starfire are right behind them in prime position to be the Moons' biggest opponent.

The Moons' Nash Green and Daly Acosta are leading in kills and blocks, respectively. They're currently playing in the United Care Center. Their next home game is this upcoming Saturday, or you can stream them free on YouTube.

## Chapter Thirty-Seven

WYATT

"Why do we have to be here at ten-thirty in the morning for lunch?" I ask as we step into a quickly forming line at a BBQ place. Nash insisted we continue my Texas lessons after the crawfish boil last month, and today is a beautiful day to... stand in line, apparently. The restaurant looks like a house with a big wraparound porch, but the smells wafting from it are unlike any home-cooked meal I've ever had the pleasure of smelling.

"Because when you're the only Michelin-starred BBQ joint in Houston, you sell out fast." Nash gestures at the line we're in. We take a minuscule step forward, and I look toward where it winds around the wooden porch. Seeing my thousand-yard stare, she reassures me. "It's worth it, trust me."

It takes us two hours to get to the front of the line. *Two hours*. I was hungry when we got here, but I'm starving now. At least you get the delicious smell of smoked meat the entire time, for free.

When we step up to the counter, I don't know what to get, so Nash orders us a little of everything she likes. We take a seat at the picnic-style tables and wait until they call her name over the speaker. When they do, I get up and grab our tray from the guy in the window. It's huge and full to bursting with brisket, pulled pork, juicy turkey breast, potato salad, and baked beans.

I set it on the table in front of her and take my seat. It's been absolute fucking torture smelling this the whole time we were in line. Not even a plate of free bread while we waited to sate my appetite. Nash has her face buried in her phone. "Nash, it's time to eat. Come on, we've been waiting for hours."

She looks up at me, her eyes full of emotion that I can't quite read until she slides her phone to me. "Look at this."

It's a clip of the Moons game last week. The last point of the game—Nash's ace serve. All of the Hurricanes rushing the court after their victory, and right in the middle of it all, with a halo of space around us like we're meant to be the focus of the video, is us. I watch as I pick her up, her legs wrapping around my waist, her face glowing with sweat and her smile so bright it could light up a city. It's like a scene out of the rom-coms Nash would always make me watch when she was feeling down.

Then I stare as we kiss on screen. I knew it was coming. I remember it with every fiber of my being, but I can't rip my eyes away. It's soft and gentle, almost surprising. It's like I'm trying to say how proud I am of her without words.

The stream of shitty comments floating across the screen breaks me out of my reverie:

*I'm sure it was easy to fill that arena selling the tickets for only $20.*
*They're really trying hard with this PVF stuff, huh?*
*I'll watch volleyball that actually matters.*
*It won't last.*

*This game is so slow compared to the men's leagues we already have. I've seen better performances at my local Sunday rec league.*

I pause the video. "You shouldn't be reading this kind of stuff."

She pulls her phone back and continues her doom scroll through the comments. "I wasn't looking for it."

"I'm sure it will blow over." I push the tray of meat toward her and give her one of the paper plates the guy in the window handed me.

"It has four-hundred-thousand likes. It's going viral."

"All of those dudes are washed-up high school heroes who never got picked for the baseball team. Or were stars in high school and didn't make a college team. They don't know anything about the PVF, or you." She's still looking at the phone, and I'm getting sick of the same fifteen seconds of the same song over and over again. I scoop up most of the pulled pork and put it on her plate. It's her favorite, and I just need a taste.

"This is exactly what I'm afraid of though, Wyatt." She lifts her green eyes to me and there's genuine hurt in them. "That nobody will give a fuck. That they would rather have one-hundred men's leagues to choose from rather than watch one singular women's game. I dragged you into this against your will for my personal gain. We filled the stadium for that home game, and still, no one cares." I wish I could take away the sting of the words from strangers, but Nash cares too much. Volleyball is her whole life. I can relate, but no one is saying the NFL is "slow" or "trying really hard."

"People care. The loud assholes on the Internet weren't at that game. I was. It was electric. You were amazing. And I'm not here against my will." I take her hand and place her fork in it. "Besides, any publicity is good publicity."

"That only applies to, like, the Kardashians and Paris Hilton."

I shake my head. "They just kicked the nest of a very passionate fan base. I bet your next home game will be standing-room only, and it won't be just because of the Hurricanes."

This is something I'm sure of. I believe in Nash and the Moons. They're going to do great things—and I will make her believe it too.

# Chapter Thirty-Eight

## NASH

## *JUNE*

Well, I'll be damned. He was right.

Our next two home games were both more packed than the last. One after another, we bring in an opponent and knock them on their ass in front of a roaring home crowd.

The video stays viral for at least five days, which is a long life in internet time. Long enough that the Gridiron sports podcast gets a hold of it. They don't know dick about volleyball, but they hype us up as athletes, which is nice. A female-focused sports Instagram page jumps on it, making a multi-slide post about the history of volleyball in the US and in other countries. It's exactly what I would want to say if I had the platform.

At every game, various members of the Hurricanes cheer us on from what's basically their unofficial section.

It was a bumpy start to the season with the scheduling issues and such, but we've more than made up for those beginning losses now. This is starting to move from 'let's just keep this thing alive' to 'we might actually make it'. Bragging rights are great and all, but so is a Tiffany necklace and an individual share of one-million dollars, which is the prize for the team that wins the championship.

We gather around Coach at the end of another tough practice. She's gotten harder on us as the season has gone on and she's seen more of our potential. I'm glad for it, though. I know we all want to win this.

"I'm very excited to tell you that for the first time in this league, there will be a televised game." Every game so far this year has been streaming live on YouTube. It's great because the games stay up all the time, so we can watch any time we want, and they put tons of work into the production, including custom commercials, but obviously you'd get more attention if you were on cable.

"Which game?" asks Temi.

"The championship," she replies, and we all titter with excitement.

There are only two games standing between us and the championship game. This is a real possibility. A real team, playing real volleyball, on real live cable TV.

Lauren looks at me. "I've never been to Omaha."

I shrug. "I have for the Big Ten championship." It's widely considered the volleyball capital of the U.S.

"At least it won't be winter." I'm not eager to return to Midwest winters.

Speaking of Wisconsin, I'm reminded that in just a few weeks, it will be June and we'll be on a plane to Poblocki, and I'll be fulfilling the last of my deal with Wyatt. The time has really started to fly since the beginning of the season. I blinked and I was home, starting on a new team and a new league. I blinked and we're in a position to now go to the championships. If I blink again, it'll be back to just being Wyatt's roommate.

I need to stop blinking.

There's a churning in my stomach at that thought. I assume it's from how little I've eaten today compared to how many down-n-backs I've run. Of course, it has nothing to do with how much more attached to Wyatt I am now than I was in February.

It couldn't be that.

Definitely couldn't be that.

---

When I get back from practice that night, Wyatt is on the couch watching baseball.

"Food is on the stove," he says when he hears me come in.

"Thanks." I move to the kitchen and grab a bowl to help myself to the spaghetti. Wyatt isn't an amazing cook, his mom did all of it growing up, but he can hold his own with a jar of sauce.

"How was practice?"

My eyes light up. I can't believe I momentarily forgot the big news. "The league championship is going to be on cable TV!"

"That's so exciting, Nash. I'm so happy for you guys."

I look at him over my shoulder while I put hot sauce on top. "I guess you were right about there being no bad press." Sure, there were hate comments, but there were also tons of comments from young women excited to continue their career after college, and girls even younger who were eager to come see a game.

"I'm normally right. Surprised you didn't know that by now."

I plop on the couch next to him with my spicy spaghetti and dig in. The game is not interesting. I find baseball to be extremely slow, especially on TV. I decide to bother Wyatt, instead.

"If we go to the championships, will you come?"

He answers without hesitation. "Of course."

"Even though it's the weekend before your brother's wedding?"

"Of course. All I gotta do is show up to the wedding on time and not make a fool of myself during my best man speech. That's my only obligation. I'll be able to do both."

I roll my eyes. *Men.* "Of course, you're in the wedding, but you'll show up at one o'clock and be ready by two."

He laughs. "I don't know what time the ladies have to be there, and I don't want to know."

"It's nice to be just a guest and show up when it actually starts." I twist more spaghetti around my fork. "But I'm going to have to sit all by myself."

"I'm sure you won't be alone. It's a small town. They don't know any strangers."

"I'll just sit and wait for you to come back." I go quiet for a second. I've been feeling the tug of nerves in my gut ever since I heard the news about the championship being televised. At first, I thought it was because I was possibly going to be on TV, but most of the games I played in college were televised. It hit me when Temi was driving us home. "I feel like this is all too good to be true. Like at the end, even if the championship is a success and maybe we even fucking win, that the powers that be could still decide this isn't worth it and cancel the whole thing. Then after all of this, I'll be forced to quit and become a coach." At the end of the day, it's my passion and my sport, but it's still ruled by capitalism. It might not matter that the Moons filled the seats. If the Las Vegas Fire, or any of the other teams can't and the league loses money as a whole, they'll still can us.

"You can't will something to happen the way you want it to, but you've put your all into this and I think it shows. If there's no league after this year, then you have to go win that championship and own the only trophy they give out before it's gone."

"That's kind of depressing." I look at the noodles in my bowl. They look limp and a little sad, but maybe I'm projecting.

"Life can be depressing," he says quietly, and I know he's talking about meeting his hero and hating him. About leaving Green Bay and starting over again in a new city on a new team. I wonder—if he had the chance to go back would he actually take it now with everything that has happened over the last few months? "Want to see something that will cheer you up?"

I immediately perk up. "Of course I do." He reaches into the collar of his shirt and pulls out his chain. It's the same one I've never seen him without, but now it's got a small silver N hanging from it. I meet his eyes and see pride in them. "My initial?" It comes out high-pitched.

"Gotta show off my girl." He lets the chain fall back against his chest and I find myself briefly jealous of a piece of metal. God, I am so catastrophically and undeniably into him.

"Who could possibly think we're faking now?" I mean to make a joke, but it comes out tight.

Fuck me.

## Moons Clench the Championship Spot
*ESPN*

The Houston Moons will be one of the two teams in the Pro Volleyball Federation championship held in Omaha this upcoming Saturday. Last week they beat Atlanta; this week they're preparing to face New Orleans for the championship trophy, as well as one-million dollars in prize money and custom jewelry.

The road to the championship game will be intense because in standard form, the next two weeks before a deciding game like the championship will be filled with hardcore practices, studious review of game tape, and preparation for the big game ahead.

Our own Victor Vega will be traveling to Omaha to cover the game. It will be on ESPN starting at 8 Eastern/7 Central.

# Chapter Thirty-Nine

NASH

The championship game is no exception to the ball throwing pregame routine.

I line up next to the other starters—Temi, Daly, Danica, Simin, and Lauren—with mine in hand. The announcer booms over the speakers, but I barely hear him as I scan the crowd. My parents would have loved to be here, but they didn't have the money for plane tickets and a hotel and everything. I know they're watching on TV, cheering me on from the living room of the house I grew up in.

My gaze lands on blue eyes in the front row as Wyatt towers above his neighbor. He's here. Just like he promised he would be.

I'm a little surprised to see him here by himself. Normally, the Hurricanes roll several deep. Where you see one, another is surely close behind. But here he is. By himself in my Moons number. Just for me.

I'm sure what I'm about to do is against the rules, but I don't care. When my name blares over the loudspeakers, I break rank and run toward Wyatt. He's so close to the court that I lean over the metal bars and hand him my ball. He catches my hand and kisses the back of it before letting me go. Stuff like that is going to make this really hard to undo when all of this is over. But I have plenty of time before I have to think about that. I have three plane rides between me and the end of whatever this is between us. Until I don't have any excuses to wear his cowboy hat or kiss him in front of everyone.

I sprint back to my place as Lauren steps up to throw her ball at her cheering parents. She was the last one to go, so we're ready to shake the other team's hands and get this show on the road.

In the last huddle before the game starts, Coach speaks, "We had twenty-two people who thought we'd be in the final. Maybe forty if you count your mothers." She looks at us each in turn as if acknowledging each individual player's contribution to getting us here. "A winning season never comes without adversity. It's what pushes you to be better. To rise above the bullshit and win. Everything we've been up against this year has led us here. Tonight. To this game. Understand? It's yours to win or lose." She puts her hand out into the circle, and we all add ours. "Moons on three. One, two, three–"

"MOONS!"

———

We are immediately out of system. The first pass takes a bad bounce forcing our setter to adapt and we lose our chance at running our intended offense, but we clean up our passing right after.

They're serving us short, disrupting my hitting route with a body in my way. We break their serve with our impeccable blocking, but ruin it again by serving to their libero. Rule number one of service—never serve to the player in the different color jersey. Passing is the bread and butter of a defensive specialist. They're there to get the hardest balls, so lobbing them a serve is basically just handing them points.

As much as we're messing up, the other team is too. We're doing a lot of throwing the ball around, pushing it and tipping it instead of the attackers killing it. Makes for a lot of scrambling on both sides. Both teams want to be able to load up their weapons and let it rain. The crowd wants that too.

We lose the first set.

The second set starts like the first except our near-perfect passing percentage drops. Now the issue to solve isn't our attack, but the basic fundamentals of play. This is embarrassing. Having done so much to get this on national television, and now my team's rocking on their heels looking for an answer after losing two straight sets.

The huddle is tense as we prepare for the third set. I can't help but speak with ardor. "Ya'll, what the fuck is going on?" I look at the ladies around me. They've been in situations like this before. I never thought when I came to play with this team that we'd be in this position. Though, nothing I thought or didn't think has turned out to be true this season.

Lauren, one of our decorated Olympians, speaks up. "We've got to get back to basics. No easy serves they can slam back at us. No bad passes. No unforced errors."

We all look to Coach who hasn't spoken again. "You all know what needs to be done. You're professionals and you know your mistakes. What's there for me to say? You can either do it or you can't. You're all capable of it. You have to want it more than the opposition wants it. You just have to go out there and make it happen."

"Yes, Coach" we say in unison. She's right. The team who wants it the most will win this. I look back up to the crowd, something I normally never let myself do, but tonight it feels necessary. Wyatt isn't looking at me, he's checking his phone, his face split with a smile like he's seeing our last kiss on video again. I wonder if he rewatches the clip like I do, but quickly shake off the thought. We have a game to win.

Tonight it has to be us screaming in victory at the end.

# Chapter Forty

## WYATT

"They really have to turn it around this set," the woman next to me says. She's either a girlfriend or a sister of one of the Moons players.

"They need to do more than that. They need a reverse sweep." Together we watch the team get ready for the third set. Already down two, the Moons need to win the next three sets in a row to win the game. This is more than a Hail Mary. That only works if you're down by less than seven. This is the equivalent of being down by fourteen or more.

I'm not sure what they talked about in the huddle that shifted their momentum, but Nash and the Moons come out swinging. Someone lit a fire under their ass, and if I had to guess, I would say it was Nash. I know this means everything to her. She's not someone who feels like she can ask for help, so for her to come to me with this "deal" all those months ago means she wants it bad. Of course, she sold it to me as a negotiation. She never could have asked otherwise.

The air is humming as the Moons come back and win the next two sets.

"Get up! Get up," I encourage everyone around us. "Everyone put your hands up when I count to three." I wait for the people closest to me to rise. "One, two, three." I throw my hands up over my head and the people to my right follow. I watch as the world's slowest wave circles through the arena. I can't believe I'm at the championship game, and these stands are so packed my wave looks more like a tsunami. When it comes back the second time, I stand again, trying to get everyone around me to participate. This time it only makes it halfway around before it dies out. That's fine, I guess. I didn't expect it to go on forever.

The score of the fourth set is twenty-two to twenty-three and the Moons need to win this point and get the serve back.

The other team's player goes back to the line to serve.

She tosses the ball up high, jumps, swings, and…

It hits the net.

They're all tied up. Twenty-three all.

Lauren goes back to serve. She tosses the ball up, but you can tell she's reeling her power in, worried about sending it to their libero who will handle it easily, or sailing it too far and over the back line.

The entire stadium holds their breath as the ball soars over the net. The left back player fields it, not a great pass, setter couldn't get to it, so she calls for help instead. The libero gets to it and bump sets the outside hitter. She goes up against the block, looking for a seam. But between Lauren and Temi, there isn't one. The blockers get a touch and the ball careens off their hands, over their heads, and toward the back row. The Moons are in control now.

Middle back—I think her name is Simin—calls for it, and the pass is perfect to the setter. Nash is already pulled back past the ten-foot line in position to swing. The set is up, and so is Nash. Flying through the air, hurtling toward the ball with momentum and power. Her hand makes contact, her entire body curling in, putting her core strength behind the hit. I feel myself screaming, the air burning from my lungs, but I can't hear it. Not over the rush of blood in my ears as I watch my best friend fly.

The other team isn't known for their blocking prowess, and Nash pushes her hit through their hands, which aren't strong enough to withstand her assault. She catches so much air on her approach that she's way on top of the ball, giving her the leverage she needs to pound it down and into the middle of the court. It's a kill.

They're ahead by one. One point away from match point and winning by the necessary two. I think every single person in this stadium is on their feet.

# Chapter Forty-One

## NASH

It's simultaneously unbelievable that we put ourselves in such a poor position at the beginning of this game and now we are in a position to win it all. I can taste victory in the air. And it smells like the woodsy warmth of Wyatt. Funny. I've never thought that before now even though Wyatt was there when U.W. beat Texas for the Big Ten championship my junior year. Maybe it's because all through college I knew I was going to leave him to go pro.

I'll have to examine that later.

For now, we have a game to win.

Lauren goes back for her second serve. This is for all the marbles. This is for everyone who left a nice comment or a mean comment on our viral video. This is for all the young girls who are watching now because we made it big enough to be on cable tonight. This is for younger me, who—as a barely functioning young adult—had to go live in another country just to have a chance at following her dreams.

I watch as the ball soars over the net. The Moons settle in to play tough defense.

Pass is up. I check on the hitter, they're moving inside to outside.

Setter gets to it. I look back to the hitter watching their nose for their attack choice.

I take one step, two. She jumps, and one second later I jump, adjusting myself according to the opening of the hitter's shoulder and the angle of her hips. I watch as she tries to redirect her hit around the block, but it's too late to change her momentum. The ball hits my hands, but I have to scramble when it starts falling on our side of the net.

I instinctively stick out one arm, fist closed, to pop the ball back up as it falls. It always felt illegal to me to be able to touch the ball a second time like that, but a block touch doesn't count against you.

I turn and bolt back to my approach position right at the ten-foot line and watch as Simin pulls the coolest libero shit I've ever seen and bump sets me facing the opposite direction. Even though she can't see me, she can hear me calling for it. She passes me the perfect ball. I can see Daly in the middle feigning a hit, the perfect decoy because she's so tall that it's hard to not look her way.

I'm in the air already, but I see the block coming. Unlike the other player, I do have time to adjust to it, opening my shoulders to hit the far cross instead of down the line.

The player in back left was ready for the deep ball, but she took her spot a little too deep and has to dive forward onto her belly, her hand out pancake style. They drill that pancake hand so deep into every volleyball player, it's probably ingrained in my DNA. That move is a last-ditch effort, but today must be that player's lucky day because that son of a bitch pops right back up, and their setter is there for a daring set from her knees to their outside hitter. They're going to come back at us with exactly what we dished to them.

This rally seems to go on as long as I've been alive, but I know it's only filled a few short seconds. This is still for game point. I'm breathing hard, my heart racing. The pace of this game is the highest it's been all night—maybe all season. The ball is already sent back to New Orleans's side. I watch as they set up the other side for a hit and I get off the net to play defense again. What does Wyatt always say? Offense wins games, but defense wins championships? Now is the time to prove it.

Their setter is able to get to it with a perfect set. Their outside hitter winds up, and I find myself in a time warp, blocking the same hit from the same player. I just *know* that she's going to try the hit she wanted last time but couldn't quite make work, and I adjust my body accordingly. At the same time, Daly's long legs bring her all the way to me in two steps, and we jump shoulder to shoulder. We push our hands over the net, not allowing the ball to fall between us and the net if we make contact.

And we do.

The ball touches my right hand and Daly's left. With our hands already headed over, we stuff it back down her throat. Right to the ground.

I watch it hit the ground.

I look at the ref who is signaling it as our point.

I look at the scoreboard where it shows us ahead and yet…

I still don't believe it.

It's not until Temi blasts into my side, hugging me, that it truly hits.

We just made history.

"We did it," Temi screams in my ear. The weight of her knocks me off balance and I'm suddenly on the ground.

She's screaming at me. I'm screaming at her.

More teammates come and pile on. Simin and Lauren. They're quickly joined by Daly.

We're all a screaming pile of limbs on the floor.

Like a vague background buzz, I can hear the crowd roaring. Confetti falls like snow over us, coating the floor and our hair.

From the bottom of the pile, one arm pinned under Temi's waist, I look over to the stands for Wyatt.

And he's there.

His face is red from yelling. He's clapping his hands. He… hugs the woman next to him?

Okay.

Even though she's a stranger and that hug is obviously platonic, it still stirs something in me. Jealousy? Protectiveness? It doesn't really matter. All that matters is the heat I'm filled with. I don't care if it's the adrenaline from winning influencing my brain, I have to find myself in his bed tonight. I'm ready to celebrate with him. I want him to know all of me. Not just my Chipotle order, not just my favorite BBQ and other things about Texas. I think I've earned one hell of an orgasm at his hands… or tongue. But we still have to make it all the way back to Houston tonight. It's going to be a long five hours between getting out of here, getting to the airport, the two-hour flight, and getting back home. I make a promise to myself right here as the confetti continues to fall around me, and I watch my team celebrate the win of a lifetime, that if I still feel this burning *need* when we get home tonight, I'll do everything it tells me to do to him.

The emcee of the night comes out from somewhere with a

mic in one hand and the trophy in the other. It's silver and huge and gorgeous. We all gather round as he sets it on a table and prepares to present it to Coach. "On behalf of this league, its sponsors, and owners, I present the first ever Pro Volleyball Federation women's championship trophy and one-million dollars to the Houston Moons." What's left of the crowd is on their feet chanting 'Houston Moons'. We group up, Coach holding the trophy first, and taking what feels like a hundred photos.

Someone comes around handing out golden scissors and setting up a ladder. I take one from him and watch as Coach steps up on the ladder and starts the first cut into the net. She saws through the bottom while music blasts in the background. When the net falls, cut right in half, we all go wild. Temi and I go to one side of the net to get ours. I hold it steady as Temi brings her gilded scissors down on the top strip, using both hands to force them shut. Her piece comes away and she holds it over her head to screaming teammates.

She remembers she's supposed to help me cut mine and returns to my side to hold the net while I hack at it. It takes me a couple seconds and it would be embarrassing, but I'm flying too high from the thrill of winning to care about what I look like right now.

After Temi and I finish with our pieces, we help the other girls with theirs, and when we're done, the net is in more than twenty pieces, proving to everyone else and ourselves that we did it. Despite all the obstacles in our way, despite coming from different cultures, countries, and backgrounds, we're champions.

The music stops and we all swing our attention to the middle of the court.

"Before we say goodnight," the announcer starts again, and

a funny feeling forms in my stomach, "we would like to invite you to tune into ESPN January 14th next year for the first game of *season two* of the PVF." Fireworks go off in the stadium, and the girls are all jumping and screaming, but for me it's like time stands still. My breath stalls out in my lungs.

*Did he just say what I think he just said?*

I turn away from my team and to the crowd, looking for Wyatt. I find him hanging over the barricade, hands fitted around his mouth, hollering. When his eyes meet mine, he drops his hands to the bar and mouths: *you did it.*

A hand touches my shoulder, and I turn to find Temi shoving an open champagne bottle at me. "We fucking made it," she screams in my ear.

I put my thumb over the top of the bottle and shake it. Champagne rains over us, sticky and wet, as we jump together and scream some more.

"Ladies," Coach calls from the sideline, and I know we've run out of time to soak it all in and celebrate. We untangle ourselves and head in her direction. When I look around, I don't see women with separate teams or titles anymore, I see us all together, the Houston Moons. "Congratulations on the win!" We scream again. "I never doubted you. And I'm so proud to have been a part of this team. Unfortunately, the bus is already here to take us to the airport. Get showered and changed. Meet in the back at nine sharp."

I look back to the stands one more time as we head into the locker room, but I only see the back of Wyatt as he heads up the concrete stairs. My eyes well with tears as I watch him go. That could be him in just a week, walking out of my life when his brother's wedding is done, our second season is scheduled, and there's no longer a need to keep up this fake relationship. I wish he had jumped the barriers like he did at that home game so he could rush to me, but the security here is way tighter, and we both don't need him getting into any trouble.

Except whatever he gets into tonight with me.

## TO THE MOON: Houston Women's Volleyball Team Wins First League Championship

*Houston Chronicle*

The Moons defeat their opponents, the New Orleans Elite, in a reverse sweep to win the first-ever PVF championship game. This comes with the title of 'the first to ever do it', along with a share of one-million dollars and a Tiffany necklace for each player.

While the game went the full five sets, the Moons never quit. Nashville Green was astounding with twenty-two kills and five blocks. The stands were packed with fans from both teams, including Nashville Green's boyfriend and fellow Houston athlete, Wyatt Vandergriff, who came to support his girlfriend. Victor Vega was there on premise for the game and reported that the "house was rockin'".

After the trophy was awarded and the net cut down, the president of the league took the microphone to announce that next season there will be three more teams added to the league's roster, and that a deal has been made with ESPN to air the games live on cable.

In just one season, the Moons have proven why they deserve to be here, why America needs a women's volleyball team, and that they are unstoppable.

# Chapter Forty-Two

## WYATT

The entire time I pack my bag, call an Uber, and walk to my gate, I'm completely lost in thoughts of Nash. Never in my life have I felt pride like I did tonight watching her and her team reach the highest level of success as a professional sports team. I saw my best friend achieve greatness, and I'm absolutely buzzing from watching her shake that champagne bottle, soaking her blonde braid and the front of her Moons jersey.

I'm losing the internal battle between my need to return to Wisconsin and my love for Nash. The love that's always been there has been set on fire and is blazing at one-thousand degrees. Like a moth to the flame, I'm ready to be incinerated.

I stow my backpack in the overhead bin above my first-class seat and settle in. Since the draft a few weeks ago, there's been no news about Jared Clark's status as a Butcher. He claims he doesn't do social media, and yet in the locker room he always knew what every outlet was saying about him. I'm sure he's knee deep in everyone's take on the Jason Amara selection. He's probably trying to decide if he's going to let his inner drama queen take over, or if he's going to try and play nice. Thank God he's not my problem anymore.

A young flight attendant with bright red hair approaches me. "What can I get you to drink?"

"A Diet Coke, no ice, please." She moves back to the kitchen area to grab it, and I scroll through my phone while I wait.

When she brings it back, I thank her and take a hefty sip.

I nearly choke on my beverage when she steps past me to help the next passenger. Nash is bent over so she doesn't hit her head on the ceiling of the plane. Her sweats are baggy and casual, but do nothing to quell the wave of need that rushes through me. "Nash." Her name is out of my mouth before I can blink.

She looks at me, her mouth open in surprise. "Oh my God. What are the chances?"

I raise a brow at her. "That we'd all be on the only return flight to Houston this late tonight?"

She laughs as she waits for the gentleman to stand so she can slide into the row. She keeps talking to me from the other side of the aisle as she shoves her backpack under the seat back in front of her. "No, that we'd be right next to each other!"

With my first NFL paycheck, I pledged to myself that I would never squeeze my frame into an economy seat again. It's been a joy and a privilege to fulfill that promise to myself. Hopefully now Nash has the success she needs to do the same.

I clock the slightly annoyed look on the gentleman in the aisle seat across from me right before he says, "Do you want to switch seats?"

I look quickly at Nash, who has a big smile on her face. "I'd love to."

The gentleman and I do the awkward sidestep around each other, and I plop down into my new seat next to Nash just as the plane pushes back from the gate. The rest of the Moons are filling in the seats around us.

"That was nice of him," she whispers to me, leaning in so close I can feel the warmth of her against my shoulder.

"He was probably worried about spending the next two hours as the monkey in the middle of us."

She shrugs. "Works for us."

The overhead speaker comes on for an announcement. "Crosscheck complete. Flight attendants, please take your seats." Wow, somehow we missed the entire safety demonstration and we're already waiting to take off.

It's damn near midnight now, so when we get in the air, the cabin lights are turned off. I lean my head back thinking the exhaustion will overtake me since this was a bit more than a twenty-four-hour trip, but I'm wide awake.

"I don't think I can sleep," Nash says.

I can't blame her after winning a championship. "I don't expect you to. What do you want to do, instead?"

There's something different about her. This Nash with her hair spilling around her shoulders looks like she's ready to take what she wants. It's making me feel too hot. I reach up and adjust my little air conditioner, pointing it straight toward my face.

I startle when Nash's phone lands with a loud clunk on the ground. When her hand lands firmly on my thigh as she leans over me to reach for it, I go completely still. I don't know what to do with her hand there, and I desperately do not want her to move it. It lasts about five agonizing seconds before she sits up straight and the loss of her hand feels like the loss to San

Francisco in the playoffs earlier this year. Like I can feel everything slipping through my fingers.

"Got it," she says with a little laugh, and it's all I can do to smile back while I try to calm my racing heart. The glimmer in her eye makes me think she knows exactly what she's doing right now.

"Ow. Fuck." I grab my leg where the metal refreshments cart hit my shin, tucking my leg back inside the space of my seat and out of the danger zone.

The flight attendant—clueless to my pain—is downright chirpy. "Do you need a refill?" She points to the empty cup in my left hand.

"Yes, please."

As she refills, she looks to Nash. "Something for you, honey?"

"Sprite, if you've got it, please."

I take my drink back from the flight attendant whose nametag says Beth. Then I lean back in my seat when Nash reaches for her Sprite. Somehow their hands don't make solid connections, and the Sprite is quickly falling…right into my lap.

"Oh my God. I'm so sorry." Nash is taking the measly napkin still left in her hand and attempting to pat my lap dry with it. Her hand is so, so close to where I've always wanted it to be. My hips fly up off the seat at her touch. When she looks at me confused, I mutter, "It's cold."

Beth comes to my rescue with a handful of paper towels, and I proceed to dry myself off. Could have been worse. Could have been hot coffee.

Until I realize my cock is pressing against the zipper of my jeans. *That's definitely worse.*

How long is this fucking flight again?

# Chapter Forty-Three

## NASH

I have no idea what's gotten into me. Nine years of friendship and all of a sudden, I don't know how to act around this man. It's like I closed my eyes when the referee blew the whistle on the last point of the game, and when I opened them, I saw everything clearly. Gone was the friend whom I'd toss popcorn at during a movie, and in its place was a man I'd love to toss my panties at. He's always been there, big and fit and sexy, but when the confetti fell, I looked at him and realized this was never fake to me.

The flight attendant moves on to the next row and I stuff the ruined napkins in the seat pocket in front of me. "Sorry about that."

"Nash," he says, and it's like he's calling me to look at his eyes and see the need there. "What are you doing to me?"

Our heads are so close I can feel the whisper of his breath move my hair as he speaks. Just the stupid little armrest between us. With the cabin lights so dimmed and the whole plane near silent, aside from the steady rhythm of the engines, it's like we're the only people here. "What do you mean?"

"I can't keep resisting you like this. Watching you tonight… touching me like this," his breath is a heavy whoosh as he struggles to find words. "I want things I know I can't have."

"What makes you think I don't want the same?" The words tumble out of me. The air around us bends and constricts as we take each other in. On the precipice of making a leap we've both been avoiding for five years since the kiss that changed my life.

Are we about to have this much-needed conversation at thirty-thousand feet? I look at Wyatt's lips—warm and welcoming—then back to his eyes, which are as blue as the sky was when I got up this morning.

I think we are.

"When you kissed me–"

"Nash, we don't have to do this." The look in his eyes is pleading, like he can't stand to hear what I'm about to say.

"Wyatt…we do need to do this. When you kissed me, it was the best kiss of my life. I laid awake all night thinking about it. Replaying it over and over in my head. Thinking about the way you felt, the warmth soaking through your shirt into my hands on your chest. I woke up the next morning, exhausted already and facing a twenty-one-hour travel day. I figured you'd be at my door the next morning, but you weren't. I figured you'd call when I landed in Rome, but you didn't. After a week went by and you never mentioned the kiss, I shoved all my feelings down. I put them away so that we could continue to have this friendship, a friendship that means everything to me. And that's where it's been ever since." I put my hand in his where it rests on his leg. "Until tonight."

I watch his throat as he swallows. "Why tonight?"

"Because now I'm in the business of taking whatever I

want." I look at our intertwined hands. "As long as you want that too."

He squeezes my fingers, bringing my gaze back to him. "That's all I've ever wanted."

"It is?"

He nods. "I had feelings for you before that kiss. I felt like I had to do it before you left because what if you never came back and I never got to experience the feeling of your lips? That would haunt me more than any playoff loss."

I poke an accusing finger at him. "*You* left me high and dry after that kiss."

"I thought *you* didn't want *me*," he confesses, his voice choked and raw. "When you still got on that plane and left, when you didn't text me that you landed safely, I thought to myself that's it. I've lost her. I put it all out there and she didn't feel the same, and now she's on another continent." He pauses, collecting himself. "Until you called. Do you remember?"

Of course, I remember. It was the first night I truly felt so homesick that I might vomit. I desperately needed to hear a voice from home, so I dialed his number. "I do."

"Then I knew that our friendship wasn't ruined. It was just the same as it had been…with no chance at ever being more. When I came to Houston, I was not in my right mind. I was not ready to be here—the place you love. I hated my prove-it contract. I missed Wisconsin. I never bought a house because I'm not committed to staying here, and I think you know that. I still don't have a signed deal with the Hurricanes. I could be a free agent in two months, forced to try out for any team that will take me." His jaw is so tense with those words, like being a free agent is a fate worse than death.

"We have some time," I start.

"If I can go back to Wisconsin, I will. So I can't offer you what you deserve knowing I could take off any day."

"But Jared Clark is still there."

"For now. They drafted a new quarterback, so who knows how long he will last with his replacement on the bench next to him."

"That's a crazy thing to be betting on."

He raises one eyebrow at me. "Crazier than betting on an unproven league?"

"I guess you have a point." I bite my lip. "So, now what?"

"We both feel something, and we're both in the off season. Let's enjoy it. At least for a little while. I could be gone tomorrow, but I could also get hit by a bus tomorrow. And I would live in purgatory forever if I died without ever having you."

"I want that. I don't want to wait any more." I pick up my hand, taking his with me, and move them to my lap. I lean over and take the sweatshirt from his lap and put it over our hands, covering us from any peering eyes.

Wyatt's mouth is agape when he looks at me. "Here?"

A smirk etches across my lips, teasing and cocky at once. "To start."

"What about your teammates?" Besides the seat occupied by the gentleman I switched with, we're surrounded by Moons players.

I peek over the seat in front of me where Simin and Daly are crashed out. It seems we're the only ones who were able to fight the adrenaline crash. "They're all asleep. No one even knows." I peek over the seat in front of me, looking at the door to the restrooms. "We could join the mile high club?"

Wyatt looks like he's desperate enough to consider it, but

he says, "There's no way we will both fit in that tiny ass bathroom."

I sigh dramatically. "You're right. I guess we'll just have to sit here and wait. Maybe look out the window."

"Or…" He starts as his hand leaves mine and touches my lower stomach, making my muscles twitch. I've never fooled around on an airplane before. The closest I've been to public stuff is in the very back of a dark movie theater, but I'm burning up for him, and I need him to take just the edge off right now until we can get home. And if the possibility of getting caught makes it even hotter, so what?

*Home.* It's a different place to me than him. We might be incompatible because of that, but that's future Nash's problem.

I suck in a sharp breath as Wyatt's knuckles pass over the peak of my thighs. I close my eyes and let the feeling of his fingers brushing against my skin wash over me. It could be five seconds or five hours of this, I'm not sure. I could do it all night. But I'm hit with a stark reminder of where we are when the captain's voice comes over the loudspeaker. "We are starting our descent into Houston. We will be arriving at terminal B."

I reopen my eyes and see Wyatt studying my face. With one strong movement, he cups my pussy in his huge palm and lets his eyes linger on mine, full of promise.

My legs react like that of a baby giraffe when we stand as the plane arrives at the gate. I try and keep my face from burning as I sling my backpack over my shoulder. I have to get off this plane and into this man's bed right now.

I've waited nine years for this and I'm not quite sure that I can wait another five seconds.

The car ride home is the quietest Nash and I have ever been. What is there to say when you know you're on your way home to possibly ruin the best friendship you've ever had, and at the same time make all your dreams come true?

We drop all our crap at the door and Nash takes my hand and drags me up one flight of stairs, and then the next, without pausing. The couch is objectively closer, but there's no way we could do this comfortably on there with both of our sizes.

We burst through my room, and she pushes me down on my bed. Thank fuck I cleaned up in here before I left for the airport.

I pat my thighs, signaling for her to straddle me, and she steps to me, bringing her knees on either side. If she was any shorter, she might not be comfortable, but her long legs are just able to adjust to the width of me. She tips her hips slightly. "Already looking for friction?" I tease and she simply moans in response.

I want to make my way to that pretty pussy, but I can't escape the call within me to thrust just a little first.

If you would have told me five years ago that I would be dry humping my best friend after she just won a national championship, I would have told you you're fucking crazy.

With the barrier of our clothes between us, I could probably do this all night. It's plenty to keep me hard, and yet not enough to bring me too close to the edge.

I take my time, sliding my hands up her hoodie and caressing her breasts. In my wildest dreams and my most secret fantasies, I never imagined it would be this good. She reaches behind her neck and rips the hoodie over her head impatiently, taking the shirt she had on with it. I pull her sports bra down and pop a petal pink nipple into my mouth, savoring the way it feels against my tongue.

"Are you going to fuck me now?" she asks, gaze up toward the ceiling, left hand holding my face to her chest. I take her in, all lean, long muscles, her hair askew from the game and the flight, her sweats riding low on her hips.

My grin is a crooked tease when I say, "I guess you deserve it now. You've been very patient, and tonight you're a champion."

"Champions get cock," she says seriously, but then snorts a laugh.

I put my fingers on her chin and force her gaze to meet mine. "My girl gets whatever she wants, whenever she wants it." I use my hand to hold her still and bring her lips to mine.

The kiss is searing. More so than any kiss I've ever had before, it's branded on my heart and in my mind. It seems to go on forever until Nash breaks away, panting. Immediately she goes for my jeans. Undoing the button and sliding the zipper down. I'm so hard I can feel every inch of the zipper's teeth moving until it's totally open, and all I can feel is the relief of not being confined.

I watch as Nash licks her lips at the sight of me, only making me harder. It feels like the right time to come clean about just how long I've wanted this. "Do you remember when we came home from the rodeo?" She bites her lip, and I know she's thinking about how she took care of herself after. "I came to your door so I could apologize after I got out of the shower and I… overheard you."

Her eyes go wide with shock. "You what?"

I massage her thighs where they straddle me while I explain. "When I realized what you were doing, I didn't stay. I swear. But I did go back to my room and turn the shower back on so you wouldn't hear me…" I look down at where we meet, our long legs tangled together.

"Touching yourself?" She finishes for me, her voice barely a whisper. I nod, my head still down. I'm not proud of my actions, but I don't regret anything that's led us to this. "Was it like this?" My breath stills in my chest as she glides her hand toward my shaft. She strokes me in one long, slow movement. "Or more like this?" She tightens her grip on me and my hips buck.

I put my head against hers, breathing the missing air into my lungs. All my thoughts hinge on the next movement of her hand, how tight or strong or grazing her next pass will be.

"Just like that," I pant.

"I have so much adrenaline—I need to take care of you. Please let me."

As hard as I am, and as much as I want that, there's a little sliver of guilt gnawing at me from the inside. I catch her hands before they can take me out of my boxers. "Before we do this, I need to make sure you know that as of right now I would still go back to the Butchers if they called me." I search her eyes for any hint of her pulling away, but all I see is sexy determination.

"I'm more worried about our friendship staying intact."

"Let's make a promise right now. No matter what happens, we'll still be best friends." I hold my pinky out to her. "Promise?"

She wraps her long one around my thick one. "Promise."

She moves from straddling my thighs and gets onto her knees. She tugs at my hands, requesting that I stand so I do. She grips either side of my jeans and pulls them farther down my hips, putting all of me on display. Another woman might need a small stool to kneel on to have a comfortable height for this, but not Nash. She's perfectly proportioned. "Like you were made for me."

She gives my dick a tug. Then another. I'm about to tell her not to push me so hard when she puts just the tip of her tongue on my head. She touches it to my slit. She swirls it around. She caresses the sensitive underside. "Nash, please." I can't take any more teasing.

She takes pity on me, sucking me down her throat until I bottom out at the back. She puts her fist around what's left and starts working me in tandem with her hand and mouth.

"Holy shit," I say because this is something I never thought I'd live to see—Nash on her knees before me. She continues her methodical sucking, and when my balls tighten up even farther, I have to stop her. I put my hand in her hair gently, so she knows I'm not going to push her any farther, but instead, bring her to a stop. "I can't take any more of that or I'll finish right now."

She licks her lips, pleased.

I help her up from the floor, and once she's standing, I

pick her up by her thighs and bring her down on the bed. I fall on her immediately like a man starved. I'm not going to be able to sleep tonight with the scent of her cemented into my sheets.

I'm kissing her neck when I feel the pressure of her hand in my hair, pushing me toward what she desperately wants. I catch her hand with a chuckle and kiss the palm of it. "I'm going, I'm going."

I don't need to be told twice. Normally, I would kiss my way down her body, revisiting her breasts before making my way over soft skin stretching lower, but tonight I find myself impatient. Maybe it's the amazing head she already gave me, maybe it's my own adrenaline from the game, or the thrill of having her in my bed, but I make a beeline for her pussy.

When I pull her sweats down, I find that I don't have it in me to tease her like she did me, I go right for it, not even bothering moving her panties out of the way at first. I put my tongue flat on her, putting pressure everywhere she needs to come.

"More," she cries, and I lap at her until she's wriggling on the bed trying to get her panties off. I help her and go right back to tonguing her, this time with more focused, tightened movements. I keep doing whatever pulls a reaction from her. "Oh fuck," she cries, but I never slow down, never change the angle. I stay there, steady and exact, until her knees are so tight on my head it feels like she's trying to pop it off my shoulders. She uses her legs as leverage to bow her back off the bed as she comes. I can feel her wetness coating me. I don't back off until she stills beneath me. Only then do I pull away and lick away her sweetness off my lips.

She scoots herself back on the bed, making room for me to put my knees down. I shuck my jeans the rest of the way off and move over her. "Do you have a condom?" she asks, looking up at me from below.

"I don't. I, ummm, I actually haven't been with anyone since you left." *Since our kiss*, but I don't say it.

"Wyatt...it's been five years? How?" Her tone is incredulous.

I look at her lips, swollen from my kisses, and then back into her eyes. "No one's felt as right as you do, Nash."

"You know that I've..."

"It's okay. I didn't expect you to do the same. You had every right to do what you wanted with who you wanted."

She pulls my face down to hers and kisses the life out of me. And I know, *I know* that things are not figured out between us. I know that we could wake up tomorrow and things might be awkward, but I'll never regret this.

Not one second of regret.

# Chapter Forty-Five

## NASH

I can't believe we've wasted all this time not doing *this* because I thought he didn't want me. He wants me and he's proven it ten different ways tonight just by being with me and supporting me at the championship game.

I can taste the musk of myself on his lips as he slides his tongue over my teeth.

When Wyatt breaks our kiss, I say, "I've been tested since my last partner and I'm on birth control."

"Okay," he replies, but it comes out choked like he knows exactly what that means.

I sit up so I can kneel over him and take in his naked body laid out in front of me. I take my time soaking all of him in. All bare skin, only his slutty little chain with my initial decorating him. His chest is not only broad, but deep. He's thick all the way from his shoulders to his chest to his torso, down to his magnificent cock standing ready for me. I love a man with some meat on him. You can keep those perfectly chiseled abs; I don't want them when there are so many other parts of this man to appreciate.

"I can't believe this is happening," he breathes, sitting up to wrap his arms around me.

"I know."

"Can I fuck you now?" His gaze is on my breasts, his hands running along the course of my back.

"Yes," I whisper.

I let myself be moved willingly as he pulls me by the thighs so we're lined up perfectly. Then with a gentle hand under my butt, he turns to flip us, laying me on my stomach. A sharp inhale breaks through my lips when the tip of him pierces me. He swipes his thumbs over my hips in a comforting motion. "You can do it. You were made to take it."

I've never felt so overwhelmingly filled in my life. There's not a man, or a dildo, that's ever compared to this. After he ruined me with his tongue, I didn't think I could get any higher, but here I am flying over the skyscrapers in downtown, barreling headfirst into another orgasm.

He punches into me from behind, and between his strength and the pleasure, it's all I can do to keep my hips up for him as he drives me farther and farther into the mattress. I keep my face in the sheets to cover the sounds of my moans while he draws almost completely out before rocking back in. A steady, perfect rhythm that drives me mad.

"Nash, I can't–" His rhythm is stilted, like he's so out of his mind with lust he can no longer find the beat.

"Faster."

He immediately abandons whatever timing he had left. I think we're actually moving the entire bed, and he'll have to push it back into place when we're done, but for now I focus on the feeling in my core where a warmth quickly grows and comes in a wave over me. I squeeze my eyes shut tightly and focus on the feeling of his cock hitting the perfect spot.

With one last hard snap of his hips, Wyatt fills me, and I follow him over the edge.

Wyatt leans his massive body over mine, covering me from shoulders to ass with his weight and warmth. I can feel his chest heave as he tries to find his breath. I bring one hand back over my shoulder and rest it against his cheek.

"Good?" he asks.

"So fucking good."

Now that I've had him, I'm not sure that I can go back to being just friends. The knowledge of how good his dick is might have ruined my ability to tease him about bringing his teammates home like I did on the first day I moved in. It's not funny now that I know it can feel like this.

Tomorrow we'll have a lot to discuss, but tonight...I have no intentions of leaving this bed.

———

When I wake up in the morning Wyatt is still crashed beside me, but my mind is consumed by exactly one thought.

*What now?*

In every single aspect of my life.

We just won the first ever Pro Volleyball Federation championship, but what now?

I just got my split of one-million dollars. What now?

Wyatt and I had sex last night, but what now?

*One step at a time, Nash.*

I'm an international and national professional champion. I'm an NCAA champion. I've been a pro for six years. What's the future for me? The eight-month break between PVF seasons is a long time. Most players fill it by playing on tournament teams to try and earn enough points to play in the

Volleyball National League, or Team USA if it's close to an Olympic year. The path to those teams is long and winding, overly complicated for reasons no player understands, but I can do all of that if I want to. No matter what, I have a team and a league to come back to next year. My one and only goal coming back home was to make sure this sees another year. I've done that. What else do I want?

What's wrong with me that I can't take this for what it is—victory—and enjoy it? Why am I wired to feel like nothing is ever enough? I wanted to play in college, and I went D1. I wanted to win a championship—I did. I wanted to play professionally, and I did at one of the best clubs in the world. I came home to play for the PVF not knowing what to expect on a new team in a brand-new league, and we won the first-ever championship. Everything I've ever put my mind to, I've accomplished. So why does it feel like I've done nothing? That it all means nothing?

My mind jumps from one thing to the next. *The money*. I'm not exactly sure how much it will end up being after taxes and other bullshit, but it will definitely be enough for the deposit on an apartment. Knowing I have that in my back pocket brings a certain level of comfort to what Wyatt and I did last night. This fake dating thing has felt more like real dating for the last couple of months...I just haven't been prepared to inspect what that means.

What happens if Wyatt regrets everything, and I lose my best friend—despite our pinky promise? What happens if we fake break up and are both in Houston and have to see each other? It's a big city, but that doesn't stop you from running into people at the grocery store. I know Audrey's family found out she was seeing Noah when her sister saw them together at the movies. I love the area Wyatt is in. I probably would get an apartment close to here. We'd have to share the same H-E-B. At least I know that if I'm not with him next season, the Moons proved themselves and the stands will still be full without the Hurricanes. The residuals from this season's win will be enough that our little stadium isn't an empty fishbowl echoing around us.

We're going to be on ESPN! My stomach does a little flip at that. At least if everything comes crashing down around me and Wyatt, I'll still have the Moons.

I steel my resolve right then. If things go south with Wyatt, I'm not stuck here. I'm not damning this immediately, but it's always good to have a backup plan.

"Good morning," Wyatt says, his voice rough like coffee grounds. I swing my eyes from the ceiling to his face. "Sleep well?"

"Very," I reply. Between the orgasms and the nice mattress and his comforting warmth, I slept way better in here then I have been across the hall.

He slings an arm over my stomach, lying on his side with a curious look on his face. "What were you thinking about?"

"Nothing," I say evenly, trying to hide that I was basically rethinking my entire life.

He smiles like he knows he's letting me get away with something, but leans to press a kiss to my still-bare shoulder. "I don't think I'll ever forget last night."

I roll over to face him. "Me either."

"What now?"

"What do you think?"

We're already fake dating, it's not that crazy to add sex into the mix. It's almost the natural next step. There's six more days until his brother's wedding, and when we get on that plane back to Houston next Sunday, this whole thing will be over.

One week of hot sex isn't going to ruin a friendship if all of this hasn't already.

Right?

"I think we should amend our rules." I can't help the flush that creeps up my cheeks. "I think we should be able to sleep together for the remainder of our agreement."

"Can't get enough, can you?" He teases, smile full of self-satisfaction.

I roll my eyes in reply. "It was all right."

He's quick as he sits up to tickle my bare ribs. "All right? I'll show you just all right." I wiggle under him trying to squirm away, my breath coming fast as I fight through my laughter. I feel a rush of air across my chest and Wyatt immediately stills. When I open my eyes, he's staring at my breasts now bared to him, the sheet previously covering them lost in our play fighting.

Neither of us breathe, and he moves his hands from my ribs back to the middle of my chest. He hesitates there. "Yes to more of this?" he asks, looking for permission.

"Yes," I whisper.

His hands move so slowly it feels like I've taken one-hundred breaths before his palms cover my already-peaked nipples.

And slow is how we make it. Last night was a whirlwind of anticipation and adrenaline. Heights fueled by celebration. This is more like lounging. Like when you know you've got all morning to lie in bed. No plans making you get up in a hurry. Leisurely. Deliberate.

Exactly how I want to spend my morning, with the man I've fallen for.

# Chapter Forty-Six

## WYATT

"Why are we here?" Jaden stands behind the chair at our table at Frisco's where we're having lunch. When I got up this morning and saw Nash in bed next to me, my first thought was that I hope I didn't ruin everything. My second thought was I need to tell someone, so I sent out an emergency SOS text to the guys asking them to meet me here.

"Yeah, didn't you get back into town after midnight last night?" I did, and I didn't go to sleep until nearly five AM, but that's not why we're here.

"I called an emergency meeting because I slept with Nash last night. And I decided on Frisco's because I thought we needed to take a break from just getting together to lift weights."

"Whoa," half the table exclaims.

I look around at them, confused. "You guys *did* want to lift weights today?"

Jaden looks at Colin. "Is this man actually concussed right now?"

Colin, who has his head in his hands, just says, "Dude."

When I don't say anything else, Noah speaks up. "You slept with Nash?"

I hang my head, not in shame, but in the face of reality. "Yes."

"And she knows you still don't have a signed contract with the Hurricanes? That you could be forced to go anywhere?"

"Yes, and I told her that."

"Is she okay with that?"

"She said she was…" I mutter.

Utensils clatter as Jaden points an accusing finger at me. "If you hurt her, I swear to–" I only have a millisecond to wonder what the hell that's about before Colin is speaking again.

"That's kind of a dick move."

"I told her before we even started that I was still planning on leaving eventually."

"You waited until you literally had her in your bed to remind her that you're leaving? And you expected her to be like 'no, wait, that's actually a deal breaker for me' in the moment?"

The waitress comes up with a huge black tray and starts doling out our meals. Jaden's looks like a dessert: pancakes piled high with whipped cream and sugary fruit. Mine is almost all meat, plus hash browns and two eggs over medium. We all thank her after she asks us if everything looks right.

Colin takes the first chance to rip back into me when she steps away. "And now you're tangling friendship and feelings and sex all together."

I try to defend myself while cutting a bite of the whites off my egg. "Only until the end of this upcoming weekend after Henry's wedding."

"Oh my God," they cry.

"This is not going to be that easy to untangle, man. You're

not going to snap your fingers and have everything go back to normal." Colin cuts his pancakes as he speaks.

I chuff. "Nash is my best friend. Has been for almost a decade. Nothing could come between us." And so what if the love I've been harboring for her for years is sitting right at the surface now? So what if I thought she didn't feel a spark when we kissed, and now I'm both blessed and cursed with the knowledge that she did and she still does? Everything is going to be fine. I pop the whole egg yolk in my mouth at once, chew, and swallow. "Not even sex. We'll get it out of our system this week and go back to normal after the wedding. We promised."

"Well, enjoy the wedding because next up will be your funeral," Colin says, taking a huge bite of his food.

"This is your pilot speaking; we are beginning our descent into Milwaukee. The weather is a sunny seventy-five degrees, and winds are coming from due north." This flight isn't very long, but it's always an express plane, which means it's tiny and there's no room for my legs, even in first class.

I lean over to Nash. "Why do all pilots sound like they're talking with the microphone in their mouth?"

Her smile is weak. "I don't know. I just know I'm ready to get off this metal death trap."

"You've been asleep since we took off." She was snoring lightly on my shoulder until this thing started shaking like a leaf in a storm. Even though the sky is a perfect blue, the landing into Milwaukee can sometimes be bumpy because of the strong winds over the lake.

"No one could sleep through this." The plane takes another dip as we round out over Lake Michigan to line up the landing, and my belly sinks along with it. Nash's hand grabs tight to the armrest between us. It's been a week since we added sex to our deal, and we haven't been able to keep our hands off each other. No surface is sacred. The big couch in my living room, the standing shower in my bathroom, the granite kitchen island. All Nash has to do is glance in my direction and I'm hard for her. Then every night this week we found ourselves cuddled up in my bed. If this is what we could be like as a real couple… The plane rattles again and Nash sucks in a stressful breath.

I pry her hands off the armrest and tuck our intertwined hands onto my lap. She eyes me from her window seat, which she always has to have so she can watch the clouds go by. "What are you doing?" she asks.

"Supporting my girlfriend in her time of need." When she keeps side-eyeing me, I ask "What? Is that a crime?"

Pink tinges her cheeks. *Success.*

As the plane makes its final descent, hitting that last horrible bump when it touches its wheels to the ground, I squeeze Nash's hand every time she flinches. I hope it takes the sting of the drop in her stomach away. Focusing my attention on taking care of her is helping keep my mind away from seeing my family. I love them, and we're super close, but they still don't know why I left Green Bay. I haven't told them because I don't think they'd understand. Ideally, I won't have to have that conversation this weekend either. I think coming home with Nash on my arm will be enough excitement—and distraction—for us all.

It's a quick sweep through the airport to baggage claim since there's only one terminal. Tough to get lost. After grabbing our luggage, we head over to the rental car area. It's about an hour drive from here to Poblocki. My family practically begs me to let them pick me up every time, but I insist on getting a rental so they don't waste two-plus hours of their day.

I step up to the rental car desk. "Name?" the check-in lady asks.

"Vandergriff."

"Okay, great. I see you right here. Can I get your driver's license and the card on file?" I hand it over, and we do the paperwork song and dance. Finally, we're done, and she says, "You'll be C32."

I take my license back along with the completed paperwork and turn to guide Nash toward the only door that goes to all the rental cars.

We hustle through the garage looking for our car, Nash easily keeping up with my hurried pace despite being loaded down with her luggage. I would love to carry it all for her, but I had to pack heavy for this trip since I'm in the wedding.

We both come to a complete stop when we see the car waiting for us.

"What the fuck?" I look at Nash. "I ordered a standard SUV for us."

"It's not that small," she grimaces.

I approach the lime green Kia Soul sitting in our assigned spot. So I do the only logical thing and stand next to it so she can see just how tiny it is. "Not that small? Look at it!"

Nash, ever practical, rounds the car, opens the trunk, and starts putting her stuff inside. "It just has to get us from the airport to your parents' house and back. We're going to spend two hours in it over the course of the whole weekend."

I grumble under my breath about how you're supposed to get what you paid for as I load my stuff in the trunk. Nash puts her hand on my bicep. "It's fine, Wyatt."

My head drops forward, fully abashed. "You're right. I have my farm truck at the house, we can drive that if we need to." I turn back toward her, wrapping my arms around her waist and pulling her to me. I still can't get over the knowledge that if we'd been more upfront with each other, we could have been having sex every time she came home to visit. I plan on making up for lost time before the weekend is over and our deal is done. "I'm sorry. I'm just nervous. My whole family is going to be here, and this is the first wedding I've ever been in. I don't know what to expect."

She kisses my cheek, which is heated from lugging bags across the warm parking lot. "This is going to be fun. I'm excited to be back in Wisconsin with you. Just like old times," she says with a wink.

Except, I don't want it to be like old times. Old times included staring at her longingly over a fried turkey the Thanksgiving she didn't have time to go home. I spent the whole day dodging pointed questions about the status of our relationship from my mom. The old times were watching her get hit on by half my teammates any time she came to a football after party. Her dancing in the disgusting living room, floor sticky with beer. Me leaning against the counter in the open kitchen where I could see her, but not be too close. I want this to be a new time. I want her to sit on my lap when we have a campfire by the lake to ward off the chill that blows off Lake Michigan even in the summer. I want to slow dance with her after my brother's nuptials. I want to be the recipient of her overly touchy drunk affection.

She starts to pull away, but I hold her in place by catching her chin. "I can't wait to show you off to my family." We should get on the road, but I want so badly to kiss her. It's like I have to have that token of her affection on Wisconsin soil to make sure this really happened, and that I didn't just imagine it in Texas.

"Yeah, your fake girlfriend. *Very* impressive." Her tone is bone dry.

Welp. That certainly kills the moment. I take a step back, into my own space again.

When I look back, there's something in her eyes, a hollowness. She blinks, and in a flash it's gone. "We'd better get going; your mom is probably already out on the front steps waiting for us."

We cram ourselves into the little Kia, pull out of the airport and onto the highway headed north.

Everything is going to be fine. I just have to be in a wedding, not upset my family by telling them why I left Green Bay even though everyone is going to want to talk about the Butcher's drafting Jason Amara and what that means—oh, and also avoid falling any more in love with Nash to ensure I don't break her heart.

Easy-peasy.

Sure enough.

Wyatt's mom, Barbara, is sitting in a rocking chair on the front porch waiting for us. She quickly covers the confusion on her face when she spots our lime green ride and jumps up to wave excitedly as we pull up to the farmhouse.

It's been so long since I laid eyes on this house. While the building screams 'farm' with its giant wraparound porch, it has tons of clean-cut lines and cozy colors. Unlike the many yellow and red farmhouses we passed by on the highway, his childhood home is painted a creamy white.

Barbara comes down the steps, arms wide open, and for a split second it does feel a little bit like coming home. There are great things about Wisconsin, like the beautiful nature in Door County, and the great summer weather. If Wyatt is so dead set on living here, could I see myself here with him? But he didn't say 'I'm going back to Wisconsin, do you want to come with me', he said *he's* going. And that's not really up to him when it's all said and done.

I'm surprised when she walks right past Wyatt and wraps her arms around me.

"Congratulations on your championship! One of many more, I'm sure." Her smile is bright and filled with genuine joy. I thought she was going to immediately start with me and Wyatt finally dating, but I'm secretly happy she didn't.

She pats me on the shoulder. "And for coming to your senses about my Wyatt." A little bead of sweat forms on the back of my neck as I continue to smile back at her.

*There it is.*

Together, the three of us get all the luggage out of the minuscule trunk and head up the steps to the front door. It's wooden and heavy, with one huge window, and black metal hardware. It squeaks when we open it, announcing our arrival to Henry, who seems like he was just about to come outside. He steps back to let us in, looking over our shoulders as we all pile through. "What the hell is that?" he says, eyeing the lime green catastrophe in the drive.

"I don't want to talk about it," Wyatt grumbles. Barb and I can't help but laugh. It'll be parked in that same spot all weekend, waiting for us to get in it Sunday to head back to Houston.

We stand at the base of the staircase as Barbara directs us. "Nash, you'll be staying in Wyatt's room." She turns to her youngest son. "Wyatt, you'll be sleeping in Henry's old room."

"That room doesn't even have a bed," Wyatt says incredulously.

"I know. That's why I put a blow-up mattress in it."

I laugh under my breath and Wyatt shoots me a look. To his mom, he says, "You know we're living together in Texas, right?"

I watch as Barbara pulls herself up to a seemingly equal

height as her son, sucking in that motherly strength as she grows. I can see how she kept these two in line all these years. I know she isn't really eye-to-eye with Wyatt, but it seems like she is with the stern way she says, "I don't care what you do when you're not here, but when you're under my roof, you'll follow my rules."

"Or we can stay with Henry."

She scoffs. "You will not. It's his wedding weekend."

Wyatt pouts and I get another peek inside what he must have been like in his youth. "Yes, Ma."

"Now, go get cleaned up. Your dad is grilling brats for supper, and he'll be starting shortly."

The promise of a grilled, beer-boiled Wisconsin brat piled high with sauerkraut and drizzled with mustard seems to put Wyatt in a better mood immediately. Hm, I'll have to try that at home sometime. Wyatt leads me up the stairs by the hand. He gestures to the room on the left. "This one is mine...well, yours."

"Thanks," I say as I drag my stuff in behind me.

I spin in a full circle, taking in every corner of the room. I stop when a wooden trunk at the end of the bed catches my eye. I point at it. "That's kind of an odd decoration for a teenage boy, isn't it."

"Yeah, it's a cedar chest. Kind of a funny story with that." He picks his chain up from where it hangs around his neck, twisting it around in his fingers, the N flashing silver.

"Now you have to tell me."

He steps closer to me into my space. "It's for you."

I crinkle my brow in surprise. "A gift?" He nods. "For winning the championship?"

"No, I actually got this a while ago. I've been holding onto it since senior year." He leans down and opens the top, which is intricately carved with flowers in each of the four corners.

"Why didn't you give it to me then?"

He chuffs a laugh. "Would you have taken it with you to Italy?"

My lips turn down in disappointment. "I guess not."

"I figured I'd just hold onto it for you until you were ready to have it."

I run my fingers along the edge, feeling the grain of the wood and inhaling its scent. "Am I ready for it now?"

Wyatt's smile is wide. "I hope so."

"Wyatt," his mom calls from downstairs. "Can you come help me carry this?"

"I'll see you downstairs for dinner," he says, planting a kiss on my lips that I think is supposed to be quick, but ends up sucking us both in. I have been insatiable when it comes to him. Is it because we knew each other so well before we added sex into our relationship, or is it just hotter when you know you're running out of time? Does it stem from the special form of intimacy that comes with sleeping next to someone every night? He breaks the kiss, flashing me a million-dollar smile. Like he knows if we hadn't been interrupted, we might be on that bed. Then he's gone, disappearing from the room and back down the stairs.

I've been to his house before, but I didn't stay the night on Thanksgiving. I drove back to school late that evening for an early practice the next morning.

The bed has the classic navy-blue bed sheets, comforter, and matching pillowcases. The shelves on the walls are filled with sports trophies and medals. Pictures of him and his brother in various Halloween costumes including Luke Skywalker and, of course, a Butcher's jersey. Other jerseys adorn the walls, all pinned up unceremoniously with thumb tacks. The biggest wall is covered in Butchers' memorabilia. A poster from their 1998 Super Bowl win, a poster of their hall of fame receiver, and in the center of it all, a huge poster of Jared Clark looking decades younger than he does now. He holds the football in one hand out in front of him, the yellow and green helmet obscuring some of his face. The number on his jersey reads twelve. What a small number. Wyatt is number sixty-nine, as he loves reminding me. He thinks it's hysterical. A small smile cracks my lips thinking about it. A man as quick to laugh and as carefree as him totally fits into a town like this, a family like this. I can see why he's so dead set on coming back. I put my big bag on the luggage rack that I have no doubt is his mom's addition to the room, and hang up my dresses.

I change out of my leggings and sweatshirt and into shorts and a t-shirt. I'm always freezing on planes, and if I'm too cold, I can't sleep like I want to, so I always bundle up no matter how roasting it is outside.

When I wander outside to find Wyatt, I'm met with the nicest weather I've felt in three months. It's the end of June now, and in Houston we are buckling in for the hottest month of the year come August, but here, just a few miles off a Great Lake, the breeze is cool, and the sunshine feels like a kiss instead of a burn. In about three hours I'll need to run back upstairs and get my sweatshirt. The small amount of heat there quickly dissipates when the sun goes down. As I settle down in a patio chair, I look at the vast land surrounding us. I think Wyatt told me once that the farm is four-hundred acres. There are cows, chickens, and miles and miles of corn. From here I can see that it's about to hit the 'knee high by July' milestone all the farmers follow.

Wyatt's dad, Charlie, comes through the back door and I stand to greet him. His smile is wide, just like his shoulders, kept strong through years of farm work. It's obvious where Wyatt gets his build. Football has just added a few more layers of muscle. His is more packed-on bulk, while his dad's is lean. Wyatt's affinity for pizza keeps him a bit thicker. "Nash, it's so good to see you."

"It's good to be here. The perfect time to escape the Texas heat."

"It's been pretty toasty around here lately. Let me know if you get too warm, I'll get the misting fans out."

He, Barbara, and Henry will probably have those fans out before the end of the weekend anyway, so I just smile and say thank you.

I laugh to myself. It was ninety-two when we left Houston this morning. Charlie didn't ask, but the rest of the family will, and they will all give me shocked expressions as if they can't fathom how any human being could live at that temperature. And I'll tell them exactly what I tell all Wisconsinites—it's no different than the winter here: you just don't go outside.

I sit on the front porch letting the lake breeze lift the hair off my shoulders. There's something about the time in small-town Wisconsin. It's like the fewer stoplights a town has, the slower the days go. It feels like you can get one-million things done, and it will still be early afternoon when you check the clock. Maybe it's the long days of summer, but even in the winter when the sun sets behind the sugar maples at four-thirty, the time still feels slow. In summer, it's like you have all day to do what you want because the sun sets so late. In the winter, it's like you have all this time to just hang around because the sun sets so early. It's fascinating compared to Houston where the rush-hour traffic starts before seven o'clock in the morning and doesn't end until after seven in the evening.

The screen door behind me slams again and I glance over to see Wyatt coming through the door holding two sodas. He plops down in the chair next to me and hands me one.

"I could sit out here all weekend and feel like I got my money's worth out of this trip," I say as I stare out onto the wide green lawn again.

"Babe, you didn't pay for this trip," he laughs, taking a long sip of his soda. Half this state calls it pop, but you lose that when you get this close to the lake and, I guess, Illinois.

"Tomatoes, potatoes." I wave my hand away, brushing off his comment.

"Do you ever miss it?" Wyatt's voice is so quiet, I almost think he's talking to himself, except he turns to look directly at me.

I have to look away from the deep blue of his eyes to answer. "Sometimes." The truth is that I was just considering it. Did he read my mind? Silence stands between us like a stranger. Today wasn't my first time thinking about coming back to Wisconsin. Every year I mail in my vote for Texas state elections only to hear the same assholes were re-elected time and time again, and that's when I consider moving to Wisconsin. They're at least a swing state. And their Supreme Court just recently upheld abortion rights. It's pretty appealing. But someone needs to stay and vote in Texas. I eye him across our chairs. "Did the Texas lessons convince you to like it there at all? Do you not see any similarities?" I gesture at the state around us.

He barks a laugh. "Oh, they're completely different. I'm just getting used to it now."

I play punch him on the shoulder. Colliding with the

corded muscle there kind of hurts my fist, but I don't let it show. He would never let me live it down.

Charlie is already on his way back up the drive with brats piled high on a platter. "You kids ready to eat?" he asks as he walks up the porch steps.

"Brats done already?" Wyatt replies, already folding his huge frame out of the regular person-sized chair.

"Have you been gone so long that you forgot they're cooked in the beer boil before they even go on the grill?" Charlie teases.

Wyatt claps his old man on the back. "Of course I haven't."

We all follow Charlie into the house which smells like mac 'n cheese and green beans with bacon. I chuckle to myself when I see the "salad" on the table. In classic Midwest fashion, there's not a lettuce leaf in sight. No, these salads are special in that they're basically a dessert. They're not big on vegetables around here.

"Wyatt, will you get the Poblocki Bakery buns off the counter and bring them to the table for everyone?" his mom asks.

"Sure, Ma."

We all settle in at the huge wooden table. It could easily seat ten or twelve people, but tonight it's just me, Wyatt, and his parents. "Where's Hazel?" I ask anyone who might know.

"Her parents are in town for the wedding, so she's out with them tonight," Barb replies.

"That's nice." Hazel and Henry got together right after I left for Italy, so I haven't gotten to know her as well as I would have wanted.

"Did you guys see the new Kwik Trip on your way in? They just built it in the spring. The food is so good. I'll pick up some Glazers for us tomorrow."

"I didn't realize they finished it so quick. We'll have to run by while we're here. Too bad it's not cold, their hot chocolate is awesome," Wyatt says and takes another sip of his beer.

The room is filled with the sounds of clanking cutlery. I watch as Wyatt piles what must be three cubic inches of sauerkraut on his brat. So much that you can't see the meat at all. Just bun on the bottom and kraut on top. This is one thing, besides my undying love of Culver's, that I brought back with me to Texas. They sell brats at H-E-B, and every now and again I get a mean craving for one.

"So," Charlie starts, and I know this is about to be the interrogation portion of dinner. "About you two…"

I knew it was coming. Anyone would be curious how two great friends ended up dating. I just didn't think there would be sex in addition to the real feelings I had when we started… maybe we'll leave that part out.

# Chapter Forty-Nine

## WYATT

I guess Pa decided that two hours was enough time to let us relax before turning on the inquisition. He might be the one about to ask the questions, but I know this push for information is coming from Ma.

"What made you guys finally take the leap?"

I wipe my napkin across my mouth and lean back from my plate. "We're both in the same place for the first time in five years."

"You didn't think long distance would work?" The questions are going strong, but I'm handling myself.

"I knew it would, but I wasn't the one going overseas. I couldn't put Nash in that position." I don't say that I tried by kissing her before she left. "That doesn't matter now."

In his proper fatherly tone, he says, "You're right, what matters now is being together." Under his breath, he mutters. "I don't know why that can't be in Wisconsin, but..."

This is what I've been waiting for since I stepped foot off the plane today. As many times as we've rehashed my leaving Green Bay over the last year, he cannot understand it. It's a sick sort of irony that from my chair at the table I can see through the living room to where my family's singular share of the Butchers rests in a place of exaltation above the fireplace. I'm sure half of Wisconsin probably displays an antique rifle that's some kind of family heirloom, the other half have that same certificate.

"We always knew the chances of me staying in Green Bay for my entire career were slim." Honestly, I'm getting a little heated at the way they're hanging onto this. It's been a whole season since I played for Green Bay. Why are we still talking about this? None of this is in my control.

"At least your child plays a sport that makes a ton of money so they can stay in their country to play instead of having to go live across the ocean from you for years at a time." Nash's tone is scolding, which I didn't expect. She's not wrong. They're sitting at the dinner table with their son, who until last year never had to go more than a couple hours away to play football. They don't realize how hard they could have had it.

Pa, at least, has the decency to look admonished. He looks to Nash, who looks like she's considering drowning herself in the thick and creamy embrace of Ma's mac 'n cheese. Not the worst way to go.

"I'm sorry, Nash," Pa says. He's a good man, he's just so entrenched in the Wisco of it all that he can't see anything else. Maybe it has something to do with me and Henry not being little boys anymore. He's losing Henry to marriage—as much as he can when they will end up living in a house on Henry's part of this land. He's lost me to professional football, even though I come home often. Times are changing, but everything in this house is the same. They don't have to worry about Henry anymore, so now all their attention has turned to me.

"It's okay, Charlie. I chose to play in Italy. I loved it there, but I'm equally happy to be home." Nash has recovered and is forking a green bean instead of wishing for death.

"We shouldn't be spending all night talking about me and Nash, we should be talking about the plans for the weekend." I gesture at Henry who has been quietly devouring several bratwursts.

"Tomorrow—rehearsal dinner at The Lodge. Saturday—wedding. Any questions?" he deadpans.

"What time should I be there on Saturday?"

"Around one o'clock. There'll be lunch when we get there."

Ma stands and starts collecting her plates. "Is everyone finished?"

A chorus of yeses come in reply. We all stand to get our plates back to the kitchen. When I put mine in the dishwasher after rinsing it in the sink, Ma stops me. "Why don't you take Nash to the beach and get a bonfire going? You can take s'mores stuff with you. We have everything for it."

I put my arms around her in a bear hug. "Thanks, Ma." When did she get so small? Is she shrinking already? I thought that was just a thing in movies.

I turn to Nash. "Grab a sweatshirt. It's not that chilly, but it's the wind that'll get ya."

A flash of amusement glitters through her eyes, and I know I've pleased her with my midwestern-isms.

Seeing her in my parents' house, back in my hometown, I realize that I want to spend the rest of my life finding new ways to please her.

Chapter Fifty

NASH

"Slow down," I basically have to yell so Wyatt can hear me over the wind. This golf cart feels like it's doing a million miles an hour down the wooded path that leads from the farmhouse to the shore of Lake Michigan. I pick his hand up off my thigh and put it back on the wheel. "At least use two hands if you insist on flying like this."

One more slight turn and we burst through the dense trees to a clearing. The dirt road leads to a grassy area to park. We pile out of the golf cart and carry sweatshirts, chairs, a cooler, and s'mores accoutrement through the grass where it stutters off into sand. The sound of the waves crashing is as loud as the wind was on the way here, but much more relaxing. The sun is just about to set over the huge expanse of water. It's crazy to see how it goes on forever, knowing that this isn't the ocean. Wyatt once told me that if you look really carefully on a clear day, you can see the lights of Michigan across the water, but I think he was fucking with me. Sounds exactly like something Henry would have convinced him of as a kid.

A lot of the shore is owned by people who have beachfront

houses, but some are connected to huge swaths of land like the Vandergriff's, and some are small parcels that are beach clubs for local neighborhoods.

I pop the chairs open, facing the water, while Wyatt busies himself with the fire. I would normally help, but I'm frozen in my spot, watching the way his hands maneuver the kindling. His hair is a bit messy from a long day of travel. He has shorts on despite the cold cut of the wind across the lake, because of course he does. If you see Wyatt in a pair of pants, it's probably snowmageddon. I've noticed you can always spot a Wisconsin native in the winter because they'll have just jeans and a hoodie on when it's literally snowing.

"There she is." He sweet talks the fire into burning just like he can sweet talk me into glowing under his hands. He stands from where he was kneeling and sits in the chair next to me. Why do I have such vivid images of me sitting on his lap as the fire dies down? Why am I questioning it? This is my last weekend as his fake girlfriend. I've already decided I'm going to cut off the sex when we get home. I don't want my heart involved with this any more than it already is, but I've got to enjoy it while I still can.

I stand quickly before I can decide against it. Then I'm just a statue in the sand. Wyatt looks at me. "What's up? Don't tell me you have to pee already, we just got here."

I shake my head. "No, it's not that. I just…"

Like he has for the last eight years, Wyatt reads me. "What do you want?"

I take a step closer to him. I can't help but lick my lips as I eye his lap. Huge thighs spread easily in his canvas chair. The perfect place to perch. It's so nice to be with someone who towers over me. I never thought I'd find that at six-foot-one. Like I can sit on his lap and not feel like a monster on the hill.

I take another step. When I put my hand on his thigh, he looks up at me from his seat. I don't let myself think any more, I just turn and settle myself. I can feel his entire body go stiff under me.

Wyatt immediately recovers, putting a hand around my waist and leaning me back against his chest. Together we relax on the chair, alternating watching the flames dance and the waves roll.

I want to enjoy the peace and serenity of this moment, but something from dinner is still on my mind. "Why don't you tell your parents the truth?"

He takes a moment, sitting very still behind me, and I know he's thinking about what might happen if he did tell them. "Everyone loves Clark."

"Okay, and…?"

He sucks in a deep breath. "You lived in Wisconsin for four years. You know what it's like here. They worship him like a hero."

"I mean a Super Bowl win, four MVPs, super high passer rating…" I list off Clark's stats.

"That's exactly what I mean. Fifteen seasons with Green Bay and he only managed one Super Bowl win, but he made sure he got those four MVPs. And don't forget his many commercials. He took care of himself. Then all but a few years he choked in the playoffs." I can feel him shaking his head behind me. "That's not what this is really about. He's a good quarterback. There's no arguing that. It's about what he was like all the rest of the time."

"I've heard not great things."

"He would teach the receivers different hand signals than what the coach taught." He ticks his fingers as he rattles off examples. "He's a drama queen. He's never in the wrong. If the pass is incomplete, it's because the other guy wasn't in the right spot."

I tap my finger to my chin, thinking. "Makes sense why you see a lot of shots of him pouting on the bench when you're losing."

"And that's what he lets the cameras see. You know how bad it got."

"But they're your parents."

"You've seen their certificate of ownership over the fireplace. They put me on a waitlist for season tickets before I was even born. They're hardcore. And besides, even if I told them, and even if they understood, they would feel obligated to tell everyone else the truth if they asked. I don't want to put my parents in a position where they have to repeat negative things to every family member. Not to mention, this is a small-ass town. The employees at the bank and the bakery and the Pig Wig and the ladies at the church all want to know. I don't want my parents to have to explain their son's actions as the hot topic of gossip. It's better this way."

"What about what's better for you?"

He looks at me genuinely confused. "What about me?"

"You're so busy saving your parents and your community from the negativity of Clark...who is saving you?"

He looks at me with so much intensity, I may as well be naked right here on this beach. It's like he's seeing every inch of me bared to him. It sends shivers down my spine that cause me to wriggle in his lap, and he takes in a sharp breath at the sensation. Without thinking, I sit up, turn, and kiss him on the cheek. The touch is so intimate that it warms me from the inside out. I start to turn to look back at the fire, but Wyatt catches my mouth in a kiss. He deepens it quickly, bringing our lips together over and over in a rhythm that matches the waves on the shore. I haven't enjoyed making out in years. It always felt like the means to an end. Getting through the kissing so we can get to the sex, but this is different. I feel like a teenager again—when I could make out for hours and never get bored of it. I could sit here on this beach all night kissing Wyatt, being kissed by Wyatt. Giving and taking in equal measure without a word between us. When I start to feel him harden under me, I know I want him right now. It's plenty secluded with no sign of any boat on the water.

I go for the waistband of his shorts. He grabs my hands and keeps them still. "You want to do this right here on the beach?"

A knowing smile splits my face. "Just the tip…" I start our familiar call and refrain. An inside joke that started from some stupid movie we watched, and we've carried with us all this time.

His pupils are blown wide, and I know he wants this, too. He responds, and what is usually playful and joking turns into a plea. "Just for a second."

"Just to see how it feels," I agree. The blanket covering my legs from the lake breeze fell to the ground when I turned in Wyatt's lap. I move to pick it up off the ground and lay it out in front of the fire for us. I turn and take Wyatt's hands and pull him with me down on the blanket.

I don't think it's the flames from the fire fucking with me, I think there's actually heat in his eyes as he lays out his long body next to mine. And I'm ready to get burned.

# Chapter Fifty-One

## WYATT

I'm living my fantasy right now. I've always wanted to bring a girl out here, make a little camp, and romance her on the beach. I'm so glad I never did it until right now with Nash.

We lie on our sides facing each other, and I run my hand down her side to her hip, giving it a squeeze. Letting her know I'm going to move lower, toward her center. In response, she hooks her leg up over my thighs and I'm so much wider than her in this position that it basically hikes her leg way up, giving me all the access I could ever want.

And I want it.

My heart is hammering, not just with the fulfillment of my horny dreams, but with the idea that this could be the last time. I love making her come, making her grip my hair in her fists like she is ready to fly over the moon with the force of it. I don't want to think about a future where that doesn't continue to happen.

Slowly tracing her body, her stomach, hidden abs there just like mine. "Perfect," I whisper as I move lower. I feel myself get harder when I see how much of her body my one hand covers. I could probably touch both of her hip bones with my one hand across them. Like they were made for me. "Does it make you wet being out here where anyone could go past us and see you spread for me on this blanket? Just like it did on the flight home from Omaha?" I ask as I unbutton her jean shorts and pull down the zipper. She shudders and whimpers in return. "My girl is a bit of an exhibitionist." I'd give her anything she wants. Bathroom of a bar, barely covered on this beach, dressing room of a department store. Anything and everything are on the table when it comes to pleasing Nash.

I push my hand into her shorts, my fist stretching them out, and begin teasing her needy core. "What else does she like?" I ask as I move from gentle teasing to finger fucking. "Does she like it rough?" Her gasp tells me that that is a distinct possibility.

I rip my hands away to shove her shorts down her thighs and off. I grab her by the waist and move her, settling her over top of me. "Does she like getting thrown around?"

"Yes," she says, and it's like that one word is all the breath she has in her.

"Does she like being told what to do?"

Nash nods in response. "Take me out," I instruct, and she hustles to slide my athletic shorts farther down my thighs than they were. "Stroke me," I say, but it comes out more choked than commanding.

"You're so big."

A devious smile splits my lips. "You've done it before. You knew what you were getting into." I grab her chin and focus her on me. "You can take it."

She lifts up onto her knees and positions herself above my already-weeping cock. I take her hips and guide her down slowly. Using my strength to keep her from moving too quickly, taking too much. Any other time I would eat her until she begs me to stop, but tonight I'm in a bit of a hurry. This beach is our private property, but the rest of the lake isn't. "There you go. You've got it." I move her hips forward with my hands. "Now rock a little." I slide in an inch. I push her hips back and pull her to me again. Another inch. "Oh fuck."

In one more move I'm fully seated. "Take what you need," I command, and she does. Her fingers move deftly toward her clit; she puts the other free hand on my chest using me as leverage to swivel her hips. It's fucking heaven.

There's ecstasy on her face as she uses my cock and her fingers to drive herself higher. She rocks again and again.

For a split second her peaceful face is torn through with a grimace and I still her hips. "What is it?"

She pushes through the grip of my hands. "Nothing, I'm fine."

I pop her right off my cock. She's tall, but she's not triple thick like me. I push grown men around for a living, Nash is nothing. She squirms in my hold. "What are you doing?"

"Tell me what hurts." My voice is steady, even though my cock is weeping at the loss of her tight heat.

She goes limp in my hands, shoulders falling. "My knee. It's still bruised from my dig last weekend." She doesn't get to finish her sentence because I'm flipping us over.

"You're not going to ride me if you're hurting." I line myself up between her thighs. From here I can see the purple spot the size of a golf ball marking her knee. If I had known it was there, I never would have flipped us to start with. "But now that you've been a good girl and told me what's hurting you," I fist myself and slide my slick cock through her welcoming folds, "you can come."

I punch my hips and slide all the way in with one stroke.

She's so wet for me, the only resistance I'm met with is from my sheer size. I guide her legs up and around me.

"Touch yourself again, Nash." I know she needs it. I watch as her hand slides back down her taut stomach. Seeing my cock disappear into her at the same time as her fingers circling her own pleasure is almost too much for me. Her free hand reaches from where it was resting next to her head as she takes one of my hands. She slides it up toward her neck and I get dizzy with lust at the idea of choking her. I put my hand around her throat, not enough to hurt or cut off her air, but just enough to let her know I'll give her whatever she wants. The fingers on her clit move faster. Her hand around mine on her neck clenches harder. "More," she pants, and I hold tighter.

"You like that? A little fear with your pleasure?" She nods, unable to speak.

I move faster, stoking her higher. As high as I possibly can. I need her to catch up with me because I can feel my orgasm starting in my lower back; it's moving at a sprinter's pace through my body.

"Oh my God, Wyatt," she moans, and I know she's letting go. I can feel her clenching down on me, the kind of tightness that I can't beat. I stroke through her orgasm until her face loses the twist of pleasure, and I fall over the edge right after.

My name is still Wyatt. That's what everyone has called me for my twenty-seven years, but when she says it now, tinged with the pleasure I'm giving her, it's like she's renamed me. I'll renounce Wyatt and obey whatever name she sees fit if that's what she wants.

The blush on her cheeks, her hair wild from sex, and the wind. She's so beautiful like this that my heart ceases its hammering and kicks one hard thump in my chest before it goes back to its erratic rhythm. I lean down and kiss her again. I don't want to ever move from this spot. I don't give a fuck that my bare ass is out on the shores of Lake Michigan.

The quick *pop* of someone shooting off their leftover fireworks startles me out of my reverie, and I realize I need to get us covered again. I guide her shorts back up her thighs before attending to my own.

"I'd love to stay inside you until I get hard again—which trust me, wouldn't take very long— but we've had a long day. We should pack this up and get back." The sun has been gone for a while now, lost to the horizon.

Nash puts on her best pouty face and gestures to the bag of goodies beside the chairs we occupied not long ago. "But I wanted s'mores."

I heave a dramatic sigh like I'm horribly inconvenienced, but quickly wink at her. "I've worked up an appetite anyway."

She rolls her lips in response, and I hope she never closes her eyes again without seeing me framed over her, my hand at her throat giving her everything I have and everything she needs. Even if I don't get a new contract with the Hurricanes, and I have to move to another new city and start over again, I hope this is what she sees at night when she's trying to fall asleep.

We stay in our blanket nest as I pull over the goody bag and disperse s'mores ingredients.

Comfortable silence stretches over us both as we watch our marshmallows toast in the flame, or watch the waves roll onto the beach.

My marshmallow catches fire, and I let it burn a bit before I pull it out to blow on it. I like mine burnt to shit. "Hold my crackers for me?" I ask, and Nash puts her roasting fork under her arm to help me transfer my marshmallow.

She wrinkles her nose at its charcoal appearance. "That's disgusting."

I shrug as I bring the treat to my lips. "Different strokes for different folks." I almost stop dead in my tracks, graham cracker gooey goodness touching my tongue when I'm hit full force with the sweetest smell in the world. Nash's wetness still coats my fingers now, just centimeters from my nose. I take a deep inhale, pretending like I just really love s'mores, and not that I'm a perv who can't get enough of his woman's sensual perfume. I know she'd be embarrassed if she knew, so I say nothing. I just eat my s'more straight faced even though I'm being tortured by the reminder of what we just did.

When we're done, I use the bucket stored near the campfire to scoop some water out of the waves of Lake Michigan to put the fire out. When I'm sure it's completely doused, I turn back to Nash. "Ready to go?"

She rubs her tummy, full of the three s'mores she ate, and says, "I'm so sleepy."

We load everything back up into the golf cart and climb in. Nash snuggles up against me to ward off the chill of the cool night. On the way here I drove like a bat out of hell. It's like I got in the golf cart and my teenage self took over the wheel. We used to speed through these woods and over the fields on four-by-fours and golf carts. It was something thrilling to do in a not-so-thrilling town. But now, with Nash completely sated and cuddled up against me, I find myself in no rush to get back to the farmhouse. No rush to say goodnight and go to our separate bedrooms. I respect my parents, but if Nash asked me to break the rules, I'd be there quicker than the Spotted Cow keg gets tapped at a Wisconsin wedding.

"Look," I point off the side of the path where little balls of golden light flash and disappear. "Lightning bugs."

Nash leans over me to get a better look, and I try and keep both hands on the wheel instead of putting one on her thigh like I'm dying to.

"They say most of Texas has them, but I have no memory of seeing them there. Only in Wisconsin. They make summer evenings feel whimsical, almost like a movie."

"You must spend too much time in the city then. This is small-town charm."

She looks up at me then with softness in her eyes. "There are lots of things I find charming about this small town."

God, I hope this weekend never ends. I hope we can stay in Wisconsin forever, frozen in time... Because we'll never go home where she'll inevitably tell me she's moving out. I'll make a deal with the devil right now. I'd give him my future Super Bowl ring in exchange for being able to freeze time and stay here in the nice weather and the loving embrace of Nashville Green.

But somehow, I don't think the devil is all that interested in football.

# Chapter Fifty-Two

## NASH

The charm of small-town life I had a taste of last night is immediately lost on me when I see the blue and red lights flickering behind us. I look at the side mirror from my spot in the passenger seat and see a county cop behind us.

"Ah, fuck," Wyatt curses. "Damn townie cops don't have anything better to do than pull people over on Main Street." When he says Main *Street*, he means it. One street through the town is their main road. You can find everything here from the local dive—Tina's—to the bank, the Pig Wig, the Poblocki Bakery, the new Kwik Trip, and a Pizza Ranch... and that's basically it.

We must look like quite the sight, two giant human beings dressed in rehearsal dinner finery riding through town in a blue 1980 Chevy pickup. Wyatt puts the truck in park on the shoulder as he grumbles, "I'm like ten feet from where the speed limit picks up." He points at a sign right ahead of us where, sure enough, the speed limit dramatically increases as you leave the town proper and move onto the country roads.

He checks his mirror, sees the cop coming, and quickly

pulls out his license and insurance. He rolls down the window and then replaces his hands on the steering wheel.

The officer who approaches us is young, and I have to bite back a smile when I get a good look at his pornstache. "Good afternoon, sir. Do you know why I've pulled you over today?"

I know better than to answer that question, but Wyatt is driving, and this is his truck, so it's his problem. He turns to look at the officer who is keeping to the back side of the driver's window. "No, sir, I–" he starts.

"Well, I'll be damned. Is that you, Vandy?"

I can see him squint, trying to recognize the person under the hat and the 'stache. "Liam?"

The cop, obviously Liam, points at himself. "Yeah, it is! What are you doing in town? Thought you were down in Texas."

"I'm here for Henry's wedding."

"No, shit! That's great. Tell everyone I say hello." He peeks around Wyatt, not easy to do with his size, and spots me. "And who is this cool drink of water? You weren't going to introduce me?" Up until this point I've just been sitting here quietly hoping that we don't get a ticket. I'm a little surprised to be brought into this conversation, but I'm less surprised that the cop who pulled us over knows Wyatt.

"Nash, this is Liam, we went to high school together. Liam, this is my girlfriend Nash." Hearing that word fall from his mouth feels like a punch in the gut. We're so close to this being real if either of us could get our heads out of our asses. He didn't have to introduce me to his parents, I'd already met them as this-is-my-friend-Nash. It hits me then that we're on our way to a restaurant full of people whom I've never met and I'm going to hear Wyatt say those words all night. *You know what, it might be good that Charlie and Barb Vandergriff are making us sleep in separate rooms.* They might be on to something. I feel like I'm twenty-seven going on seventeen with how much I enjoyed last night, and how easy it is to turn my thoughts in that direction.

I do a little wave at Liam. "Nice to meet you."

"Didn't know ol' Wyatt had a girlfriend. Would have been the talk of the town seeing as he's Poblocki's most eligible bachelor. Hell, he might be all of Wisconsin's most eligible bachelor," Liam jokes and Wyatt goes a handsome shade of red.

"Knock it off," he says, but he's smiling.

"It's nothing, man." In a split second, Liam seems to remember the circumstances of this reunion and pulls on what I assume is his lawman face. "I pulled you over for doing forty in a thirty-five." Wyatt opens his mouth to argue, but Liam keeps going. "I know you can see the sign for the speed increase from here, but you can't hit the gas until you pass it. You grew up here, you should know that."

Wyatt nods. "I understand."

I hold my breath waiting for Liam to decide if he's going to write us a ticket or not. "I'll just give you a warning today, since I know you've been gone a while and are just getting back into the swing of things, but another guy on the squad may not next time. Some dudes get their rocks off giving guys like you tickets. So be careful." He leans back around Wyatt to look at me. "Nice to meet you, Nash. Enjoy your time in Wisco."

I smile back. "I definitely will. Thank you."

Liam heads back to his cruiser, and Wyatt rolls up the window. "Liam is very charming," I say.

"Yeah, yeah," Wyatt replies as he cranks the AC back up.

"I haven't met many of your high school friends." I watch

him as he pulls us off the shoulder and back onto the main road. I wonder what kind of people Wyatt hung out with in school? Other jocks, I assume. I guess I'll find out tomorrow.

"You will tomorrow at the wedding. Most of the town will be there."

"That will be super fun."

Can't wait to get asked about the Kwik Trip for the millionth time.

# Chapter Fifty-Three

## WYATT

I'm trying to shake off the bad mood I'm in from not only getting pulled over, but from Nash's comment: *Liam is charming.*

If Liam is charming at all, then I'm Prince Charming himself. The man has a mustache straight out of the seventies. He obviously doesn't have a girlfriend, or he'd shave that thing off. He's not going to get one with it either.

Nash and I walk hand in hand into Graze—the nicest steakhouse in a fifty-mile radius (read: not *that* nice) and are immediately greeted by my various relatives. I try to keep hold of Nash's hand while my Aunt Shirley hugs me, but it gets too awkward, and I have to let go. She holds me by my shoulders, "You're a bit late, aren't you?"

I am not going to admit to getting pulled over, so I say, "Just running a bit behind is all." She winks at me and is going to say something I know will make me blush, but my cousin Matt steps in first. "He's late cause he got pulled over on the way here."

My eyes flash to him. "Where did you hear that?"

"My mom told me as soon as she got here. Said she drove right by you on her way over." Matt's mom is my aunt who lives literally one right turn from my parents. "I swear this town..."

Nash takes my hand again, pulling me out of my embarrassment. The look of amusement in her eyes is worth every barb. I'll take getting caught breaking the law one-hundred more times if I can see her smile in such obvious appreciation of small-town gossip. *Wait until she hears about the phone tree.*

"Sorry for my rudeness," I say to her as I turn back to my many family members gathered around us. "This is my girlfriend Nash." She takes each family member's hand, or hug, in turn.

"Have you guys been to the new Kwik Trip yet? I've been killing those mini tacos." Matt talks about the gas station like a new five-star restaurant just opened up.

Nash's smile is full of grace. "First place we stopped on the way in." Matt beams back at her.

I decide to save us from more questions. "We're going to go find our seats."

I lead Nash through the room, heading for the front where the bride and groom are already standing by their table greeting their guests. The bridesmaids and groomsmen are all at one long table for the rehearsal dinner. Apparently, when the restaurant asked Hazel if they wanted a sweetheart table for just the two of them, she said 'why? I eat dinner with him every night'.

Henry spots us first and rounds the table to greet us. "You clean up nice."

I hug him back. "You're not so bad yourself." I turn to greet his wife-to-be. "Hazel, beautiful as always."

Nash takes her turn, then we take our seats. I look at the dinner menu, the options are beef… or beef. That's Wisconsin for you.

Nash leans over to me. "Are they really serving torte for dessert?"

"It's a staple," I say, looking at the item she's referring to. Torte is like a dessert lasagna. A layer of cookies for the crust, a layer of ice cream, a layer of sweet sauce like chocolate or caramel, usually some kind of nut, then whipped cream. My personal favorite is Oreo cookie crust, vanilla ice cream, chocolate fudge, caramel, crushed peanuts, and Cool Whip.

"Hey, guys," someone says behind us, and I turn to see who it is. "Hey, man! It's good to see you." I get up to greet Henry's friend Grant. I introduce him to Nash. She stands and hugs him hello. I love that she's a hugger when meeting new people. She's hugged everyone I've hugged, but shook the hands of people I did as well, letting my familiarity with them steer her. I look at Nash. "We palled around in high school. Henry and Grant played baseball together."

"Been to the new Kwik Trip yet," he asks. It's not his fault. He doesn't know we've already had this conversation ten times. When not a lot happens in a town, something like this is a big deal.

"Wyatt," a feminine voice calls and my stomach hits my feet. With fake dating Nash and going to all the Moons games, then being gone for the championship, I totally forgot that Grant is with…

"Layla," I respond. "Been a long time." She approaches me for a hug, and I hope she can't tell how stiff I am.

"Years," she answers as I look down at her. Way down. My high school sweetheart is only five-foot-two. Her dark hair is down around her shoulders, longer than she used to wear it when we were together. I can see Nash looking between us, catching onto the surprise in my voice, but not really understanding the connection.

I'm stunned a second too long because Layla reaches by me to offer Nash her hand. "Nash, right?" I watch as she nods. "Nice to meet you. Wyatt and I dated in high school." She laughs a short, tinkling laugh. "Well, basically all of high school."

"That was a long time ago," I say, hand on my chain, twirling it between my fingers, the shape of the N poking me.

"Not that long. We just had our ten-year reunion. This guy didn't even bother to come." She thumbs at me but speaks to Nash.

"I was busy with football." I hope they're sitting on the other side of the table from us tonight.

Layla whacks me playfully on the shoulder. "That's always your excuse." It's meant to be teasing, but I hear some of the hurt behind it. I was not a very good boyfriend. I never cheated or anything, but she never came first in my life. It was always football, then the farm, and then her. I'm glad she's with Grant. He's not a farmer or a football player, so he likely has the ability to put her first in his life.

Thankfully, we're interrupted by Henry before I can bury myself in this conversation any further. "Can everyone please take their seats? The wait staff is about to come around and take drink orders. Thank you."

The room fills with the mumbling noise of thirty people all moving at once. I take my seat next to Nash again, putting my napkin in my lap. When the waitress comes to our table, I order us both a Spotted Cow, my favorite beer that's only available in Wisconsin.

Henry sits down directly across from me, done making his guests feel welcomed. "When are we rehearsing?" I ask.

"Tomorrow before the ceremony."

My brows raise up. This is my first wedding, so I had no idea. "Then what are we doing here?"

He chuckles—yep, this is my older brother who seems to always know how things work and has all the answers to the mysteries of life. "People used to do them the day before and then eat dinner, but now most wedding venues only let you have the day of because other people are using it the day before. So we just smash it all into one."

"That's cool. Either way, we get to eat and I'm good with that." I thank the waitress as she sets down our drinks.

Nash points to the first beef selection on the menu. "You get one, I'll get the other?"

"Sure. We can trade if you don't like yours."

"You guys are so cute," Hazel coos.

Nash looks suddenly extremely interested in the beer glass in her hand. "Thank you."

They go on about the dresses they're wearing and how Hazel is going to have her hair styled for the big day. Before the entrees come out, Henry interrupts them. "Excuse me, but Hazel, it's time for us to thank everyone."

"Oh, right," she says as she pushes her chair back to stand.

Henry picks up the glass in front of him and clinks it with a knife, getting everyone's attention. "Hello, everyone. Before dinner comes out, Hazel and I just wanted to thank everyone for coming. We know it's a long way for some of you coming from different states." He looks at Nash. "Some of you are fresh off a championship game, and we are so glad to have you." My heart practically bursts with pride. "Wyatt, I'm glad you're with a woman who has lived in Wisconsin and understands the eccentricities that make this place special. I'm so honored you agreed to be my best man."

"I'm honored you asked. Though," I fake look around me. "I don't see any other brother here who could do it." The crowd laughs.

"That's true. I always said you're my favorite brother, and my only brother." He offers his glass to me, and I clink it with mine. "Cheers."

"Cheers," I say back.

Henry turns back to his bride. "And cheers to my bride, who has been with me for every celebration and every hardship for the last five years. I hope to have more celebrations than hardships in the future, but I'm happy to have you by my side because I know I can survive anything." They clink glasses and kiss, phone cameras flash and the crowd *awwws*.

Despite all the happiness surrounding us, I feel a little sick to my stomach. My crush on Nash hasn't been as strong as my call to come back home, but now that I'm here with Nash...I'm not sure this place is what I need anymore.

Chapter Fifty-Four

NASH

I'm full of mixed emotions as we say goodbye to everyone at the rehearsal dinner even though we will see them again tomorrow at the wedding.

On one hand I've enjoyed being back in Wisconsin, enjoyed seeing Wyatt back in his hometown, and I've been thinking about what it might be like if I moved here. Madison isn't that far from here, and they could have a team next year. All his family is here, so we're going to have to travel. How would that work? It would be the same if I convinced Wyatt to stay in Houston. Plenty of people live away from their families.

On the other hand, meeting Layla rocked my confidence in what Wyatt sees in me. She's the opposite of me in every way. She has luscious, dark hair to my dirty blonde. She's petite in a way that brings back all of my high school insecurities. I bet she's never had a problem finding jeans that weren't high waters, or cute shoes in her size. She probably wasn't dateless to her high school prom because all the guys were too intimidated by her height to ask her.

I'm sure she's a very nice girl. Obviously, she and Wyatt

got on well, at least for a while. It's unfair of me to put this on her, but it was like seeing her made me the awkward, too tall, brace-face, sixteen-year-old again.

When we slide into Wyatt's old truck to head back to the farmhouse, Wyatt asks me, "Did you have a good time?"

I did, and I want to be able to brush this odd feeling off and move on with our night, but I'm terrible at hiding what I'm thinking. "Everyone was really nice."

"It was good to see some of the guys again. Usually when I come visit it's just to see family and get back."

"Layla was especially nice." I am cruising for a bruising.

"I'm sorry for not forewarning you. It slipped my mind that she's with Grant now. Seems like every time I come back, who's together and who's not has changed. This town isn't very big, ya know? The dating pool is about the size of a bird bath." He takes my hand in my lap across the bench seat from him. "Layla and I were kids. She means nothing to me now." He looks out the front window of the truck to the other guests piling in their cars. He puts his other hand on his neck, rubbing something away. The stiffness of this conversation, maybe. "I'm glad you and I weren't friends in high school."

"Why do you say that?" I ask with a laugh.

"I wasn't boyfriend material." He shakes his head at the thoughts of his younger self. "I never put her first. Football and the farm always came before her."

I wave him off. "You're being too hard on yourself. You were both just kids."

"You didn't hear her jab at the table? When I said I hadn't been back in a while because of football, she basically said that was always my excuse." He pauses, then continues. "And maybe she's right. Football is always my excuse."

I lean back against the worn leather bench seat and gaze up at the ceiling. "I've probably done the same thing in my life."

His eyes flash to me. "You have?"

"Uh," I start playfully, "does running away to another country to play volleyball after kissing you ring any bells?"

"You already had the flight booked and you were saving our friendship by never bringing it up again." His eyes look sad as he thinks back on the memories. "You let me down easy."

I reach over to take his hand. "Now you know that's not true. You're still the one I always turn to when I was overwhelmed with homesickness."

"That's true."

"And the only one I wanted to live with when I moved back."

He shrugs. "That was just for convenience."

"No, it wasn't." I shake my head. "I wanted to be around you. And that's not going to change."

I desperately hope I'm right about that.

———

The day of the wedding, Wyatt, his parents, and I eat a huge late breakfast together. There's coffee, pancakes, and breakfast casserole—which is basically a full breakfast mixed all together and baked in a dish.

I watch in awe as Charlie pours himself a cup of hot coffee from the pot and immediately takes a sip of the scalding liquid. He never blows on it, doesn't put any milk or creamer in it that would cool it—just down the hatch.

I lean over to Wyatt and whisper, "Your dad's taste buds must be fried."

He barks a laugh that gets his dad's attention, and Wyatt attempts to cover it with a cough into his own mug. "I did not get that gene." His coffee has a splash of half and half and two sugars.

"I'm glad; what a shame to lose your sense of taste." It comes out sultry, and Wyatt's pupils go wide at my suggestive tone.

Weddings always get me all riled up. I think I'll take to teasing him all day. Anticipation is the best foreplay, isn't that what they say? I thought the other night on the beach was the last time, but I'm determined to fit in one more.

I smile back at him unapologetically, letting him know the game I'm playing, and his smile turns hungry.

We clean up from breakfast and make sure Wyatt has everything he needs to head to the wedding venue. "If the other guys are taking shots, do not take one," I warn. Wyatt's a big guy and he can hold his liquor, but wedding days are a marathon, not a sprint.

He pauses, shoving stuff in a backpack to look at me. "You think I'd risk coming home to you with whiskey dick?"

My cheeks burn at the idea of him thinking about that already. But wasn't I doing the same thing at breakfast? I'm encouraging this. And I like it.

If I let this keep going, he'll miss his arrival time. "Do you have everything?"

"Almost. Just one last thing." He closes the gap between us in less than a second, his long legs eating up the carpet, as he begins to kiss me slowly, like he doesn't have anywhere to be. His hands move down over my leggings to palm my ass. He kisses me until I'm leaning so far into him, I'm not sure I could stand on my own. When I'm almost ready to peel his

Hurricanes shorts down and suck his soul out before he goes, he breaks the kiss. "There. All ready to go."

I swat at his chest playfully as he shoulders his backpack, picks up his garment bag, and walks through the door heading down the stairs. I follow him because what else am I supposed to do? I stand on the porch and wave, watching his truck as it ambles down the long dirt path leading to the road.

Now I'm all revved up with nowhere to go.

*Damn him!* He may have won this round, but I will have the last laugh today.

# Chapter Fifty-Five

## WYATT

I've been to plenty of weddings, but I've never been *in* a wedding. Much less the best man. Much less for my big brother. I can't fuck anything up today. I couldn't bear the look in Hazel's eyes if I ruined their photos or their ceremony or their dinner.

When I arrive at the wedding venue, a huge building with a brick-walled groom's suite and farm chic reception area upstairs, I hang my suit up and someone immediately puts a beer in my hand. It's been an hour and I'm still nursing that beer. Not only can I not lose any of my wits until I do my speech, but I can't disappoint Nash. She's obviously got an idea in her head of how tonight will go, and whatever she wants, I plan on giving it to her, goddamn it.

I hold a pool stick in one hand and my half-drunk beer in the other as Grant circles the table looking for his next shot. It doesn't really matter, though; we're all shit at pool.

Our phones all collectively go off with the ESPN app notification chime and we dig through the pockets of our shorts. It's an hour and a half until go time, and none of us are even dressed yet.

Henry is the first one to read it. "Holy shit."

The other two groomsmen and I are too slow to see the headline before he says, "Jared Clark is gone."

"He's dead?" Brad, the third groomsman, asks, baffled.

"No, idiot. He's going to the Jets." Henry runs his hand through his hair. "We're never going to win a Super Bowl now."

I put my hands up in an effort to calm him. "Dude, chill out."

"I kinda never liked the guy," Henry adds. And the room starts spinning around me.

"It's embarrassing as a Butchers fan when he's on the big screen pouting. Like putting a towel over his face hides anything," Grant agrees. I've only had half a beer, but all of a sudden, my feet don't feel steady on the ground, like I'm already twelve deep. I stare at my brother and his two friends in kind. My eyes physically look at them, but don't really see them. Instead, I'm seeing my first day as a Butcher when I met Clark and was immediately dismissed by my high school hero. I play defense, what reason did he have to talk to me? My last day as a Butcher, emptying out my locker at the end of the season for the last time, a huge hole in my heart knowing that I've already peaked in my life. I made my dreams come true at twenty-three and they came crashing down around me at the ripe old age of twenty-six. What do you do with the rest of your life when you've already shot for the stars and fallen depressingly, embarrassingly, back to earth with nothing to show for it? I stall on that moment, on those feelings I had as I took my name plate off the locker. If I think really hard and dig all the way down to my toes, there's a tiny hint of excitement. There's hope the size of my pinky fingernail. And that hope is Nash. That if I came to Houston like Coach was telling me I was going to, she might be there. We'd be together again. The one person who always understood me.

I break out of my reverie and pull my shoulders back from where they've slumped since the other night at dinner when my dad said he didn't understand my leaving—just in time to hear Henry say, "Well, he's their problem now."

I look at Henry. "You didn't like Clark?"

"He was great in the early years, but we all know he's gone downhill lately. Old school football is out. All the new guys coming out of college are playing with lots of motion. Sometimes I'd see him play and think 'he just can't keep up'."

I'm not sure whether it's a relief to hear him say this or it's terrifying to know how fast your fandom can flip on you. Did the people of Wisconsin do the same for me when I left? Would Houston do the same?

"I never liked him either," I blurt.

There.

I said it.

Six eyes turn to look at me, but Henry is the first to speak. "You didn't?" he asks. "But you played there for four years."

I shrug. "Yeah, and I left. And he was the main reason why."

"What did he do?"

"Everything you've ever seen him do on TV, but one-hundred times worse." I finish my beer. Finally, I've said it out loud. And the sky didn't fall, and I didn't spontaneously combust for daring to speak out against King Clark in his own territory. A wave of relief washes through me as I look back to my brother and his friends.

"Why didn't you say anything?" Henry's face shows he's a little hurt by my lack of trust.

I gesture to Brad who is literally wearing a Butchers t-shirt and hat. It's not even football season. "How could I when you all love him so much? The entire state does."

"I don't love anyone more than I love my brother," Henry says, and Grant pipes in, "Except Hazel." Henry points at him. "Right."

I look at my shoes, the right lace is a little loose. "Sometimes that's hard to know when the fans are so loud."

Henry steps in front of me and puts both of his hands on my shoulders. "That's my fault, little brother. I should have never let you feel like a football team was more important than you." He pauses. "It's not. Just so you know that. From right now until we die. I'm your number one fan. No one else's."

We hug, both patting the other one hard on the back.

The baseless hope I had when I saw them draft Jason Amara returns with a rush. Before today there was a shithead in my path back to Green Bay. Well, that path has been cleared. I could float away from this spot. Things are working out exactly the way they were meant to. This is why I haven't signed with the Hurricanes again. I saw that draft pick and I read Jared Clark's ego like a book. He was never going to stick around and train his replacement. He's too important and special for that. No. You can't fire him because he quits. Classic asshole move.

I pull my phone back out and click on my agent's contact to shoot off a quick text.

Before I hit send, the wedding coordinator calls, "Okay, gentlemen. Time to get dressed. I'll be back in five minutes for photos of Mom pinning your boutonnieres." With that, she's back out the door.

Grant jumps to me and pounds on my back, knocking my phone out of my hand. "Let's go, boys! Showtime!"

There will be time tomorrow when we're waiting at the gate to finish that text to my agent. It's Henry's wedding day.

I mean, it's not like everything is going to change overnight or something.

Chapter Fifty-Six

NASH

I take the program from the young man in a suit as I walk in through huge glass doors. "Thank you."

The inside of the venue is white with brick flooring. The ceiling is dotted with chandeliers casting a subtle glow.

I drove the little green Kia here since Wyatt took his truck, and his parents came before me. So it will just be me in the audience by myself.

*Great.*

Only two hours until I can reunite with Wyatt and not feel like such an outsider.

My heels click on the brick flooring as I walk toward where the ceremony will happen. The sounds of a softly playing string quartet meet my ears as I enter the large space, music carrying in a graceful way through the wandering guests looking for their friends or family.

The flowers are bursting from vases at the beginning of the seating where the aisle leads to the altar, and I stop to smell them as I walk past.

"Nash…" I turn to see who could be calling me. I know almost no one here.

"Oh, Layla," I say and walk toward her. I guess sitting with my fake boyfriend's ex-girlfriend for the ceremony is better than sitting alone. Like Wyatt said, they were kids when they were together, and she seems happy with Grant now. There's no reason for me to believe she has any misguided notions about Wyatt or me.

She pats the empty seat next to her. "Come sit by me."

I collapse into the chair she offered. "Thank you. I don't know anyone else here."

"Oh, I know everyone," she laughs.

I smile back. It was wrong of me to instantaneously dislike her for being Wyatt's ex. I need to get control of my jealousy. After all, it will be misplaced when we go back to Houston and back to being just friends.

Why does that thought make me want to barf?

My quick issue with his ex, my jealousy over the idea of any other woman looking his way… I'm in this deep.

I'm about to find out just how deep because the music has changed, and the officiant is heading down the aisle. I watch as Henry comes next, dressed to the nines in a navy-blue suit with matching tie, his parents on each arm. The music changes again and we turn back in unison to watch Wyatt come down the aisle alone as the best man. When he takes his first step around the corner, my breath is stolen from my lungs at how handsome he looks. His big frame and his broad shoulders draped in the rich navy color perfectly offsets his blonde hair and blue eyes. I never want to see him in anything else again. I thought the football pads and helmet were hot, but this is another level. I'll never be able to unsee this. Every night when I dream it's going to be seeing him dressed like this. I watch with rapt attention as he strolls down the aisle to the slow melody of the music. He smiles at people he knows as he passes, looking like a natural. Like he's the center of attention every day—and maybe in Wisconsin he is.

When he's even with our row, the smile and wink he throws my way has me melting in my chair. How long is this walk? It feels like it's been minutes since I took a breath, but it's probably only been seconds. I would happily suffocate if it meant spending every moment in his presence.

Finally, he walks up the three small steps to the altar, clapping Henry on the back and politely greeting the officiant. He takes his place next to his brother and clasps his hands in front of him.

Everyone around me turns back to see the rest of the bridal party walk down the aisle in pairs, but I cannot force my eyes away from Wyatt. I haven't had enough of him. It's like he can feel the heat of my gaze on him because now he's looking back at me. Somehow through this sea of people his ocean blue eyes find me. He looks down at my dress, a red number he's never seen before, giving my whole body a slow and sensual perusal that makes my stomach swoop. When his eyes meet mine again, he mouths just one word, *wow*. I smile so hard it hurts my cheeks, and I cover my face with my program so I don't disturb the other guests. There's something in his eyes I don't recognize. Like he's looking at me through a different lens. Maybe it's the soft summer glow glancing through the trees and filtering in from the windows casting everything in heavenly light. Maybe it's my dress. I don't normally wear red because I find it too flashy, and that it clashes with my height for attention, but for this I figured *fuck it*. Go big or go home.

Hazel's sister looks stunning in the sage-colored, off-the-shoulder gown she chose. The earthiness of the green brings out the darker streaks in her brown hair. We follow her with our gaze as she moves down the aisle and to the altar before turning back to see the ring bearer and flower girl coming down together. The crowd chuckles as we watch the young girl attempt to throw the petals, but managing to only put down about three the entire way.

The music stops for an abrupt moment as it switches to the correct song for the bride. "All rise," the officiant asks, and we do. The sound of all of your friends and family standing to greet the bride, the anticipation of the moment right before you see the star of the show for the first time, is my favorite part of weddings.

I watch as two enormous wooden doors are opened to reveal Hazel and her dad. I never imagined myself in a dress like that, but the organza with rouching across the chest looks so stunning on her, it might convince me. The luxe fabric flares out just above her knees, and a five-foot train trails behind her as she walks. It's breathtaking, elegant, and looks like it would be found at a Hollywood event rather than in Wisco.

I look my fill of the bride quickly so I can turn and watch the groom as he sees her for the first time as I normally do at weddings. The bride looks beautiful, but the emotion on the groom's face is always the best view. Except this time my eyes barely graze over Henry, who is, in fact, crying because they're drawn into the overpowering orbit of Wyatt. He's here to witness the marriage of his older brother, but his eyes are on me again. I hold his gaze. I feel the heat build behind my eyes as tears pool in their corners. I don't want to be the one to keep Wyatt from where he wants to be, but after all this time, I don't think I can do life without him. There has to be a way for us to both get what we want.

If I were a better woman, I might feel guilty about the

amount of time throughout the ceremony Wyatt spends watching me instead of the literal vows being professed in front of him.

But I'm not. And I don't.

"I, Henry, take you, Hazel, to be my lawfully wedded wife…" I'm only half hearing the vows as the officiant guides them through the ceremony.

Before I know it, the officiant is announcing, "And with the power vested in me by the great state of Wisconsin, I now pronounce you husband and wife. You may now kiss the bride." He steps aside so the photographer can get the perfect photo of their first kiss, and I appreciate the man's attention to detail.

From a few steps to the side, he calls out, "It's my honor to introduce to you, for the very first time, the new Mr. and Mrs. Vandergriff." The crowd roars with excitement, and I clap my hands and cheer along. A punchy rendition of a classic rock song on the string instruments plays as they traipse down the aisle. Henry stops them about two-thirds of the way to sweep his new wife into a low kiss, sending the crowd into a frenzy.

"Well, that was beautiful," I say to Layla, who is standing beside me as we wait our turn to make our way out of the ceremony room and into the hall where cocktail hour will be hosted.

She dabs her eyes with a tissue and says, "So beautiful."

I step out of our row and motion for her to slide past me. "Let's go get a drink."

The bridal party is swept away for photos by a stressed-looking woman in all black while Layla and I are herded out onto the porch for cocktail hour. A tray with bruschetta passes by me and the smell makes me realize how hungry I am.

"Get in line for a drink?" I ask Layla. I'm going to need one if I'm going to get through this night without pulling Wyatt into a coat closet.

"Yes, please."

She greets everyone as we pass by, introducing me to those I have yet to meet. The rehearsal dinner was pretty intimate, so there are quite a few friendly new faces. I meet the baker and his daughter, who briefly dated Henry in high school. I meet the owner of the local bar who invites us to have a drink after the wedding tonight, and I politely decline because I plan on drinking plenty of free booze here.

"Wow," I breathe after the last person ambles away to say hello to someone else.

"It's a lot, isn't it?" Layla plays with the toothpick of the bacon-wrapped water chestnut she just finished.

"It is, but it seems like Wyatt loves it."

Layla's smile is small and reminiscent. "There're great things about living in a small town. When my dad had his hip replaced, we didn't cook a single meal for weeks. But when I got a minor in possession ticket at a bar in the next town over, my parents knew about it before I even crossed the county line."

"*You* got an MIP?" But she's so smart and put together.

"Everyone has their days. There's not much to do around here."

It's my turn to inspect the toothpick in my hand. "What was Wyatt like in high school? I mean, I met him shortly after graduation, but..."

"He was a lot like he is now. Big hearted, big bodied," she laughs, then continues more seriously. "I remember the first time he came home after he met you."

My eyebrows meet my hairline in surprise. "You do?"

She nods. "He talked about you the whole weekend. By

that time, three years later, he was calling to order a cedar chest."

My mouth turns down at the corners, confused. Wyatt didn't say anything about where the chest came from. And why would Layla know about it? How could someone's furniture purchases be the hot gossip of a small town? "I don't understand."

"He didn't explain it to you?"

I shake my head. "He just showed it to me this weekend."

She laughs and it sounds like bells tinkling. Her hand lands on my shoulder as she says, "In Poblocki, gifting a girl a cedar chest is the equivalent of a promise ring. It's making your intentions known."

My entire body goes still, but my mind spins. He had that chest made *years* ago, but I just saw it for the first time this weekend. What does that mean?

I realize how long it's been silent between us, and I stumble over my thoughts trying to find the right words, but she saves me from having to speak. "You didn't know." It's not a question.

I sigh. The weight of this fake relationship with undercurrents of my real feelings is dragging me down. "There's a lot I don't know."

"Next," says the bartender, shocking us both out of our conversation. I'm grateful to Layla for stepping up to the bar and ordering first, giving me a second to breathe and collect my thoughts.

When Layla steps away with her drink, I step up to the bar.

"I'll have the house red, please." The bartender starts to pour me a glass of wine in the small plastic cups they always have at weddings. I check the time on my phone and am bewildered to see that it's only been twenty minutes. Another forty minutes of cocktail hour, then wedding party entrances, then some weddings I've been to go right into the first dance before dinner is served. Which means I'm not going to be able to get any clarification from Wyatt for a while.

Realization hits me—this is Henry's wedding. Wyatt is the best man. It is absolutely not the time or the place to have this conversation. Plus, if Wyatt wanted me to know about the meaning behind the cedar chest, he would have told me himself. But he didn't because as of today, I have a feeling he is planning on leaving me after the breaking news that came out about Clark—well, leave Houston, to come back to Wisconsin. He made that perfectly clear. He has through this entire fake relationship. It would do me good to remember that that's all this is. What it has been for him this entire time.

Fake.

Seeing Nash through the crowd felt like being struck by lightning. Or at least what I imagine it might be like. Sudden, scary, thrilling, and painful all in a flash. I tried to concentrate on the ceremony, but the entire time my heart was aching from the strike. I tried my best to keep this fake like Nash needed, to make sure she gets everything, and that I had a chance to get what I desperately wanted to, but the thing about being struck by lightning is nothing is ever the same after.

And the same goes for what we've been doing because nothing will ever be the same after this. I looked into Nash's green eyes, and my instinct was to wink at her. Playing my part as the always teasing friend, but when I got up to that altar, I had another life-changing moment, a second lightning strike. I saw a sliver of what it could look like to stand at the altar on my own wedding day, waiting for Nash and her dad to walk toward me. Waiting for my bride to meet me there and confess her love for me like I was ready to confess my love for her.

When the ceremony was over, and we were shuffled into

different positions for pictures, all I wanted to do was get to Nash. Thank God I never had a chance to send my agent that text. Because I realize that I want to see Nash in white. I want to be with her, wherever that is. At this point, if she changed her mind about wanting to go back overseas, I would quit football altogether to follow her. After spending this much time with her, living together, and fake dating, I can't go back to a life without her being beside me.

I'm going to tell her. Tonight.

Fuck my brother. The wedding ceremony is over, and this is the party. It's free game.

Standing just outside the double doors to the reception area, I can hear the bass of the music thumping as the DJ hypes everyone up for the entrance. I'm set to enter with Hazel's sister, the maid of honor.

"What should we do for our entrance?"

"Just follow my lead," she says as she takes my arm once again.

The huge doors open, there's a pop song blaring as we start. It sucks that we have to go first, but someone's gotta do it.

We've taken about three steps in, the crowd roaring their applause, when she looks at me. "Go long!"

"What?" I ask, thinking I mistook her over the noise of the music, but she just holds her bouquet up by her shoulders and motions me away from her. Oh my God, she's going to throw those flowers like a football. I don't have any better ideas, so this is what we're doing.

I take off and make it about five steps before she throws it. I don't know much about her, but she fucking launches that thing. She even leads me in steps, throwing it to where I'm just about to be. An absolute dime.

I catch it and hold the bouquet over my head, cheering like I just scored the game-winning touchdown. She runs up to me and jumps up to chest bump me. She's so short, I don't have to jump. If I did, I would have probably knocked her over backward. We celebrate together, and then like nothing happened at all, we calmly collect ourselves and head to the side of the dance floor to await the new Mr. and Mrs.

It feels like forever as we stand and watch them be announced. They dance their way into the middle of the floor, and the DJ cuts it to a slow song. "Please give your attention to the new couple as they have their first dance."

I watch as my brother and his new wife turn in slow circles to a country song. I'm glad everything went off without a hitch. No one got too drunk, no one was late, no one's rental pants were too small. It was perfect. All that's left of my job for today is the speech.

The song ends and everyone claps as we make our way to our seats. I head straight toward Nash and lean down to speak to her, not even bothering to take my seat first. We might have just a few minutes. "Nash, can we go somewhere and talk?"

She opens her mouth to respond when the DJ cuts in over the speakers. "Dinner is ready to be served. If the head table will please stand and go to the buffet line first. After them, someone will come around to your table to let you know when it's your turn."

The whole table rises, and we're swept away toward the food line.

"What did you want to talk about," Nash asks.

The buffet line waiting for dry chicken or overcooked beef is not where I wanted to have this conversation. "Ummm…I don't remember. But I'm sure it will come to me later."

During dinner, we make amicable conversation with the

other members of the bridal party as we eat our mashed potatoes.

I try to enjoy my food, but my stomach is all twisted up with nerves. The only order of events I was informed of for the entire night is my speech being right after dinner. I'm in desperate need of a drink, but I have to refrain. I'm going to get up there, I'm going to do my speech, people are going to clap, and then I'm immediately beelining it to the bar.

Nash's hand resting on my thigh pulls me out of my anxiety. "You're going to be great." Her eyes are full of encouragement. It's like her hand is soaking up all of my worries.

I kiss her on the cheek before rising. "Thanks, sugar."

When the wedding coordinator approaches me, she asks, "You good to go?"

"Yeah, I'm ready."

The DJ gets on his mic and introduces me. "Let's welcome Mr. Wyatt Vandergriff, the best man!"

People clap and I can't help but think about how much clapping you do in one night at a wedding. More than any other night, but probably less than a concert. I'm just thinking about stupid shit to distract myself as the DJ hands me the microphone.

"Hello," I say, and immediately it's way too loud. My eyes flash to where Nash is sitting, and she moves both her hands down in a stay calm gesture. "For those of you who don't know me," I start, and God, why hasn't anyone invented any other way to start this speech? "My name is Wyatt Vandergriff and I'm Henry's younger brother. I could talk about Henry and what a good guy he is and how much fun we've had throughout our lives as brothers, but tonight I want to focus on who we all know is the star of the show," I turn more toward her, and away from the audience so I can address her. "Hazel, hi."

"Hi," she says back.

"Welcome to the family."

"Thank you." A light wave of laughter ripples through the crowd.

"I'm assuming you'll be living in Henry's house on Vandergriff Farm, so I've selected a few things I think you'll need to make your life easier." I hold my hand out and Grant plops a wooden spoon in it. I take it from him and hand it to a surprised Hazel. "Growing up, Ma and Pa popped us with one of these when we were misbehaving. I just thought you'd like to have one of your own for when Henry steps out of line. Check the handle." She does and a laugh bursts out of her. "I had Vandergriff engraved on it so you don't confuse this one with any other wooden spoons you might have in your kitchen." I address Henry now. "So next time you want to have ice cream before dinner, or a beer when it's too early to start drinking, you'd better think twice." I hold my hand out for the next item. It's just a sign the size of a regular sheet of paper. I hold it facing out so the crowd can see it, and there's another round of laughter. *Hell yeah.* I'm killing this. I let the crowd laugh their fill and then turn so Hazel and Henry can see it.

"Dude, what?" Henry asks incredulously.

"We all know that when Henry gets to talking, it's sometimes hard to get him to stop. That's why I drew you this sign that just says 'shut up'." Pause for laughter… "I also got it laminated so he can't "accidentally" spill his drink on it. Next time he's going off about the newest crypto he's going to invest in, or how badly his fantasy football team is losing, you can just whip this bad boy out."

Henry puts his head in his hands.

"And for my final gift…"

"Thank God," Henry moans. I don't know what he expected. Everyone knows that the perfect best man speech pokes fun at the groom and compliments the bride.

One last time I gesture to Grant to hand me the cherry on top of my perfect speech. "Finally, I have for you a Wyatt Vandergriff Houston Hurricanes game-worn jersey, signed by yours truly. By marrying into this family, you are granted immediate entry to my personal fan club." Pause for effect. "I am also promoting you to vice president of said fan club. Behind my wonderful girlfriend, Nash, who is, of course, the president." I pretend to cover the microphone and talk just to Hazel. "We'll iron out the details of what that will mean for you later," and then back to everyone, "but for now, I know you'll *love* wearing a Hurricanes jersey in Butcher territory." My grin is FDA certified because I've got this crowd eating out of the palm of my hand. Grant pulls a second jersey from behind the table and hands it to Henry. "Don't worry, bro. I got you one too."

When the laughter dies down, I bring it home. "But seriously, you guys are so great together. I know this is going to be a long marriage full of joy and laughter. I'm so happy for both of you." I raise my water glass, "Cheers to the new Vandergriffs."

"Cheers," the crowd says in reply. The sounds of delicately clinking glasses fills the space and the DJ comes on the mic to welcome Hazel's sister to do her maid of honor speech. I stand and listen to her talk about how wonderful her sister is, and how everyone loves her, and cringe a little when I realize that she didn't fully prepare for this. She's kind of just up there rambling. She ends her speech the same as mine, asking everyone to raise a glass for the new Mr. and Mrs.

The DJ announces that the dance floor is now open, and I make a straight shot to the bar.

I jump when Nash comes up to me from behind and rests the side of her face on my back. "You were amazing! Everyone was cracking up."

I suck in a deep, dramatic breath knowing she can feel it in my chest. "I'm just glad my job is done." I take my beer from the bartender in one hand, and turn Nash around me with the other. "Is now a good time for that talk?"

The first notes of "YMCA" play over the speakers, and Henry appears besides me taking me and Nash both by a hand as he pulls us onto the dance floor. "Come on," he says, "it's your job to help get the party started."

I look at Nash, just for a second. She's already letting Henry bring her onto the dance floor, head bopping to the beat. And I let myself be pulled too. Now's not the right time.

We groove to whatever songs come on, family members and friends moving in and out of our little dance circle, but the whole time I'm watching Nash. She looks so free tonight. Like the weight of the Moons and our fake relationship are off her shoulders. Like she took everything on her own and made it succeed with the sheer force of her will, and now she's out here dancing like she's celebrating more than just Henry and Hazel.

"We're going to take it down now, folks," the DJ says in a sultry voice, and the first few notes of a slow song comes on. I put my empty beer down on the nearest table and pull Nash into my arms. I've barely had a chance to talk to her today. "I missed you," I say, my breath coasting over the shell of her ear making her shiver.

"I missed you, too."

"I saw you sitting with Layla."

"Yeah," she nods. "She's really cool. I was wrong to be jealous of her. That was immature of me."

"What about taking it out on me?" I ask petulantly.

She kisses me quickly on the cheek. "I was wrong to take it out on you, too."

I move us slightly to the right to avoid running us into my aunt and uncle as they dance. "Did you see the news?"

"About Clark?" I nod and she continues. "I did. You were expecting it, right?" Hearing her speak so plainly on what was once my second biggest secret (behind being in love with her for years) makes me regret not saying anything sooner. Everyone would have understood. I nod and she continues. "What did everyone say?"

"They basically said 'good riddance'. They feel the same way I do: that he got his MVPs and his sponsorship deals and his commercials and choked in every championship game."

Her brows shoot up in surprise. "Henry said that?"

"He did. And Grant agreed." The song changes from one slow song to the next. I'm relieved. I was not ready to let Nash go.

"Did you say anything?"

"I told them everything I had been wanting to say." I shrug. "They were totally cool with it. I'll have to fess up to Ma and Pa tomorrow, but I'll deal with that then."

"I'm so happy for you," she says and rests her head against my chest as we sway in small circles.

"I'm sure Chad or Grant have already told their parents, who have probably already told my parents. Those two can't keep their mouths shut."

"What does this mean for you?"

"I haven't signed a new contract with the Hurricanes but I'm–" Someone taps me on the shoulder, and I could scream right now. How many fucking times is someone going to interrupt me.

"Can I steal her for a dance?" Henry asks, and I can't say no to a man on his wedding day.

I step back from Nash. "I'll be right over there," I say to her before heading toward our seats and leaving her in the hands of Henry.

Before I step away, she says, "I'll support you no matter what." Her face is warm with encouragement and something else… Determination? Weird.

For the rest of the night, no matter how hard I try, I'm interrupted at every turn. By the time they're ushering all of us out of the venue so the bride and groom can have a private last dance, I'm out of patience.

I'll just wait until we get back to the farmhouse where no one can interrupt us.

# Chapter Fifty-Eight

## NASH

It turns out the grand exit was quite the show. There was a big hullabaloo when Uncle Jamie attempted to light his cigarette with his sparkler. Aunt Shirley had to take it away from him, but he got the damn thing lit. He looked like a cat who caught the canary the rest of the time we waited for Henry and Hazel to come out. Their mom had decorated Henry's truck, which was nearly twenty-five years newer than Wyatt's, with a just married sign, as well as flowers in the truck bed and empty cans tied to the bumper. It sat in the drive at the end of the walkway waiting for them.

When they came out everyone shouted over Hazel's wardrobe change. Gone was her elegant, flowing, yet fitted, floor-length gown. Replacing it was a short number with tassels of pearl beads around the hem. It glittered in the sparklers and the camera flashes as they walked down the middle, pausing only for another dipped kiss. It was so sweet to watch as Henry helped Hazel into the passenger seat of his truck. Wyatt had told me that the wedding coordinator had already packed up all their stuff and loaded it into the backseat. They'll go straight from here to the hotel in Milwaukee to catch their flight to their Florida honeymoon tomorrow.

After we could no longer see their brake lights, people broke off into small groups to talk and make plans for breakfast tomorrow.

Wyatt turns to me, and I can instantly read the heat in his gaze. "Ready to go?"

"I'll meet you back at the farmhouse." He seems reluctant to leave me even to drive his own car home, but I don't think they want us leaving cars in the parking lot overnight.

I take my time driving back. I'm in a tornado of emotions. The pull I had toward him this morning, the one I've always had for him, is still there. His strong arms call to me, telling me that once I'm wrapped up in them, everything will be okay; he'll make me feel good. My kitty is being tugged in that direction. My heart is beating a bruised rhythm. Every beat of it sounds like *fake, fake, fake*. It hurts knowing that at one point, years ago, he was possibly in love with me. When he purchased that chest, he wanted more from our relationship. How could he have sex with me on the beach in front of the fire just two days ago when he knew his ultimate goal was to come back here? *Why did I kiss him back knowing the same?*

The answer is easy, but disappointing. You don't have to be in love with someone to have sex with them. You can be attracted to their body and not interested in anything more than friendship. I just have to decide if I can accept that from Wyatt. Right now, we are fake dating with benefits. Will I be okay to return to just being friends with benefits, or not even friends at all, when we go home tomorrow?

If we'll be nothing when we return to Houston, what do I want from the rest of tonight?

Him.

His body.

One more time. I'll take the feeling of his warm skin beneath my hands and keep it tucked away for the rest of my life. I'll smile when he says, 'this was fun' and wait to let the tears fall until I'm back in my own room.

I start the car and pull out of the venue parking lot.

Let's go get my one last time.

———

Before I know it, I'm pulling down the long dirt driveway to the farmhouse. When I shut the door to the chartreuse disaster, I spot Wyatt leaning over the porch railing, his forearms thicker than the plank of wood they're leaning on. He watches me as I come up the steps, and greets me with a kiss when I'm in arm's reach. "Are you hungry?" he whispers.

"No, I had my fill of wedding cake."

He moves to open the door for us. "Ma and Pa already hit the hay. They'll see us tomorrow morning before we go to the airport."

"I hope they had fun," I whisper back as we walk through the main area and to the stairs.

"I think they did. Maybe they're in a bit of shock that their oldest is a married man, but I think that will quickly turn into excitement for grandbabies."

I laugh and he shushes me. "Sorry," I whisper.

When we get to the landing, we just look at each other for an eternal second. Wyatt's been trying to tell me something all night. Now's his time to fess up to whatever it is. My stomach twists at the thought that he might be about to tell me he's somehow already made a deal with the Butchers and is headed home to pack his bags.

He heaves a breath that's big even for his size. "We need to talk."

Okay, so we're going to figure this out now. Perfect. "About what?"

"You know now is my chance to go back to the Butchers," he starts.

"So you've said." Anger rises up, choking me. After letting me fuck him, getting a taste of what it feels like to really *be* with him, he's telling me—what is he telling me?

"But when I saw you tonight from the altar, I knew that's not what I wanted any more. I don't have to come back to Wisconsin to be happy. I've been chasing the wrong thing. I was so mad about the way I left Green Bay, I let it affect my relationship with my team," he takes my hand and holds it, "and you. I won't do it anymore. I can't. I thought I'd get clarity coming back here, but I haven't. You know what I have thought about?"

"What?" Is that all I'm capable of saying in such a big moment?

"The way you fit in my parents' kitchen. The way you laugh with my brother and his friends. How beautiful you look when the sun strikes you the perfect way. It's the same sun here and in Texas. And it's the same you."

I want to sink into everything he's saying. Take it all and shove it in my pocket, but something doesn't make sense. "Layla told me what the cedar chest means. It's more than just a common gift between friends." I look at him, but he says nothing. "Isn't it?" I urge.

"Yes. Like I'm sure she told you." He looks at his sock feet.

"My mom keeps the clothes Henry and I wore on the way home from the hospital in her's."

"You said you bought it years ago."

"I did. At the end of our senior year." His voice is rough, like the gravel road that leads to Vandergriff Farm. This is starting to all add up.

"So what? You loved me then, kissed me before I left, but didn't love me enough to do anything about it for five years?"

"No." There's genuine hurt in his voice. Like it's painful to think back on that time.

"Then you agreed to fake date me for six months," I continue.

"It's not like that," he pleads.

"Now you're saying you don't want to come back to Wisconsin? What does all of this mean, Wyatt?" My eyes search his face, looking for signs of the truth. I don't want any more miscommunication between us. I can't do another five years of holding my tongue.

"It means I want this to be real, Nash. It means that it's felt real to me this whole time. It means the years we were apart I was *suffering* without you."

"The mixed signals are going crazy, my guy." I try to laugh but it comes out weak.

"You already admitted that you felt something after we kissed and didn't say shit about it either," he says back, like that's checkmate.

"*You* kissed *me*."

"And *you* ran away." He crosses his arms as if that helps him prove his point.

"I had a flight the next morning." How dare he. My first instinct is to be mad, but there's a small part of my heart that's breaking at the idea that we've both lost five years because we were both waiting for the other to do something.

"You had time that night to stay and figure things out, but you took off," he says accusingly. So what if my bags were already packed and all that there was left to do was wait for it to be time to head to the airport? I didn't want to say a real goodbye to him.

"So, what? You agreed to fake date me because you've been in love with me this whole time?" I wave my arms around like a crazy person.

"Yes," he whisper-yells.

"Oh." I pull my hands back to my chest.

"I loved you when I got you the cedar chest, I loved you when I kissed you that night, I loved you the entire time you were in Italy, I loved you when you asked me to be your fake boyfriend, I loved you when we slept together after the championship game, I love you right now in the house I grew up in."

"What does that mean for us? Tomorrow? When we're supposed to go home and go back to being friends?" My instinctive anger is fading away, getting harder to hold onto in the face of my desolation.

He shakes his head. "I don't want to go back to being just friends. We don't have to change anything we're doing right now. We can just stay the same and be real like we've been telling everyone it has been." I don't remember what it feels like to have a hold on your emotions. It seems like I haven't for days now, weeks even. The high of winning a league championship, the high of sleeping with Wyatt for the first time, the low of him telling me his plans to go back to Wisconsin remain intact despite everything between us. If I had been honest with Wyatt at my going away party, would we have stayed together those five years? Would I have made it five years being long distance with him? Or would I have cut it short and come back, possibly hindering my career?

It must have been a long time since he finished speaking because he says, "Nash? Say something."

I can't yet. I don't want to break this moment with what if's and what about's. Yesterday I was thinking maybe I could see myself leaving and coming to be with him in Wisconsin, and now he's telling me he's ready to give up on coming back? What does this man actually want? And can I trust him when he says he wants me?

"I want to be with you, too, but I can't make you stay. Are we going to flip a fucking coin and whoever gets tails has to give up on their dreams?"

"I said I'm willing to do it."

"And I said I'm not willing to let you." I take a step toward him and let him fold me into his arms. Tears sting my eyes both from the thought of losing him like this and keeping him like a caged animal. I won't clip his wings and stuff him in an aviary. Even if it's gilded with a nice townhouse downtown and a new contract that will likely be worth millions.

"Why?"

I don't look up at him. I let my words hit his chest where I keep my head tucked. "Because I love you, too. I have since before Rome. And since Rome. And right now. Which is why I can't let you give up."

"This is the way it has to be, Nash. I will be happy with you no matter where we live."

"You can't possibly know that. After a few years you'll resent me because of this. We'll come visit your family for the holidays and you'll be depressed when we leave. In the heat of the summer every year you'll be miserable and wishing I didn't drag you into all this." I look up at him. "And I can't bear the thought of that." My Wyatt. "Isn't it better that we're best friends for the rest of our lives than something more until things go south?"

"So what are you saying?" I can feel him holding his breath as he waits for my response.

"I love you too much to let you give anything up. You're too funny and kind and hardworking to not have everything you want." The tears stinging my eyes are freely pouring now. He wipes them away with his thumbs.

"I want you." I breath him in, cologne mixed with sweat. The smell of comfort, of home.

"You already have me." We stand still at the top of the stairs waiting for time to come back to us. To remember where we are, the feeling of the carpet beneath our feet. The house holds its breath, too. Waiting to see what we'll do. I love him. I *want* him. I make up my mind right this instant. If we can't figure out how to make this equal in reward or in sacrifice…at least we will have had one last night.

I put my mouth on his, breaking the tension between us. I exhale into him, and I feel the house exhale around us, too. I moan at the feeling, and he quickly pulls me into his room, never breaking our kiss. The smell of him in here is so overwhelming, it's like I'm drowning in it. I love it.

He pushes me back on the bed and I yelp with the force. He's always so gentle with me that I forget he's capable of that kind of power.

"You've teased me all fucking day," he whispers and somehow, it's sexier than if he had said it aloud. "I hope you're ready to pay for it." Just like that, we're back to teasing, playful friends. Friends who fuck.

I sit up on my elbows, the fire in my body starting to burn

higher in anticipation of finally, *finally* getting what it wants. "It's not a tease if I always intended to follow through."

"What does that make it then?" he asks, and my smile goes from playful to devouring.

"Foreplay."

He growls as he pushes me back down on the bed, wasting no time in flipping up my dress, revealing my lace thong. Wyatt pulls it to the side in his rush to get to my pussy. He drops to his knees and starts tonguing me though the gap.

It feels like my clit has been halfway to swollen all day. Waiting for someone to come by and give me the sweet pressure I need. He pulls back for a split second to blow on it gently, and the coolness of the air against my soaked panties has me bowing off the bed. He dives back in like he's scuba certified. The power of his body apparently extends to his tongue because it pummels my clit in the short, fast movements I need to meet my climax. "Wait," I whine, "I want to come on your cock. It's so much better when you're inside."

He quickly shoves two fingers in me and gives a couple of rushed pumps. Foreplay is not at the front of my mind right now considering I've been waiting for this all day. When he stands, I reach for his cock, but he pulls my hands away and up his chest as he kneels on the bed and leans over me. I feel the warmth of his skin as I wrap my legs around him. There's layers and layers of muscles there, but no ridges to his abs. I love the thickness of him. He's broad to my narrow, and the idea of taking his thick cock again has me squirming under him.

He reaches down to take hold of himself and lines us up, but pauses excruciatingly close to entering me to ask, "Can you be quiet?" I only nod in response, showing him how quiet I can be. "If you're too loud, I'll have to stop."

I shake my head and nudge at his hips with my crossed feet, trying to urge him on like some kind of fucked-up steed.

His hips push forward and he's inside. I take in a sharp breath at the punishing size of him. He finds his rhythm quickly, and I let myself revel in the feel of his cock sliding deep inside me and then all the way back out until just the tip of him stays. He snaps his hips forward and is all the way back in. "Oh, fuck," I cry out. He stops instantly, mid stroke.

"I thought you could be quiet?"

"I'm sorry," I beg, my voice a whisper. "Please don't stop."

He picks up his speed again and I move my hand down to touch my clit while he rocks into me. I'm honestly not sure I can be quiet. The build of my orgasm is coming so quickly, I don't know if I'll have the wherewithal to hold it in. It feels so good, so right, that I don't want to have to hold it in.

The combination of his strokes and my light caress is too much to handle. I start whimpering again, but this time Wyatt's hand covers my mouth. "I'm too close to stop."

Cutting off my airway just drives my need higher, pushing me closer to my edge. "Wyatt," I speak through his palm, his name comes out louder than my last cries. With the hand not covering my mouth, he grabs the shirt I slept in last night and pushes it in my mouth. The cotton instantly soaks up every bit of spit, and I bite down on it, the whining coming through my nose instead. Wyatt holds my nose closed with one big hand, and I've never been so denied of air. Never let my penchant for a little choking go as far as this. My back curls off the bed and I cry into the shirt as I come. Wyatt's blows become stuttered and uneven, and I know he's falling with me.

The second I come down from riding the wave of my orgasm, Wyatt pulls the t-shirt from my mouth. "Too far?" he asks with a seriously concerned look in his eyes.

"Just far enough." I pull his head down to mine and kiss him. I hope I kiss the breath out of him like he withheld my breath from me. I hope he likes it half as much as I did.

I know I'm the one pushing him away emotionally, but I want to keep him with me physically. "Stay?"

"You know Ma and Pa's rules…"

"They won't even know," I counter.

"We literally live together," he pauses, then huffs a dramatic breath. "Okay. You win. But I'm sneaking back to my room before they get up."

"You're a grown man," I laugh.

"I still respect my parents' rules," he shrugs.

My heart aches with how much I love him. Waves and waves of it overtake me. Like I'm a grain of sand on the shore getting pummeled. He's too pure for this world. Is that a Midwest thing? A Wisconsin thing? Or is it just how this wonderful man was made? After living here for four years, I think it's a Vandergriff thing.

And who am I to take him from that?

———

The next morning starts relatively early after a long night of dancing, drinking, and getting cracked. When I wake up, there's no Wyatt. His parents get up super early to start farm chores, so he'll have been long gone by the time the sun came up.

I roll out of bed and set to getting dressed and packing up to head back home. I love visiting Wisconsin and getting a break from the heat, but I'd be lying if I said I wasn't nervous to get back home.

I put the t-shirt Wyatt gagged me with last night in my

suitcase and a shiver runs down my spine at the memory. I mentally kick myself. I can't keep sleeping with my best friend who's in love with me knowing I don't have a solution to both of us giving something up. It's not fair to him. Is it still leading someone on if you have feelings for them, too?

When I'm presentable, I head down the stairs. The smell of coffee brewing hits me first, and I'm hoping for a piece of leftover breakfast casserole before we leave.

I'm about to round the door into the kitchen when I hear something that stops me in my tracks.

"What about your place on the farm, son?" That sounds like Charlie.

My heart stops beating in my chest, like it can't continue pumping blood until Wyatt responds. "It'll be here waiting for me, won't it?" I hear the rattling of a spoon in a mug as he speaks. "When football is done, I'll be able to come back?"

"Of course. But how many years will that be?"

"As many as possible. I love football. If I can play an unprecedented amount of years, I will." I hear a chair scraping the floor. Wyatt must be sitting at the kitchen table. I can see him in my mind's eye—hair mussed from sleep, Hurricanes t-shirt on, coffee cup clutched in both hands.

"Now that Clark is gone, would you consider coming back to Green Bay?" his dad asks.

"Henry told you?"

"No, Grant did. That kid's a loudmouth." He pauses, looking for words. "Listen, I know this state has had Clark up on some kind of pedestal, but he's not from here, and now he doesn't play here anymore. People will move on from him now, but you? You're one of us. Corn stalk. Born and raised. You belong here, and I hope you never forget that."

"Thanks, Pa. That means a lot."

*His place on the farm…*

A parcel of land just like Henry's. A place of his own in Poblocki… I set that thought in the back of my mind so I can work on it later.

I step around the doorway and Wyatt's eyes snap to mine. "Good morning," I say as I move through the kitchen toward the coffee pot.

"Good morning," both men respond.

I use the couple seconds it takes me to get a mug down and fill it with coffee to hide my face and school my features. Emotions whir in my mind, questions without answers. Does Wyatt see himself coming back here when his football career is over? If he's so dedicated to Wisconsin, why hasn't he done anything with his land? When his parents are too old to work at the farm anymore, will he feel obligated to come back and help Henry? It's kind of pointless to think about where I could be in the future. I'll go wherever volleyball takes me. But when that's over… *is* Houston my forever home? Could I be happy retiring here if that's what Wyatt wants?

I've got even more questions to think about than before.

# Chapter Fifty-Nine

## WYATT

The unfettered joy I felt at returning that lime green Kia could only be matched by plopping my ass on my own couch. The trip from Poblocki to home was smooth sailing but I'm glad to be back in my own house.

Nash and I are still in this alternate state. Two people who have admitted their love for one another, but aren't together. The bottom line is, I believe love is enough. I'm not giving up on Wisconsin, on getting to be with Nash for real. Despite the odd circumstances between us, she didn't immediately pack a bag and dip, so things are okay for now.

Nash comes back in the room as I'm sprawled out on the couch. "Did you see the weather?"

"I never pay attention to the weather. It's June, it's hot. What is there to check?"

"Uh, it's hurricane season?"

I chuff. "The Hurricanes season doesn't start until September. Training camp is late August." I jump as she whacks me with a rolled-up magazine like a naughty dog.

"No, you oaf. Actual hurricanes. Not your football team."

"What about actual hurricanes?"

"There's one coming," she says, and it's so unbothered that I have to do a double-take.

"Come again?"

"They're tracking a hurricane in the Gulf." She shows me the Weather Channel post on her phone. "It looks like it's going to hit us."

"When?"

"Tomorrow night."

I sit up straight from the couch. The news of an imminent natural disaster catapulting me from my reclined seat. "Tomorrow night? Why are we just now hearing about this?"

"We weren't here, so I wasn't really paying attention. We were lucky to even get in today." She flips her wrist like *damn, I can't control the weather.*

I stand up because I think better on my feet. "What do we do?"

She eyes me for a split second and her eyes go wide. "Holy shit, this is your first hurricane." She moves and takes me by the shoulders. "Don't worry, we still have plenty of time to get ready. Plus, right now it's only a category two."

"That's good?"

"Well, it goes to five, so two is lower than five." I nod, but she keeps talking. "It will likely gain some momentum before making landfall, so it'll probably be a three by the time it hits us."

"Three?" I put my hands in my hair. "That's closer to five!" What a horrible welcome back gift. Almost like the city is punishing me for coming back. Maybe I was wrong— Houston sucks, I don't want to stay here. I knew everything would be ruined when we came back to Texas. She's about to see how unprepared I am for a natural disaster and decide that she doesn't love me because I don't know how to protect her.

She reaches up and pulls my hands out of my hair. "I know what to do. We are going to do it together and everything is going to be fine."

"Everything is going to be fine," I repeat.

"Does your truck have gas in it?"

"I don't know; it's been a couple days since I drove it."

"We'll take it to go get some water and you can fill it up at H-E-B if you need to."

Hours later we're back at the house with two vehicles filled with gas, one gallon of water per person per day (which I learned is the math for prepping water for a storm), a loaf of bread, and a jar of peanut butter. We unload everything onto the kitchen island. I look at all of it and then look at her. "Now what?"

"Now we wait." She shrugs and reaches for the peanut butter pretzels we stocked up on.

"But a storm is coming, and in the three hours we've been preparing, it hit category three."

"Yes, but now there's nothing left to do but wait to get hit."

"That's insane." She strides over to the couch and plops down. Now she's as relaxed as I was earlier, and I'm strung up like a live wire.

"That's just how it is. Get comfortable."

"We're supposed to just make dinner, and watch TV like it's another normal night?"

"Yup," she pops the $p$.

I grab the bag of purple Doritos I got for myself—a Wisconsin classic that H-E-B occasionally has—and take a seat next to her on the couch. I go for the remote. "What do you want to watch?"

"Whatever Gordon Ramsey shows we need to catch up on."

I turn the show on for her, but I don't really watch it. Worries about the storm just keep running through my mind. Should we have evacuated? Nash packed us a go-bag in case this gets out of control and we have to be rescued or something, but maybe I should have taken the initiative and just packed us up? There are blizzards in Wisconsin, but since the snow is solid, there's no chance of it flooding your house. This seems a lot more serious between the wind and the rain. I wonder if we'll be on the 'dirty' side or not? *I really need to stop googling.*

All I know is Nash is the most important thing in the world to me and I would literally fight Mother Nature to keep her safe.

## Chapter Sixty

NASH

Coming home to a hurricane isn't ideal, but it's been nice to take my mind off where Wyatt and I are and focus on getting us prepared. Hurricane Arthur is quickly approaching the Texas Gulf Coast.

Growing up here, I've been through Hurricane Ike and Hurricane Harvey. The former left us without power for two weeks, the latter dumped forty inches of rain over Houston in three days causing record flooding. This ain't my first rodeo.

If I've learned anything in those years, it's that it's better to be safe than sorry. So even though people online are saying this isn't going to be as bad as Ike or Harvey, I still put new batteries in the flashlight and set it next to the ship to shore radio I insisted Wyatt buy.

By the time we're settling in on the night the storm is supposed to make landfall, I'm exhausted, but I feel like I've got everything done. Now we wait and see how the Texas power grid holds up. (HA—what a joke! It's not going to hold up.)

I start piling extra blankets on the couch. "I think we

should sleep down here. It's probably safer than being on the top story."

"Okay, I'll go get all the pillows from upstairs."

After we make our hurricane-certified blanket fort in the living room, we settle in to watch more TV. It's hard not to just watch the weather reports, but I make us take a break from it every now and then. It's not going to change that much from now until the storm has moved past us anyway.

The anticipation of something bad happening makes the time feel as thick as molasses. The TV plays show after show and we watch and wait.

Around midnight I can hear the start of the wind whistling through the trees. "Do you hear that?" I pause the TV so Wyatt can listen.

"Is that it?"

I nod. "It's the beginning of the winds hitting us."

We sit, huddled together, Wyatt's arms fully wrapped around me, TV paused as we listen to the incoming storm.

It's kind of ironic. There's a storm inside me, and now there's one at our front door. Is it still our front door? Will I still stay here after this is over? If nothing else, I'm glad that I can be here for Wyatt during his first hurricane, and that he can be here for me to keep me from being so afraid because of the past hurricanes I've experienced.

The rain starts up slow at first, a few big drops hitting the roof, but it quickly turns heavy. Rain pounds on the shingles, plinking against the glass windows. We watch as the wind blows the rain in sheets. The maple tree that normally stands tall and proud outside of Wyatt's front door is shaking like a rattlesnake's tail. *Danger*, it says, and I know when to listen.

"Consider this your Texas lesson's final test," I joke, trying to find some humor in the situation.

"That's not fair, they don't get hurricanes in Dallas."

I giggle at his seriousness. "That is true, but they get tornadoes, which are worse, in a way, since they can come unexpectedly."

"I guess you're right," he sighs, his head heavy on top of mine as he holds me.

I want to tell him that I'm going to find a way for us to be together where no one has to give something up, but it doesn't seem like the right time. Depending on what kind of damages we wake up to tomorrow, that might not be the right time either. If the power is going to be out for a couple days or a week, this will be the best of days for a while. It'll only get hotter after the storm is gone, and without any way to get cool. I've lived it after a couple other hurricanes. The only real guarantee is that it's going to go out with a category three storm.

"Wyatt," I say, not really knowing how to start. How to change the pace and the topic of the last forty-eight hours in anticipation of this weather event. But I feel like, at the very least, I should apologize for my anger the other night.

"Nash," he says back, imitating the way I said it. Even now in the face of his first hurricane he's teasing me.

My next words die on my lips as the power flickers once, twice, and goes out. The light goes away, taking my words with it. The darkness with no glow from the electronics or the streetlights outside is so complete, I bump the coffee table on my way to standing. "I'll get the flashlight."

I set the flashlight on the coffee table in front of us. I settle back down on the couch. "It's probably better to try and get some sleep now. With the AC not running, it's going to get toasty in here quick."

"Fun," says Wyatt sarcastically. He scoots his back up

against the back of the couch and pats the space in front of him. I lie down where he wants me, and he throws a light blanket over us, then lets his arm rest across my hips.

You never realize how much noise electricity makes just by being on. Outside of cars driving by, music playing, the TV on, everything makes a slight humming noise, and the overwhelming silence of it when it's gone rings in your ears. The house is heavy with it. A millisecond later the air is filled with the hum of people's automatic generators switching on. It's like the drone of a thousand worker bees humming in the background.

"Goodnight, Wyatt."

"Goodnight, Nash," he whispers.

With his strong arm around me I'm not afraid of the hurricane that's coming. I trust Wyatt would never let anything bad happen to me, but I definitely thought my first night back with Wyatt would go differently than this. I worried he would tell me to pack my bags. That I hurt him too badly for him to stand the sight of me any longer. Or maybe I would be the one who wanted to leave. Living with him after refusing to let him give up Wisconsin for me would be cruel. If I kept myself away, he would get over me eventually. Now we'll never know because…here we are.

Tomorrow we could wake up to the devastation of thousands. Some people might need to be rescued from the roofs of their houses. There's a chance there will be no damages besides the power that goes out whenever a fly sneezes or the devastation of our relationship once we finally talk, but we won't know until the sun comes up on another day.

# Chapter Sixty-One

## WYATT

The nights in Poblocki can be quiet. There's no traffic noise or rowdy neighbors besides the animals, but the type of quiet with the power down is different. The generators are still running all around us. It seems like my house is the only one that doesn't have one. I'll have to fix that immediately. Don't know why no one told me that I needed one or that it was even an option.

Nash is hot on my arm since the air conditioning isn't working, but I'm relieved to see her there. We didn't get swept away by flood waters; the wind didn't tear the roof off my house. She's safe. I'm safe. That's all I could ask for on the morning after my first hurricane.

My stirring wakes her. "Good morning," I whisper. It feels like talking will be yelling in this silence.

"Good morning." She stretches her hands over her head. I'm sure sleeping on this couch wasn't the most comfortable, both of us being giants and all. But if it's the safest, I'm glad we did.

"Should we get something to eat?" I'm starving even after

both of the burgers I ate last night. All that worrying worked up an appetite.

"How's peanut butter sandwiches sound? The power has been out long enough that everything in the fridge is already trash. But the freezer should last forty-eight hours."

"What are the chances the power will be back on by then?"

She thinks for a second, surely considering all her previous hurricane experiences. "Medium."

"What does that mean?"

"It means some areas might get power back quickly while other's will be in isolated pockets of outages for longer. You're not that far from the big hospitals, so hopefully you get it quick."

"Hopefully."

I check my phone. There's still cell phone service, so we huddle around it trying to see the damages. There was enough rain to flood low-lying houses in the Houston area, of which there are many. People are putting together volunteer crews to go help those who need it. Fallen trees need to be cut up and cleared away; any house that has water inside it needs to have everything wet ripped out in less than forty-eight hours so mold doesn't start growing.

I look at Nash after reading the extent of the damage. "Do you want to go help?"

"I would love that. Maybe we can get the Hurricanes and the Moons together."

"Let me send a text to the group."

Is anyone interested in finding a place to volunteer?

COLIN

For sure.

JADEN

Do you guys have power?

We don't.

COLIN

We have a generator.

NOAH

We don't either. Went out at about one AM.

JADEN

Same

MACK

Lucky bastard.

COLIN

Anyone who wants to can come stay here.

I'll reach out to and find someone who needs volunteers.

"Okay," I say to Nash. "Colin is going to find somewhere for us to help out."

"I'll text the Moons and see who wants to come."

"Do you want to go stay at Colin's? They have a generator."

She shrugs. "Sure, that sounds good. In about six hours, it's going to be miserable in here."

A couple hours later my phone pings.

COLIN

There's an elderly couple who ended up with a few inches of water in their house that need help. Their address is 5678 North Washington Avenue. Can everyone be there at two PM?

JADEN

I'll be there

NOAH

We'll be there

See you then. Some of the Moons might come.

I copy the address and text it to Nash. "Send this address to the Moons and see who wants to meet us there at two o'clock."

———

I'm amazed by how blue the sky is. It's like the dark gray clouds from last night never existed, like I imagined them all. How could the sky be so calm after 140 mph winds whipped through it just twelve hours ago? The trees that are still standing are a little short on leaves, and a lot of the trees that fell across roads have already been cut up and hauled away. All my neighbors are outside cleaning up falling sticks and debris when we pull out of the garage after having to manually open it. Nash and I waved on our way out, and to be honest, I don't remember the last time I did that. Since I never planned on staying, it didn't seem important to get to know anyone. But now…

I slow my truck down as the GPS says we're approaching the address of the house of the elderly couple. The street is lined with cars already.

"Just pull up to the curb." Nash points to a spot a few houses down. "We'll walk it."

So I do and we hop out. Colin got this sanctioned as an official Hurricanes thing, so I've got my Hurricanes t-shirt and ballcap on. Nash is wearing a Moons t-shirt and rainboots.

We walk up to the house and the rest of the guys are already here.

"What's up, man?" asks Colin.

"Nothing much," I say back as we clap hands and each other's backs.

"All good?"

"Yeah, not too bad. Just no power, but we'll take you up on your offer and camp out at your place until it comes back."

"Okay, dope. Chrissy is at home cooking for everyone."

Nash is greeting her teammates as well. They're all hugging each other and laughing. I don't think she's seen any of them since they won the championship. Everyone kind of took a break and then we were out of town. This is one hell of a reunion.

I say hello to Jaden and Mack before a man I've never met comes through the front door of the house and speaks to us. "Good afternoon, ladies and gentlemen. Thank you all for coming. My name is John, and I own a clean-up company. Today we are here pro bono helping out the Pattersons. We started early this morning and are glad to have you here to help this afternoon. Half of you will be relegated to helping rip up the floors, and the other half will be helping to haul debris outside to the curb. Please come take a mask before you go inside."

I look over my shoulder and back at the curb where piles of trash are already forming. Who is going to come get all of this? How long will it take to clean up?

We line up and take our mask from John. The inside of the house is like nothing I've ever seen before. The water only went up a couple inches, but the drywall is cut out to almost the bottom of my knee all the way around the house. There are probably ten other people in here all carrying shovels full of wet carpet, or handfuls of ruined walls.

Someone puts the local classic rock radio station on a speaker as we get our teams. Nash and I are put in separate groups, so for the next couple hours we just pass by each other. It's a quiet type of labor. I don't know if it's the reverence of being in someone's house that was basically destroyed, or if it's from the backbreaking work. My muscles aren't just for show, but everything weighs a thousand pounds when it's wet.

Colin stands with his hands on his knees sucking in air, something we're not allowed to do on the field. Jaden is taking a break on an upside-down bucket guzzling water. I scan the room for Nash and spot her with Mrs. Patterson who is showing her the pictures that haven't yet been taken off the wall.

At around six o'clock, John calls an end to the day and asks us to gather around him. I stand in a semi-circle with Nash, and both of our teammates and friends and look at what we were able to accomplish in just one afternoon with the help of so many hands. "We so appreciate your help today. If you're available and interested, you can come back tomorrow to help us finish the tear out and start spraying bleach. We'll start at eight AM."

"Thank you for letting us come crash your work site," says Colin, reaching out to shake the man's hand.

"We're lucky to have you." He points playfully at Colin. "Thanks for the signed Hurricanes hat."

"It's no big deal."

We all wave as we head out the front. Nash says goodbye to the Moons who are all staying at Simin's parents' place that is far enough out of the city that it still has power.

Colin takes a headcount of who is going to his house, and basically everyone else raises their hands.

I head out to my truck to grab a sports drink from the cooler we packed for ourselves, not knowing what would or wouldn't be provided here.

"I'll take one, too," Nash says from behind, startling me. I hand her the blue one—I know that's her favorite flavor. We lean against my truck, drained.

"I'm glad we could help, but I'm exhausted."

"Big bad football player can't stand some actual work," she teases.

"I've been keeping up just fine, thank you." I gesture to the ever-growing pile of furniture, fabric, carpet, and wood at the curb. "I did part of that."

"I brought it out here," she chuffs.

We sip our drinks in silence, both of our eyes roaming around. The street is alive with people going to and from trucks, in and out of houses. Few homes were saved from the water damage, on this street, in particular. I've never seen anything like it. I've also never seen Nash like this. Sweat? Yes. But dirty from a day of hard work in the heat? No. She looks ethereal even with her hair sticking to her neck. I soak in being in her presence because who knows how much longer I have?

I lean casually against Wyatt's truck, but I'm so filled with excitement I can hardly stand still. While we were taking a break, Mrs. Patterson took me on a tour of their framed photos and told me about their life together. They were high school sweethearts and had rushed to get married before Mr. Patterson was drafted into the war. They looked so blissful in their wedding photos—and so young. It stirred up something that was already swirling in my chest. It felt like I've seen that look on a man's face before, I just couldn't pinpoint where it was. Maybe my own parents' wedding photos? They've been happily married thirty years, so it's possible.

When Mrs. Patterson was telling me about their delayed honeymoon, it hit me. I've seen that look more than once in my life. The look of a man totally lost in a woman. I have a picture of it on my phone from the day we played flag football with the Hurricanes earlier this year. I pulled it out right then to look at it, pretending to check my text messages. When Chrissy sent me this photo and I saw it for the first time, I thought it was just chance that Wyatt was looking at me like that. That he missed the countdown on Chrissy's phone telling everyone when to look and smile, but as I scroll through the photos we've taken at the NFL Honors, at the PVF championship, at Jaden's crawfish boil, and at Henry's wedding—Wyatt is looking at me in every single one of them. There's not a photo on my phone where he's looking at the camera.

This couple's home is full of water. They're having to stay with their daughter until it's fixed. I'm sure there's other times where they've had to be away from home and that's never kept them apart. I feel the realization in the back of my throat. A house is not permanent. Volleyball might try to take me away from Houston, and if I want to keep playing, I might have to go. Wyatt and I need mutual ground. Somewhere to meet that we both love. A place that's neither Hurricanes nor Butchers nor Moons.

Now I'm here. Leaning up against the best man I've ever known's truck, drinking my favorite flavor of sports drink, having brought it unprompted by me. I'm covered in muck and sweat. I must stink to high heaven, but I can't help but smile. I have a plan. I use my left foot as a pivot to spin around and settle myself against him. The truck supporting him and him supporting me. I put my chin on his chest to look up at him.

"Hey there," he says surprised at my affection.

"Hi." The universe has been on my side bringing us here, forcing me to see. I was cleaner then and objectively much cuter. But I've seen what my future could hold with Wyatt in the salt and pepper hair of Mr. Patterson as he carefully packs away their wedding photos with a reverence that's rare. They've been together literally through hell or high water, and I know in my heart I want that with Wyatt.

He interrupts my thoughts by saying, "Do you want to go for a walk?"

I shrug. "I guess." What I'd really like is to lay him down in the back of his pickup truck and–

*ARF!*

I stand perfectly straight, no longer leaning against Wyatt's hard-packed body. "Did you hear that?"

# Chapter Sixty-Three

## WYATT

"I think it came from over here."

I peer around the side, and sure enough, there's a little dog sniffing my tire. It's probably ten pounds and the exact color of rainwater and mud mixed together. I look back to Nash, but she's already rounded the corner calling to the dog. I grab her wrist to stop her. "It could be rabid."

"It looks lost."

There's no stopping Nash from saving this dog, I know. She's always had a soft spot for animals, but with volleyball, she hasn't ever had a chance at getting a pet of her own. "Just be careful," I say, releasing my grip on her arm.

I watch as she crouches down and approaches the dog slowly. It's a little hesitant at first, but she coos at it, and it eventually steps up to sniff her outstretched hand. She strokes its head gently. "I'm going to pick him up." I watch as she moves her hands under the little dog's chest and lifts it into her arms. "That's a good boy," she murmurs. "I think it's a boy, at least."

She stands and turns to me, and when her eyes meet mine,

I about keel over at the softness and care I see in them. Her face is warm as she takes in the dog's matted fur. The dog seems to relax in her hold like he's been wandering a long time and is finally able to rest under her care.

*I know the feeling.*

"We should walk around with him and see if any neighbors recognize him or know the owners," I say. I can see Nash's attachment forming to this dog in real time, but I have to make sure we do our due diligence so she doesn't get her heart broken when she has to give him back.

Colin is still here, talking to John, so I call to him, "We found a dog. We're going to try and look for his owners. We'll see you at your house later."

"See you then," he says and goes back to his conversation.

We head in the direction we were originally going to walk in. Anytime we pass someone, we show them the dog and ask if they know him. Again and again the people of the neighborhood tell us no.

The walk is not a pretty one. The streets are full of trash from the flooded houses waiting to be picked up. Yards are full of people's undamaged property covered in bedsheets. Some have 'we will defend' spray painted on cardboard signs or on the sheet itself. Others have signs that say 'do not take'. It's crazy and a bit disturbing to see. Not only seeing what should be inside houses out here on the front lawn, but the idea that there might be altercations over property. The sun is quickly setting over the trees, and with the power still out there won't be any streetlights. I suddenly feel the size of this city, the amount of strangers who live here pressing in on me. "We should head back. It's getting late."

"But we didn't find his owner."

"Tonight we can give him a bath and some food. Tomorrow

we can take him by the vet and get him scanned for a microchip."

"Come on, Arthur. Let's get you something to drink."

"Arthur?"

"Yeah, after the hurricane." She smiles at her own cleverness, and I have to admit, I'm basking in it too. I eye Arthur, who looks perfectly content being carried around in Nash's arms. Lucky bastard. Like he knows we won't take him to the pound. What do they call it when you just find an animal and they decide they're yours? *The animal distribution system.* I think it's mostly cats, but dogs aren't unheard of.

I put my hand on her lower back to guide her back in the direction we came. I'm surprised to find how far we've walked. It hits me just a little ways back how nice it is. To be out for a walk with Nash and a puppy. Maybe it won't be this puppy if he belongs to someone else, but in the future, it could be a different dog. Maybe during the two months we both have off we could walk down the street to the coffee shop by my house on Sunday mornings to get a latte and a pastry. Us holding hands and taking turns walking the dog.

I don't have any problem being a big man walking a little dog, if that's what she wants.

# Chapter Sixty-Four

## NASH

It's close enough to dusk that most people have left for the day. We take a second to pour some water out of a bottle for Arthur to lap at before we head home. We're about to put him in the back seat and climb into Wyatt's truck when a lady in an SUV pulls up beside us. "Excuse me, but do you guys have food to eat?" Wyatt and I must have had confused looks on our faces because she explains. "I'm looking for people who haven't eaten dinner." She holds up a fast-food bag full of what I assume are chicken sandwiches. There's probably twenty of them in there. I guess the flooding was worse than the damage done to the power lines since they already have some power on the main road where the grocery stores, gas stations, and restaurants are.

Wyatt answers her, "Yes, ma'am. We do have plans for dinner this evening, but we just came from that direction," he points down the road we just walked, "and they had some people outside still, so you might ask them."

"Thank y'all. Have a good one."

"You too," we say as she rolls up her window and rolls away.

I get into Wyatt's passenger seat and point all the air vents directly at my face. Every year I forget how truly hot it gets in the summer, and every year I'm violently reminded.

"Is it always like that here?" Wyatt asks as he turns the key in the ignition.

"Like what?"

"Like *that*. A random person out looking to feed people?" He puts the truck in drive and pulls away from the curb.

It's never struck me that it could be considered weird or different. I've lived here two thirds of my life, so I'm just used to the Texan friendliness. I think back to my earliest hurricane memories. "When I was a kid, we had a hurricane that knocked the power out for two weeks. We went outside the morning after, like you and I did today, and there was a tree leaning on the little canopy over our front door. In just a few hours, my dad and some of the men from our street had the whole thing off the house and cut into pieces. To thank them, my dad cooked whatever meat we had in the fridge on a camping stove and fed everyone. It wasn't going to last long without power anyway, so we just cooked everything and fed people."

"Just like that?"

I nod. "Just like that."

"Wow."

"Another year, a different hurricane knocked tons of trees into the streets of our neighborhood. My dad filled his chainsaw up with gas, took the four-wheeler around and helped clear the roads. After hurricanes it's like anyone and everyone who owns a chainsaw is out helping." I laugh at the memories of being a kid and being able to just do whatever because our parents didn't want to entertain us at home. "I think that was the same storm that I was old enough to just hang out with friends after. No power, no school, and nothing to do at home. I would call my friends who lived in the neighborhood on the landline, can you believe it? And we would meet up near the bike path and just ride around for hours until it would get close to dark."

"What did you do?"

"I don't know. All sorts of stuff. Watch turtles swim in the creek, poke at a dead snake with a stick. Maybe we would walk someone's dog. Just killin' time."

"That doesn't sound like a bad childhood."

"It's not like that growing up in Wisconsin?" There's basically no traffic, so it's not long before we are close to Wyatt's house so we can shower, change, and grab some stuff to stay over at Colin's.

"It is to an extent. The town is so small you can't get away with anything, like you saw. Imagine everyone knowing you got a speeding ticket before you even show up to the function, but like a thousand times worse. They knew when you snuck out, when you were partying, who you were going out with. There was no privacy. A high school class of two-hundred kids means there's nowhere to run."

"But it also means the town takes care of you."

He nods. "It does, but look at Houston. Two-million people in the city limits and everyone is out and about helping. It's like the small-town kindness with the big-city benefits."

I never thought I would hear Mr. Wisco himself talking about Houston like that. It kind of warms my heart. Makes me feel like maybe he's not going to hate my guts in ten years for giving up on Wisconsin to be with me. Maybe he can appreciate this city for what it is. I don't think my Texas lessons had as much of an impact on him as this experience. There's part of being a Texan that you can't teach. The media makes us out to be a bunch of dumb hicks who ride horses to school, but when push comes to shove, my big blue dot in a sea of small-town red is accepting, welcoming, and caring. People wonder why young women like me with big careers and big dreams haven't fled Texas in the wake of the horrible politicking going on here, but this is why. When I was a kid, we had Go Texan Day, and I always felt so proud to live here. As I got older and started paying attention to politics, I lost that pride, but that's what they want. When you realize how diverse and beautiful this city is, you appreciate the Texan state of mind even more. It was built on the 'come and take it' attitude, and that's the same mantra I use for staying and fighting.

I put my hand on Wyatt's arm. "That's a really nice way to say it."

We pull into his garage, and I step out of the passenger seat to the back to get Arthur. I carry the dog while Wyatt carries the cooler back inside. "Holy fuck. It's disgusting in here," Wyatt cries as we walk in.

The heat has taken its toll on the temperature inside the house. It's probably a muggy eighty degrees. "Thank God we're not sleeping here."

"True, but I don't think Colin would appreciate a dirty dog running around his house."

"We can't leave him here." If someone sees the pictures I posted on the local social media pages, they could be wanting to come get him any minute.

"Let's put him in the tub and get him clean. Then I won't feel bad about bringing him."

We bring him to the guest bath, setting up our phones as

flashlights. I hold my wrist under the tap, waiting for the right temperature.

It's a good thing we're both disgusting because we would have ended up that way anyway trying to get Arthur bathed. He wasn't super happy about being wet, and he let us know it by shaking his dirty water all over us while we tried to wipe him down. "Hold him still, Wyatt," I shriek as Arthur shakes again, coating me in sudsy water.

"He's so small I don't want to hold him too still and hurt him."

I pick up the extended shower head and start to rinse him. "It's okay, little guy. We're almost done."

I spray him all over, the water that was running gray starting to finally run clear. When all the soap is gone, it's like an entirely different dog is looking back at me. "Oh my God. He's white."

Wyatt bursts out laughing. "Arthur the color-changing dog."

"He was cute when he was brown and dirty, but now that he's clean he's adorable." I wrap Arthur up in a towel and hold him to me. With one hand I wipe him dry on one side, then turn him around in my arms and towel dry the other side. "I'll hold Arthur; you go get cleaned up. We're already late for dinner at Colin's."

Wyatt gets up and starts to head toward his bathroom but stops abruptly just short of the door. "Wait. How do I take a shower in the dark?"

I can't help it, I crack up laughing. I laugh and laugh with little Arthur in my arms. I don't know why the image of Wyatt fumbling around in the dark trying to turn on the shower is so funny to me, but it just is. "The same way Arthur just did. Take the flashlight from the living room with you," I answer between bursts of laugher. "Then bring it out to me so I can use it when you're done."

While Wyatt's showering, I head to the kitchen to find Arthur something to eat. I was hoping that Wyatt would randomly have dog food from dog sitting or for feeding the raccoons, but I can't find anything to safely feed him except white rice and a can of mixed veggies.

I set a pot on the gas stove and fill it with water to boil. I set Arthur on the ground to explore and lean against the counter.

My phone doesn't have much battery left, but if I can make this call before it dies, that's all that matters.

"Yellow…"

When we get to Colin's, the house is already packed. People are lounging around the couches and on the floor. There's a game of cards going, and Mack and Jaden are playing chess on Colin's ridiculously fancy stone chessboard.

"I saved you guys the last room, since you're a couple. I gave all the single guys the couch or a blow-up mattress," Colin says as he leads us up the stairs to dump our overnight bags. I wouldn't say he was thrilled to see Arthur in my arms, but he let us in anyway.

"Thanks, man," Wyatt says as he dumps our backpacks on the bed. "This is way better than my place."

"It's not as cool as I normally keep it, but it's not as hot as it could be, so we'll take what we can get."

My phone pings in my pocket, and I check it while Wyatt is distracted by Colin. God bless that woman. She got me the information I need so quick…like she was expecting it. Her note confirms my suspicions: "Good luck." I'll tell him tomorrow. Tonight, we should just hang out with friends and revel in how lucky we are to be sleeping in a house with lights, air conditioning, and no flood waters.

We head back down the stairs as Colin says, "There's grilled chicken, broccoli, and baked beans downstairs. The generator runs the AC, the fridge, and a couple outlets to charge phones. But not many lights, so we've been using candles and flashlights."

"We brought our own flashlight, so we'll be good up there with that, and we'll take a turn with the charger once everyone else is done."

"Sounds perfect." He gestures to the kitchen. "Please help yourself to dinner and refreshments."

"*Refreshments*," Wyatt says teasingly. "Who are you? Chrissy has rubbed her hostess with the mostest all over you, bro."

I elbow him. "They're literally feeding us a hot meal when we have no power. Be nice."

He hangs his head like a reprimanded puppy.

Chrissy has returned to the couch, surely exhausted from feeding several football players and a sleepless night with the storm. I walk over and offer her Arthur. "Could you watch him while I eat? I'm starving, but he's too cute to not be held."

She holds her arms out for him making grabby hands motion. "Gimme," she commands, and I hand him to her. She leans back against the couch, and he immediately settles in her lap. "Are you going to keep him?"

"We have to at least *try* to look for his owners."

"How long will that take?"

I look at Wyatt for any idea of how long is long enough to look for Arthur's owner. "I don't know. Two weeks?" he says.

I look back at Chrissy. "Two weeks."

"That's so exciting for you guys." She pauses and then adds, "And sad for his people if he has any."

"I'm trying not to get attached to him just yet," I say.

"You guys are making a little family," she coos with her hands clasped in front of her like that's the cutest thought she's ever had in her life.

"Maybe we're moving too fast," I laugh.

"What do you mean? You've already been together six months and you've known each other for years."

I pause, the lying from the last couple months bearing down on my conscience in front of Wyatt's teammates, who I consider my friends. We look at each other for just a second like we're deciding with telepathy who is going to be the one to own up. In a split second I decide it has to be me. It was my idea. I strung him along. I don't want Wyatt's friends to hear about our deception and think of him differently. Everyone deserves to know the truth.

"Actually," I hedge, and all seven pairs of eyes land on me —eight, if you include Arthur. "Wyatt and I were faking it."

Mack gasps like I just revealed the killer on his latest telenovela.

Colin looks to Wyatt as if in confirmation. I hurry to explain. "It was my idea. I wanted to fill the stands for the Moons games, and I thought that using Wyatt's access to the Hurricanes' popularity would help."

"You used us?" Mack exclaims, shocked. Almost too shocked?

I hold my hands out to him wanting him to understand. "No! Of course not. Unless you guys only came because Wyatt asked you to and not because you wanted to see me play?"

Colin steps in and signals to Mack to calm down. "That's not true, Nash, and you know it. We would have come to support you even if you and Wyatt were just friends forever. If you're important to him, you're important to us. No label needed."

"But," Wyatt starts.

My head whips in his direction. "But what?"

"I had to tell them."

I look at all the people around me. "You knew?" It comes out an accusation, not a question.

Chrissy raises her hand. "I didn't." But everyone else in the room nods.

Wyatt takes a step toward me, and I take a step back. The hurt in his eyes makes it almost not worth it. "I needed their help," he says as if that's a perfectly good explanation.

"So they watched us kiss and hold hands and they knew it was fake the whole time?"

Noah clears his throat. "We knew *you* thought it was fake." He points at Wyatt. "We knew he was actually in love with you the whole time."

My first instinct is to be mad, but I take a deep breath and one second to think about what this really means. Wyatt brought his teammates into this because he needed them to know what the stakes were for me. He confided in guys he didn't want to like for me. Now look at us, all crammed in Colin's house like sardines.

"You did this for me?" I ask Wyatt, tears stinging the back of my eyes. He just nods in response.

Mack speaks up, interrupting our moment. "How do we know you weren't just using Wyatt this whole time?" Colin shoots him a silencing look, but the words are already out.

"If everyone's telling the truth here tonight, I guess I will, too. Our deal was that we were going to find a way to mutually end the fake dating after Wyatt's brother's wedding last weekend, but…" the words get stuck in my throat, which is too clogged with emotions to speak. I swallow hard and look at Wyatt. His friends all know, but he needs to understand. "It turned into something real along the way. I was in denial, but something has always been there for me. Wyatt told me he loved me in Wisconsin, after his brother's wedding, and after I told him I loved him back, I told him he couldn't give up on the Butchers for me." I turn to face him now. This isn't how I imagined telling him what I did, but it's now or never.

"And?" Mack asks on the edge of his seat on the couch.

I smile, knowing the answer already, and everyone else erupts into hoots and hollers. Colin claps Wyatt's hand and pulls him in to pat him on the back. Chrissy prances over to me still holding Arthur and wraps her arms around me. "Welcome to the WAGs. You were an honorary member before, but this is your official welcome. Hmm, I should start making goodie bags to give out." Knowing Chrissy—she's completely serious.

"That's not necessary," Wyatt says, and I shoot him a look. If she wants to give me a goodie bag for fucking my best friend, who am I to stop her?

"Wait," I say, and it comes out way too loud for the space. I feel like this is the perfect moment to reveal my plan. Everyone can hear it straight from me, and there won't be any games of telephone. I take Wyatt's hand in mine. "I might have made a phone call." His brows raise at my admission. "Since the night you told me you love me and I told you not to be so selfless, I've been racking my brain trying to figure out how to make something work for us that doesn't involve self-sacrifice. And today, when we helped the Pattersons clear out all of their personal possessions, it hit me. So I called your Mom."

"You what?" Wyatt sputters, but I march on.

"I know you have a designated parcel of Vandergriff Farms that you haven't bothered doing anything with yet. I now have my share of a million dollars from winning the PVF championship."

He steps into my space, putting his hand on my cheek, giving me the wherewithal to continue. "Turns out, it's just enough money for the fee to get on a custom builder's calendar."

"You didn't," shouts Jaden from his spot next to Mack on the couch.

I shoot him a smile over Wyatt's palm. "Oh, I did." When he pulls me gently back to look at him, I see everything in his eyes. I see our years of friendship, I see our time apart, I see all of our fake-dating adventures, but most importantly, I see the future. "I want to live in Wisconsin, in that house, on your family's land every June and July. I realized that our careers could always take us elsewhere, but with that house we'll have a permanent place to call home. Something that isn't controlled by a sports team, and doesn't have rules about whether you can mount a TV on the wall. A place that is just ours."

"You really didn't have to do that. I have the money and–"

I place a small kiss on his lips to quiet him. "I wanted to. Consider it my equity in the house. You provided the land, I provided the builder."

He smiles, and then he's kissing me again, and I want more. I want it all. With him.

Audrey stands up from the couch. "Well, all these confessions have exhausted me." Wyatt and I break apart like two kids caught making out in the school hallway. I can't believe we're sleeping in a house full of people on what could have been the most romantic night of my life. Oh well. We have all of eternity now, and soon we'll have an entire Wisconsin cabin to be as loud as we want, anywhere we want. She looks to Noah, "Babe, are you ready for bed?"

He nods and stands, taking her hand. "We're going to hit it." They walk together through the living room, heading for the stairs. "'Night everybody."

"Goodnight," we all say back.

## Vandergriff Signs New Deal with Hurricanes
*Texas Football Today*

After a long and tenuous off season, defensive lineman Wyatt Vandergriff has finally signed a new contract with the Houston Hurricanes. The six-foot-five graduate of U.W. came to Houston after finishing his rookie contract in Green Bay. His first year with the Hurricanes was a one-year deal where he had to prove his worth to the team. It seems after going to the playoffs and winning the Sack Leader of the Year Award, Vandergriff has been successful.

We are looking forward to a year packed full of Houston sports from January to December now that there are multiple H-Town teams to root for now.

## Chapter Sixty-Five

### WYATT

## *TWO WEEKS LATER*

"Do you know what today is?" Nash asks me in a singsong voice that is much too chipper for this early in the morning.

I rub my hand over my face and ask, "What?"

"It's officially two weeks since we started looking for Arthur's owners. That means he's ours." The scruffy white dog looks at me from his spot on her lap. It doesn't seem like he ever had any intention of leaving. Her eyes go wide and her head perks up. "We should celebrate!"

I smile at her enthusiasm for this even though she and that dog have been inseparable for the last two weeks. "What do you have in mind?"

"Let's go to the pet store and officially get him a tag for his collar." She pets his head and talks to him, "We wouldn't want you to go getting lost again, would we?"

"Whose phone number should we put on his tag?"

"I think we should put both of our numbers. We both travel a lot; it'll be easier that way."

I've been trying to let her have the time she needs to start this conversation, but I think it's time that I take the metaphorical bull in this relationship by the horns and step up. "How will we decide who gets Arthur when?"

"What do you mean?" she asks, still stroking his little head.

"If you get your own apartment like you originally planned when you came back from Rome, will we trade him back and forth every week like divorced parents sharing custody of a kid?"

"Or by our sports season?" she says, thinking out loud. "I'd have him August to December, and then you'd have him January to May? Eventually we'll be together at the cabin for June and July."

My chest aches at the idea of watching Nash pack her stuff up and leave me. Even if she's not leaving the relationship, it still feels like that would be a step back. My voice is tight in my throat when I say, "Is that what you want?" I lean against the countertop, my hands on either side of my back, gripping the granite with all my strength.

For a second, she's quiet while she pets the dog, running her fingers gently over his soft ears. Her answer comes out in a voice so soft I almost don't hear it. "No."

"Wouldn't it be easier on the dog if we were together?"

When she looks back up at me, her eyes are filled with an emotion I can't identify. "Is that the only reason?" She holds my gaze, and I watch her take a deep breath and gather her courage. "Ask us to stay, Wyatt."

I cross the room to where she sits on the couch and drop to my knees in front of her. I'm willing to beg. "Nash," I look at the dog, addressing him, too, "Arthur. Please stay here with me. Please don't move out. Don't leave. I don't want to just have a drawer in your dresser at whatever new apartment you get. I don't want to spend a single night without you next to me in bed and Arthur curled up between us. I know this might seem fast, but we've known each other a long time. Hell, we already have the architectural planning meeting scheduled. We've been moving toward this life at a snail's pace for nine years, and I'm ready to grab on with both hands and hold on tight to us. People might say we're crazy, but they don't know us, Nash. They don't love like we do. It's different with us, isn't it, sugar?"

She sits up to wrap her arms around my shoulders, startling Arthur out of her lap with the movement. "Yes, it's different. Better than anything else I've ever known. Easier than breathing and just as natural."

"So you'll stay." It's not a question because it doesn't need to be one. The way her breath is coming faster, and her eyes are taking in every inch of me kneeling before her tells me everything I need to know.

"Yes," is barely out of her mouth before I'm wrapping my arms around her legs, under her thighs where she sits on the couch and hauling her easily into my arms. She wraps her legs around me as I rise and head toward the stairs. "Where are we going?"

"I'm taking you to your room to get the clothes out of your dresser. You're moving all your things into my room. Right now." The last word comes out as an unintentional growl. "Then I'm going to take you to bed, and make you come until you're begging me to stop. After that I'll wash your tight body with a soft cloth until you're melting in my hands." Her hips start moving against me, desperate for friction. I'm climbing the stairs as fast as I can while still being careful not to hit her extremities on anything. Arthur weaves around us, rushing up the stairs to be first so I have to dodge his little body, too.

I put her on her feet in the room that for the last six months has been hers so I can look in her eyes when I say, "I've been waiting eight years for this. I physically cannot wait another day. Not another day for you to call my house your home. Not another day to wake up and have breakfast with you. Not another night where you don't fall asleep in my arms after getting absolutely and thoroughly fucked. So yes, it has to be done today."

I turn her by her shoulders and smack her on the ass. "Now get to packing. I'll start in your bathroom; you start with your clothes."

She turns back to me, putting her hands on my chest. "I think we should start with sex first." She pushes on me, and I let her guide me backward though the door and across the short hallway that separates our bedrooms.

My door is closed, and she pushes me up against it. "Fuck, I love when you push me around."

She leans against me, running her hands over my chest, over my stomach. "You don't wish I was small and meek? That you could put me in your pocket?"

I start pulling her Nike shorts down her hips and off. I toss them behind me into the hallway. "I like knowing I can throw you around and not hurt you. I like that you like it a little rough. I like knowing you can take a pounding."

I hook my hands under her thighs and lift. She squeaks as her feet leave the ground, but keeps going. "I like that I can wear my heels when we go out. I like that I never feel like I'm too much for you, too much athlete, too competitive, too big, too much woman."

She puts her hands on either side of my face and pulls me to her, meeting me with a searing, open-mouth kiss. She's ravenous in her affection, lips clashing against mine. When she reaches for the waistband of my shorts, I pant, "Wait."

She stops short. "Is something wrong?"

"I don't want to just fuck you."

"You don't?"

"No, I want to make this last." I bring us away from the wall and through my bedroom door which she helps me open. I lie her down on my bed, taking in the sight of her pretty pink pussy. I plant a kiss on her forehead before making my way down her neck to her chest, still clothed. I don't even care. I'm going to deliver on the promise I made downstairs, and every promise I ever make to her for the rest of our lives.

# Chapter Sixty-Six

## NASH

After he makes it to my belly, Wyatt crawls into the bed next to me and we lie like we have been every night when he cuddles me before we fall asleep. "I want to hold you this time."

Two fingers, then three rock hard into me and I involuntarily move my hips with his push and pull. "That's it, sugar. Are you ready for me?"

I can feel his hardness pressed up against my back, needing my attention. He palms it and brings it between my legs, sliding it through my slickness.

I feel my hunger for him and him alone. "I was ready on the couch downstairs."

He laughs, and it's loud and full of something like disbelief that this is us. This is how it feels to be *us*.

I'm so wet he basically slips inside.

"It feels so good," I say, turning my head so he can kiss me deeply over my shoulder. Everything tunnels down to this moment, these feelings. Nothing else in the world exists, not even my words. Wyatt rubs my hip in a comforting way while we move slowly together like both of us are being carried along on the same wave.

I cry out when he takes my thigh in his hand and wraps my leg back around his hip, opening me wide. I take in a sharp breath at the feeling of his finger circling my clit. His left arm is under me, wrapped tightly around my chest, the right laying over my stomach playing the perfect notes I need.

"I'm gonna come," I moan.

"I've got you." His voice shakes despite his calm façade, and I know he's going to follow me over the edge, but not until I get every last second of this orgasm. Held in his arms we find ecstasy together, binding us in a way that we weren't before. By more than friendship, more than lust. By commitment and mutual gratification in love and life.

And I know I'm never going to leave the safety of his arms.


## SEEING DOUBLE: A New League on the Rise
### *Just Her Sports*

In the wake of the PVF's extremely successful first year, a new league has popped up. Just a month after the first-ever PVF championship game, owners of the new league announced that the U.S. Volleyball Club will be open and ready to play their inaugural season next year.

Volleyball fans all over the country are thrilled to have twice the games to watch, but we can't help but wonder what this kind of competition might look like. Are there enough players to go around? Enough fans? Enough cable time slots? Could this boost pro volleyball up with the likes of the WNBA, or will it spread the talent, money, and fan base too thin?

Only one way to find out. Stay tuned as we keep track of trades and the newly drafted class of players headed for their dreams in a professional volleyball league.

WYATT

## ONE YEAR LATER

"I can't wait to see it." Nash is practically jumping out of the golf cart and onto the grass.

"It's just a bunch of concrete and two-by-fours right now." I turn the key and step out of the cart.

She takes my hand and drags me toward our spot, Arthur bounding along beside us. "But it's *our* concrete and two-by-fours."

I smile back at her, hoping my nerves don't show through. A tiny black velvet box is burning a hole in my pocket. I wanted to tie the ring to Arthur's collar and have him greet her at the front door, but when the builders called and said the framing of our cabin was complete, I knew it needed to be here.

The house doesn't look like much now, but when they're done it will be a two-story cabin with the big logs and green roof. There's a fireplace in the living room and heated floors in the primary bathroom. This is a forever home more so than when other people use the term. My family has owned this land for over a hundred years. We're never selling. This is it. The permanence of it all made me feel like it was the perfect place to propose.

Nash is running her hands along the wood where the front door would be, chattering on about how big of a window she wants the door to have. Something about wanting more light. I watch as she takes another step into the house, Arthur on her heels. I follow behind her, taking a step forward.

I can feel my blood rushing in my ears. The anticipation of this has been killing me. With my next step I'm close enough to get down on one knee. Earlier this week I practiced which knee I was going to get down on, but I can see now that all of that planning went right out the window as soon as I had the ring in my hand.

I clear my throat. "Nash."

"What are these blankets doing here?"

"Nash," I repeat.

When she spins to look at me, her eyes go wide, taking me in, as I kneel before her. The concrete is hard under my knee, but I'll stay here forever if that's what it takes. I hold the box up to her while I try and rack my brain for my speech, which I also rehearsed earlier, and which has also disappeared from my brain.

She gasps, putting her other hand over her mouth when I hold it up in front of her, the reality of what's happening fully hitting her. "Nash," I begin again. "There hasn't been a day that's gone by since we first met that I didn't love you. When I first met you, I loved your laugh, I loved your fire. As we got to know one another, I loved the softness you rarely let people see. I love that you're always there for the people in your life. As hard as I tried to fight it, my love became romantic. Slowly at first, and then all at once. I loved you close up during our junior and senior year while I watched you win a Big Ten championship. I loved you from five-thousand miles away while you chased your dreams in Rome. I loved you when I thought you were faking it for everyone else, even though I never was. Because I never was. It was always my reality. I loved seeing you win your first championship at home. I loved seeing you dance at my brother's wedding looking like you were exactly where you were meant to be." Tears stream steadily down her cheeks now, but I push through. I pull the ring out of the box and take her hand. "Every time I thought a version of my love for you was the best it would ever be, we changed, and it got better. I thought when you said you'd stay here with me and Arthur that that was the happiest I'd ever be. I finally had everything I wanted, but then it changed again. Loving you together in our own place was better than loving you as a roommate. I expect," I pause as I hold the ring against the tip of her finger, "that after I put this ring on your finger, I'll find a new level of bliss as your fiancé. And after that as your husband. Will you, Nashville Taylor Green, do me the honor of discovering if that's true by marrying me?"

She chokes a laugh through her tears and cries, "Yes." I don't need to hear anything else. I slide the ring on her finger and stand, wrapping my arms around her. I hold her up and she puts one hand on the side of my face. "Of course I'll marry you." She kisses me once and pulls back. "Is this why you've been so weird the last two weeks?" Her eyes light up with the realization, and I can see her putting the puzzle pieces together. "Is that why you insisted on meeting my parents for dinner a month ago? And why Temi took me to get my nails done before we left?"

"And why my parents happened to be busy today instead

of being on the farm like they normally would," I add. She smacks my shoulder, and I rub where she hit me. "Ow!"

"I'm so surprised and so excited I want to hit you and kiss you and run away all at the same time."

"Well," I take the hand that wasn't on my face and guide her farther into the house. "I hope you will stay and have a picnic with me."

In the middle of what would be our living room sits a setup right out of a reality dating show. Thick blankets lay on the concrete, topped with decorative pillows, and a low table holding an assortment of Wisconsin cheese and a bottle of nice champagne in an ice bucket.

She dances a little in place when she sees the setup. "Our first meal in our house," she squeals.

I let her go to move toward the champagne flutes and fill one, handing it to her, then another for myself. I put my hand on her arm, guiding us down to the blankets. The front of the house looks out toward what will be our driveway. Two acres away is the front of Henry's house. The back of the house will have huge windows so you can sit on the couch and watch the deer move through the forest, or watch the snow fall silently on the leaves.

It's everything I dreamt it would be. I hold my flute out to Nash. "To us." She touches hers to mine, leaning in to kiss me at the same time.

"I love you," she says when she pulls back.

"I love you, too. You're the most important thing in the world to me."

She straightens her left hand out over my shoulder and admires the ring. "You did good."

"Yeah?"

"It's perfect."

I smile because hearing those words makes it feel like I've done everything in my life up until this moment to lead me here. I left Green Bay heartbroken and mad at the world having lost my faith in destiny after believing in it my whole life. But now that I'm standing here in front of my girl and our dog, who was also brought to us by destiny, I can see that this is where I was headed the whole time. The guiding stars in the sky and the gravitational pull of Nash never led me astray. They were leading me not to a place, but to a person. I think we both realized that life isn't about where you're from, but who you build it with. And for me, it's her.

My best friend.

The love of my life.

Then and now and always.

THE END

**Want to see more of Wyatt and Nash? Sign up for my newsletter to read their bonus prequel short story.**

**Enjoyed Love on the Block? Please leave a review on Amazon and/or Goodreads!**

# About the Author

Emily Rex is an author living in Houston, Texas with her dog and husband. She wrote a chapter book around age twelve about guinea pigs saving the world, but *Love on the Block* is her second full length novel. In high school, she used to stay up late at night writing poetry in iambic pentameter for funsies. She thinks there's nothing better than a book that makes you feel the emotion in the back of your throat.

When she's not writing, you can find her reading voraciously, spending time with her family, walking the dog, playing ARC Raiders or diamond painting.

You can find her website here or through the QR code below:

Acknowledgments

This book was so much fun to write and I'm so glad it's out in the world!

I cannot do this without the love and support of my family, especially my husband who is my best friend and my biggest cheerleader. I'm so proud to be your wife.

Thank you to my editor and cover artist, having you guys to steadily rely on has been priceless in this process.

To my writer friends who have helped me along the way with problem solving, encouragement, input, critique and company— thank you.

Thank you to all the professional female athletes. You'll likely never read this, but I am so inspired by your strength, beauty, and confidence. Even though the world continues to laugh at you, to underfund you—I believe in you.

*Also by Emily Rex*

Red Zone Realizations